Loner

THE BOYS OF WELLES BOOK ONE

by USA TODAY bestselling author
GINGER SCOTT

LONER

The Boys of Welles Book 1

Ginger Scott

For Ace.
You are stronger than you think.

Chapter 1

Lily Beachem

The only reason we're friends at all is because I pulled them both out of the river.

The sun is at its peak, and the part within my hair burns, a permanent ultra-violet line slowly being tattooed onto my scalp. At least two more trips to my car to go before I'm done. I think I have too much stuff. My belongings are a mere fraction compared to my roommates, though. Morgan's family came in two vehicles, one of them a truck—the fat kind with a king cab and doubled-up wheels in the back. Brooklyn has *literal help,* as in people who call her "Miss" and have uniforms on, hauling her things up the walkway and into our dorm room for our final year at Welles Academy.

Our worlds are miles apart, and it's foolish to think we'll be able to exist in this small room together for an entire year. My blankets and pillows are knotted up in a black trash bag. Their expensive bedding is new, the tags still dangling from the packaging. Their families are seeing them off, while mine doesn't see the reasons why I'd want to come to a place like this. I don't fit in here. I never have. Anika wanted us all to be together, but that was when there were four of us instead of three. She was the nucleus. She brought the harmony.

I miss Anika.

My doubts haven't slowed since the three of us agreed to follow through with the original plan at the end of last school term. I got caught up in the moment, I guess. Moved by the instant bonding that comes with trauma and a promise to the only friend you've ever really had. A summer apart, though, made me realize the three of us were acting out of guilt more than anything. My small-town home in Ohio is a joke compared to their Boston penthouses and sprawling homes on the Cape. But being here in Ashwood, just outside of Boston, is better than being at home. A world built on guilt trumps one crawling with shame.

"Look, someone actually wrote Triple B on our white board," Morgan says when we reach the landing just outside our door. She lifts the cloth tacked next to the board and erases it with a faint laugh at the memory. I force a tight-lipped smile on my face, one I imagine looks just like the fake smile Brooklyn is wearing, and then head into our room toward the small corner that is mine.

Our last names had always put us in groups together whenever we had to line up for ice breakers and social events, and that's the only reason we knew each other at all before last semester.

Lily Beachem.

Morgan Bentley.

Brooklyn Bennett.

Triple B, as some of the first form boys called us during physical education our seventh-grade year. They were making commentary on our breast sizes more than our names, even though triple B is not a bra size, and if it were, none of us were hardly enough to fill an A cup. That was before the guys of McKinley Hall had even seen a set of boobs other than in the pages of the magazines some of the older boys snuck into the dorms after trips back home.

Those boys who teased us in their crackling voices while wearing baby-faced grins turned into men wearing suit jackets and ties over washboard abs and smelling of expensive booze they'd snuck in for underground parties. Triple B had disappeared by the time we reached fourth form, when students were no longer forced into proximity with one another based on things like alphabetical order. We chose our own friends. And until last year, I had one, barely. Angela Fischer and I were roommates and more academic arch-nemesis than we were friends. I suspect she liked living with me because she could keep tabs on my progress in all things academic—to make sure her papers and projects were always just a step above. She will, without doubt, be graduating top of our class, and there have been nights I thought she would hold a pillow over my face if it came down to me or her just to make sure she wore the gold honor cords at convocation.

I've never been able to figure out why she was so threatened by me. I don't really care about being valedictorian, or even performing in the top percent of our class. That honor comes with duties like public speaking and mentoring younger students and serving as a prefect. I didn't want to live with first and second forms when I was one, let alone now that I'm a sixth form. So, while Angela spent our time together worried about ways to defeat me, I put all my effort into doing just poorly enough on my studies to never edge her from the top.

Being above average is enough for me. It's where I thrive,

just off the page out of the spotlight. I don't exactly fit the "Welles mold." I don't own a piece of Burberry or Chanel or Louis Vuitton, and I'm basically academically ambitionless. I'm on the swim team, and if I applied myself, I'd probably dominate. I'd rather just enjoy the silence that comes from the water, though. Don't get me wrong—I am full of potential. I just don't want to go to any of the destinations that potential leads to. It's quite a thing to be so smart that one can outwit the system and fly perpetually under the radar.

That's what led me to Anika Rothschild, the girls of Hayden Hall, and the night that would change my course forever.

Anika was everything I idolized. She was bold and maybe a little pushy, but in a way that people responded to. We were all fighting for our places in this maze built of limestone, tradition, and rules; meanwhile, Anika acted as if there weren't any walls around her at all. Her hair was a different color, cut and style every few weeks. Platinum rings pierced her ears in seven different places, and she had a septum ring in her nose that she merely pushed out of sight while in class whenever one of our instructors made mention of her dress code infractions.

If I had the tiniest bit of Anika in my bloodstream, maybe I wouldn't have run to this place—and away from my problems at home—to begin with. But I wasn't Anika. I was Lily. Quiet, shy, reserved, timid, awkward Lily with curves and breasts she was desperate to hide under school uniforms and thick tights, and headbands meant for little girls.

It was Anika who brought us all together. We all admired her for our own reasons. And I spent my entire summer wondering what would have happened if our bond was allowed to grow naturally, free of the brute force thrust upon us the night we all got in that car and crashed into the Solemn

River. Trauma has a way of forging connections that go against the grain. I am nothing like Morgan, and she is nothing like Brooklyn, who is nothing like either of us. We are three opposites on the friendship color wheel, yet here we are, entering our sixth and final form at Welles Academy, moving our things into the big corner room to live together.

As friends. Just like Anika wanted.

"My brother can help carry the rest of your things from the car." Morgan spins and falls back on her bed, her gorgeous auburn hair splaying out and her Welles skirt flaring above her knee-high socks. I would give anything to look like that—not her body or hair or skin, just the way she's always put together. I'm in constant shambles. Even now, my uniform skirt is too big for my waist, leaving it to sag on my hips, which means I must wear a blouse one size too big to make sure it stays tucked in.

"Thanks, but I'll get it. I think I'm going to visit the pool for a little while. I'll grab the rest of my things on my way back up." I flatten my hand on the slick fabric of my suit, scratching my fingertips along it but opting to push it deeper in the drawer. I'm not ready to put it on and get in the water. Not yet.

"Do you want us to come?" Brooklyn's words are uncertain, matched by the flashing glance Morgan shoots her as she lifts on her elbows. They don't want to do this with me, which is fine because I don't want them there.

I smile.

"I'm okay. Thanks, though."

I wait for Morgan to fall back against her bed and for Brooklyn to return her attention to setting up her desk, arranging the tiny, framed photos of shared moments between her, Morgan, and Anika together. I'm not in a single shot. I wasn't part of *them* yet.

Pausing just outside the door, I draw in a deep breath to fill my lungs. They haven't felt full in months, not since that night. The room remains quiet behind me, and I get some satisfaction from the fact Morgan and Brooklyn can't easily talk without me.

I opt for the stairs, knowing the elevators are going to be packed with parents and fourth and fifth forms moving in. Minus a few slamming doors to the floors below and the occasional rush of footsteps ducking into the stairwell to avoid the crowds like I am, I'm alone. Off the grid, in a space on the fringe—exactly how I like it.

Maybe I'm not ready to visit the pool. Coach doesn't expect me on a timeline. Everyone's giving me grace. They get it.

My feet drag down the steps and my palm slides along the wooden rail, feeling the knicks and grooves from years of wear. My vision hazes and I mentally go back to the river, to the screams and the crunch of metal, the moaning echo of the sedan losing the battle against the water rushing in, taking the car under. The waking nightmare is jarred to an end with the slam of a door below, and I scramble to my feet and check to make sure my eyes aren't watering.

My palm leaves my face and my eyes open in time to meet his eyes staring up at me from the bottom of the steps. The familiar vision stabs at my chest. Theo Rothschild's eyes look just like his twin sister's did, a steely gray-blue that could mirror the sky or water, only the joy I always found in hers is replaced with resentment and pain.

"Change your mind and decide to transfer out?" Theo drops his hands in the pockets of his dress pants and leans against the wall of the stairwell, which suddenly feels smaller.

I match his stare and ignore the thunder in my chest threatening to knock me off my feet.

"No."

I try to hold my mouth in the same straight line his is showing. Theo Rothschild hates me. Yet I have been in love with him since I arrived at Welles five years ago. We rarely spoke to one another before that night, our worlds two entirely different realms. Anika was the bridge. It's not why I became her friend, but he would never believe that. And now she's gone. Because I couldn't save her.

Theo's mouth ticks up on one side and his eyes blink slowly as he looks down to his palm, pulling a small tin of mints from his pocket. He stands up straight, leaving the wall's support, and pulls a mint out and places it in his mouth. He begins to flip the lid closed with his thumb but pauses with a grin. He holds the mint between his teeth and for some reason, it looks threatening. He lets the small metal lid fall open again and holds the tin out toward me, glancing up with one arched brow.

My eyes move to the offering then back up to his waiting expression. This feels like a test.

"No, thank you," I say, just wanting to move past him and out the door so I can drown my pain without his observation and opinion. He doesn't move immediately, instead holding the tin out for a few long seconds as his teeth crunch down on the mint in his mouth and his stare holds me captive.

"My apologies. Didn't mean to interrupt . . . whatever it is you do here." He flips the tin closed and drops it in his pocket along with his hand. His head tilted to one side, gravity pulls his hair across his forehead, ghosting his eyes. Hostility radiates from him despite the cool demeanor he is working so hard to perfect.

I'm sorry! She was my favorite person. I wanted to be just like her. Please forgive me. Talk to me! We could help each other. I hurt, just like you hurt. Please!

I can no longer take the heat of his presence, and rather than answer, or worse, cry, I dash past him and push out the main door to head out onto the lawn and toward the aquatic center, where I plan on hiding out in the dark locker room until I'm forced to get back to this life.

Chapter 2

Theo Rothschild

By the time I push open the stairwell door, all I can see of Lily is her long brown hair swaying against her back and the flash of white from her knee-high socks.

I never noticed her before Anika introduced us. Maybe we've had a class together but I'm not sure. It was probably my fault—my lack of awareness, as Anika used to say—that Lily and I never spoke before the party down at the abandoned barn. My sister had to drag her to it. And even then, it took Lily two hours to finally come sit out by the bonfire with me.

She was shy. I'm . . . *definitely not.* A few beers in, I figured I'd do my sister a favor and talk to the girl for a while. If getting to know me was that big of a deal to her, I didn't want to let her down and make her think I was a total dick.

Then the strangest thing happened. Once we started talking, we couldn't stop. I sobered up during the time because I had no interest in leaving our conversation to get more to drink. Lily didn't drink at all. I probably would have made fun of that if my sister hadn't warned me to be gentle and openminded. Actually, *polite* was the word she used. Because of Anika, I had one of the best nights of my life. Lily and I talked music, college, travel dreams, childhood memories—at least the good ones. There were things she was guarded about, that I could sense were off the table, which I understood. I've got shit of my own. But the more hours that ticked by, the more I relaxed and let my mind embrace the idea that maybe, someday—*someday soon*—I'd share some of that baggage with Lily in hopes she would share hers back.

She had light brown eyes that played tricks on me all night, teasing me with the bits of green and gold. Her hair was pulled into ponytails on either side of her head, and the strands that didn't fit constantly tickled her face. Her mouth was wide, and when she smiled it lit her up with this unmistakable energy. I liked the way she kept pulling her sweatshirt sleeves down over her hands to keep them warm, and the way her ankles showed under her rolled-up jeans and sockless shoes. She was everything my sister talked her up to be. She was also so much more.

Then they got in that fucking car.

Lily was supposed to be my sister's friend. Instead, she was one more person who let Anika down. I let her down, too, but not that I didn't try. Anika never wanted to talk to me the way I wished she would have. Maybe I should have pushed harder. Maybe then I wouldn't wonder if it was really an accident when she veered off that bridge last spring or if she drove through the barricades on purpose. She shouldn't have been behind the wheel. That's one detail I know for sure. Everyone fucking knows thanks to a very public medical history report and the damn gossipy local press. The story was so salacious, Boston picked it up. Scandals like underage drinking at boarding school parties go viral. Add in a stolen car hijacked by a seventeen-year-old girl with a serious seizure disorder and you have the perfect formula for one of those four-part miniseries.

I wonder if Lily ever thought about not coming back. I guess it's easier to show up at a place that thinks you're a hero. She probably doesn't get the same empty glares I get, the frozen O-shaped mouths that don't know what to say to console me. I've been here for less than twenty-four hours and already the murmurs have picked up steam.

His sister just died. How can he come back to this place?

I heard they have a terrible home life. I wonder if they really got along or if it was just pretend?

Why didn't he save her? Where was he when she got in that car? I didn't know she was so sick! He never should have left her alone.

I pinch the bridge of my nose and squeeze my eyes shut as I back into the stairwell and let the door slam closed, the echo of the metal falling into place loud enough to shake the voices from my head. If I'm going to survive this place—this year—it must be business as usual.

I'll be lucky if a single company invites me for an internship interview this year. It's the only reason I came back to this place. A Welles recommendation gets me closer to going to college somewhere far away from my mother and her never-ending toxic relationship with my stepfather. It's hard to not think of Neil as *our* stepfather. That's what he was for so long. Anika and I uttered that word with every bit of disdain we could, the kind reserved for the evil stepmothers in fairytales. Neil put them to shame every time he was in our house. The man emanates a certain air of evil. I don't know what he did to Anika exactly. As her brother, I probably should have insisted on knowing. Maybe I didn't push for details to protect myself—or maybe I did it to keep Anika innocent. Whatever it was that happened over our last Christmas break at home, it was enough for our mom to finally kick him out of the house.

All I need is one good year. Football will help. Not because we're good but because extracurriculars count for more when classes are so rigorous. I only need to convince the coach I'm ready to play.

I give my shoulders one final roll and blow out the toxic anger that continually simmers in my chest, drawing in clean air that I hope makes me seem convincing for the next few minutes.

Coach Wallace's family lives at Hayden Hall as the dorm parents. Of course, his family's quarters are more like a first-floor penthouse than the tight dorm rooms we all live in. It's one of the ways Welles can get such amazing professors and coaches. His family lives here rent free, and his daughters will get a Welles education for nearly nothing.

I rap my knuckles against the door then straighten my tie. I got used to life without this uniform over the long summer. Every year I'm here, the chokehold is tighter.

I'm practicing my opening line mentally as the door opens and I make it as far as, "Coach, hi. I'm sorry to barge—" before I realize the face I'm staring at is an entirely different man than I was expecting.

"Peters? Or . . . one second." This man is about six inches taller than Coach Wallace and about sixty pounds lighter. He has a full head of hair where Wallace had none, and a forearm that flexes with the simplest movements. He pulls glasses from the collar of his shirt and slips them on as he glances down at a clipboard in his hand. "It should be Peters, but you don't look like a lineman, so Raskin?"

"No, I'm Rothschild. I mean . . . Theo. Wait. Where is

Coach Wallace?" I shake my head, wondering if I'm dreaming this.

"He decided to take a job at a public school. And Rothschild, let's see. Oh, right. Yes, you're the young man who—"

I cut him off before he says something that will, I'm sure, disrespect my sister's death and everything we've been through.

"I'm the tight end. Senior, sixth form?" I'm still confused as to who this guy is. And why am I instantly threatened and trying to sell myself to him. If my expression is half as affronting as it feels, I must look pissed as hell.

"Right, Theo. I'm sorry. This is probably not what you were expecting. You know what? Come on in. Peters isn't due to be here for ten minutes yet." He opens the door wider, and I step in still feeling a little dazed by it all. Nothing in this apartment is the same as it was last year. Every trace of my old coach is gone. I didn't know he was leaving. We weren't incredibly close, but I'd like to think I would have heard about the staffing change.

Nobody thought I'd be back.

I walk toward the dining room, glad to see that at least the layout hasn't changed. I'm about to pull a chair out to sit in when another guy my age steps into the room from the other end. He's wearing one of our jerseys already, and I know they haven't been issued yet, which means he's someone with special privileges. I'm guessing by the near identical build and height; this is the new coach's son.

He sets his soda can on the table and wipes the moisture from his palm against his side before reaching across the table.

"Hey, man. Didn't mean to sneak up on you. I'm James. I've been sitting in on all the intro meetings with him so I can get to know the team." We're still shaking and staring at each other when Coach walks in.

"Right. Uhm, sorry. I'm Theo. And you're . . ."

"Coach's kid. Yeah. I know, but I swear I work my ass off." James smiles, guilt dimpling the corners of his mouth. He read my mind, and I'm sure he senses a lot of entitlement whispers behind his back. He seems all right.

"We're all a bunch of entitled assholes here, so they'll move on to resenting something else by next week," I quip, noticeably easing his tension. It seems to go a long way with the new coach standing to my right, too, as he pats my shoulder with a heavy hand before gesturing for a shake.

"Dave Fuentes," he says, his shake firm. I'm still skeptical . . . and thrown off my game. I had a plan coming in here, but now?

I pull a chair out and Coach sits next to me, turning his sideways. His son takes the seat directly across, and I glance at him, smiling through my teeth.

"Oh, should I— Is this private?" He points to his dad, then to me. Really, though, might as well get this out of the way before he gets fed the entire tale of me and my life through the Welles rumor mill.

"Nah, it's fine." I relax into my chair and fold my hands in my lap. Crossing my legs, I twist to face Coach more head on. "It seems you've been filled in on my situation. And I know I was not here for the summer camps and haven't been on the text strings or in the email group."

"Understandable," he cuts in. "You're still a part of this team. I mean, I hope that's what we're getting at here?"

I laugh out and my shoulders drop down more. He gets it.

"It would mean a lot to me." I nod.

"Of course. You'll have to compete for your starting spot like everyone else, including this asshat over here," he pauses, nodding toward his son, who rolls his eyes. Yeah, both are growing on me.

"Absolutely." Having played the last three years and started at tight end every year, I'm not too worried. Welles competes against the other privates and boarding schools in the Mass Prep League. Competition isn't exactly fierce, though we could maybe win the title this year with James throwing the ball. Our last quarterback was about half his size.

"And listen, I know I'm the new guy here. You guys probably had a tight relationship with your former coach. But whatever you want to talk about—*or not talk about*—" He stands, and I follow his lead, our eyes meeting in a mutual understanding of what he means. "My door is always open. It's just me, James, and my wife, Penny. Our house is your home, anytime you need it."

"You mean our dorm apartment," James corrects. Without pause, Coach tosses the pen from his clipboard at his son, hitting him in the chest.

"See? Asshat."

I laugh through a brief smile. This feels good. Maybe being here is good for my future *and* my present.

"I appreciate that, Coach."

We shake hands again.

"Running a little seven-on-seven today. If you feel up to coming out, we'd love to have you. Tryouts and practice don't officially start until next week." My chest tightens at first, and I hesitate, not sure I'm quite ready for camaraderie today, but James interrupts my doubt.

"I'll pick you first. We'll make history." I glance at him in time to catch his smirk, and that tightness morphs into a dose of adrenalin.

"Screw that, I'll make him captain if he comes out today,"

Coach interjects. James' mouth hangs open in pretend shock and I let out a genuine laugh.

"Well, now I've gotta come out, don't I? Can't let my fellow history-maker down. I got you." I reach across the table, and we slap hands twice as if it's something we've always done. There's immediate comfort there. A brotherhood.

It will never replace Anika.

Chapter 3

Lily

I barely slept. I spent most of the night looking at the other girls' corkboards and beds and desktops. They're cluttered with photos and postcards and torn ticket stubs—memories. I don't think Morgan changed her pinboard from last year. She just took it down and rehung it above her new bed. My walls are bare. Even my comforter and pillow are bland and without character. It's as though I purposely work to leave zero footprint of my existence. I'm aware of it more than I used to be. I'm trying not to dishonor Anika's lack of existence by being too present in my own.

I'm not sure how the other girls are doing it, how they're . . . *coping*.

Anika is in so many of their photos. I only have a few with her. We weren't friends as long. And the more time that passes I wonder if we really *were* friends. It all happened so fast. Our talks morphed into morning coffees and then lunches and study groups. Eventually, I found myself invited to things with the three of them. Was that simply pity, though? Was I Anika's project?

I'm an outsider here.

My hair still wrapped in a towel from my morning shower, I sit on my prison-like bed clutching my shower caddy as Morgan and Brooklyn get ready for our internship interviews. This is the reason people come to Welles. It's a guaranteed path into whatever career you might want. Ivy Leagues? Yeah, no problem. Politics? For sure.

Until last spring, I wanted to work for *The Affiliate*, Boston's premiere sports magazine. They take one intern from Welles every year. The student from five years ago was just hired as one of the youngest editors on staff right out of college. I'm still going to show up and try, but that fire isn't in me like it was. I guess I feel like I don't deserve this chance.

Anika doesn't get one.

"You're going to be late, Lily. You don't even have your outfit picked out yet." Brooklyn glances my way before walking toward my section of the closet. She begins to shift my hangers in search of suitable interview clothes.

"No. No. No. Lily! Didn't you bring anything professional with you?" Her hand on her hip, the straight edges of her suit jacket jut out like knives.

"I have dresses." My brow pulls in at the realization that my dresses look more like Sunday church wear than power meeting executive attire.

"Come here," she huffs.

I set my shower caddy to the side and stand, letting my towel unravel. When I reach Brooklyn she eyes me sideways and audibly sighs.

"What?" I'm starting to feel like going back to bed is the best option.

"You're going to have to dry that!" She points to my head, and I look up, practically under my eyelids.

"I was thinking of twisting it into a bun or a braid." *To be honest, I was thinking about bombing my interview and just coasting my way out of this place.*

"Here, put this on. Then sit at your desk. You are not giving up. Not this early." Brooklyn has a dominant tone that makes me obey. I slip on the silky gray blouse and catch the black pants she tosses against my chest.

"I don't have shoes for these," I warn, slipping out of my sleep shorts and into the slim-fitting pants. They're definitely tighter on me than they are on her, and I'm instantly self-conscious about how things look from behind.

"These will be a little big, but you can stuff tissue in the toes." She drops a pair of closed-toed black Manolo Blahniks on the bed next to me and I gulp. I'm pretty sure my food plan costs less than these shoes. She drops a tissue box at my side next then takes a seat behind me, sitting up on her knees. I'm about to protest all of this when I'm cut off by the sound of a hair dryer and the sharp thwack of a detangler against my scalp.

"Start stuffing," she orders, pointing over my shoulder at the tissues and shoes.

I do my best to make the shoes fit, and after an aggressive blowout of my hair, I feel a little more willing to follow through with the interview process.

"Here, you should wear it for luck," Morgan says, finally getting involved with Brooklyn's project—*me*. She hands me the thin silver bracelet with a clover leaf pendant that Anika gave me last year. I'm sure it's ridiculously expensive, just like the shoes, but this piece of jewelry means more to me than any value could ever capture. Anika gave it to me about a week before we went to that party. She knew I liked it.

Standing and spinning slowly with my hands out at my sides, I expect my dorm mates to tell me I look like a kid playing dress up, but instead, Morgan lets out a slow whistle.

By the time I turn to face her, she's nodding with folded arms and eyeing me approvingly.

"Really?" I quirk a brow.

"If you don't get an internship offer, you're definitely getting asked out."

"Gross, Morgan!" Brooklyn pushes her arm and forces her off balance. "We're not all into dating *way* above our age range like you!"

Morgan has a thing for older men. At least, she did last year. I'm not sure whether the hook-up rumors between her and Coach Wallace were true or not, but since she's the one who always dropped the hints, I'm guessing there was some truth to it.

As complimentary as they're both being, I still feel like a little kid compared to them. They've been exposed to so much of the world, and I've seen the highlights of Ohio and everything along the highway between Cleveland and the outskirts of Boston. I haven't even ventured into the actual city on my own. I'm afraid to take the train without an organized class trip to guide me, and I've only had my car since last year. Driving has little appeal since the accident. I was forced to drive myself to school this year because my mother refused to take me, and she forbade my stepfather, Drew, to do it. My stepbrother, Levi, is sixteen and their precious little rule follower, so I didn't even bother to ask him—*not that I'd be able to stand nine hours in the car with him and his ego.*

"You do look nice," Brooklyn says, her hands soft on my shoulders as she brings her chin down to rest by my neck as we both look into the full-length mirror on the back of our door.

"Thanks," I eek out, managing a half smile to go with it.

I follow them both out our door and struggle to keep up due to my ill-fitting shoes. Lines are already forming outside the auditorium. I'm sweating for all sorts of reasons—*I don't look like myself, my confidence is non-existent, people are looking at me as if I'm a celebrity, and I feel guilty for getting to be here.*

Oh, and one more thing: Theo Rothschild is two feet to my left.

"I was really surprised he came back for his senior year." I'm not sure who half-whispers that statement behind us, but both Theo and I hear it; I can tell by the way his jaw clenches.

"Hey, Theo. Good to see you," Morgan says, stepping across me and moving in to give him a hug. *How is this so easy for her to do?* Maybe years of knowing each other helps. Or the fact she was rescued and not the person doing the saving. She's not the person who failed his sister. *I am.*

"Hey, Morg. How are your parents?" His voice is smooth, caring—the same one he used with me that night as we talked. *Before.*

Our eyes meet briefly over Morgan's shoulder as they hug. I swallow down the discomfort that chokes me as the flash of hate colors his expression, forcing me to look down at my feet stuffed in shoes that aren't meant for them.

"They're all right. You know the Bentleys. Always something to brag about." Morgan's parents are utterly dysfunctional but incredibly rich. I don't know her well enough to be certain, but from the little I do know I get the sense that she came to Welles to escape her family as much as I did.

"I was surprised I didn't see your dad on the list for interviews today. Not taking any interns this year?" Theo's gaze drifts to me as he speaks, and I hate that he catches me looking back. I blink rapidly and turn to face the line of students ahead of me.

"That's because he assumes he has his intern already

locked down. But she's going to see what else is out there today and maybe he'll be stuck scraping the bottom of the barrel."

I was wondering why Morgan isn't simply taking her family's internship. They own a company that owns lots of little companies. For a business-minded person, an internship with the Bentleys is a golden ticket.

"That's a family fight I'll pay to have a front-row seat to," Theo says through laughter.

He's so light, so comfortable. I refuse to turn around and ruin it by making eye contact with him again.

"You won't need to buy a seat. The world will hear, I'm sure. Carl Bentley doesn't really have an inside voice."

They both chuckle, but I can hear the nerves behind Morgan's. The lines move forward, so I focus my attention on the only table I'm interested in. On the tips of my toes, I size up how each intake person appears. Business suits are usually for the law firms and major corporations, so I drift to the right through the crowd of students to scope out the remaining tables. The military uniforms are easy to spot, so I keep weaving through people, trying not to notice the way everyone is looking at me. My superhero status makes it a little easier to bear the brunt of a crowd, but I'm still uncomfortable in my own skin.

I spot the cardinal red hat first, which pulls me in for a closer look. *The Affiliate's* branding is that red along with silver and black. When I get a glimpse of the polo shirt on the man holding a clipboard, I suck in an excited breath. *This is it!*

It takes me a few more seconds to work my way toward him, but I finally do, practically tripping toward *The Affiliate* table in Morgan's damn shoes. I manage to save myself from landing palms first into the man wearing the company colors.

Glimpsing his name tag—*Scott*—as my eyes drift up to his face, I straighten my spine and hold out my hand for him to shake. He grins, amused, *I hope*.

"Sorry, I'm a little eager. I'm Lily Beachem, and I have been reading *The Affiliate* since I could tread water. Your coverage of the last US Championships for swim and dive was exceptional. Truly." My heart is thumping in my chest. I know I'm babbling and oozing compliments that make me sound like a fangirl, but it's all from the heart.

"Lily, nice to meet you. You're a reader, then?"

We're still shaking hands, so I loosen my grip and roll my shoulders to pull myself together a bit.

"Yes. Your magazine is the reason I want to get into sports reporting. I love the idea of getting to write long-form pieces. Your feature on Jenny Crane last month . . . *wow*."

Scott smiles genuinely at my answer and holds the clipboard against his chest, crossing his arms over it. I should feel relief at this connection, but it's ruined all too fast by the snicker masked by a fake cough behind me. I glance over my shoulder out of reflex, knowing who I'll see.

"Sorry, I was laughing at something else. Continue," Theo says, waving his hand dismissively.

One tiny interaction with him and my excitement has turned into shame, my belly feeling as if it's full of sludge.

"You're in luck, Lily. Last spot!" Scott finishes scribbling in my name as I turn my attention back to him, and he rips the final ticket from his booklet and hands it to me. "I think you'll do quite well," he adds, leaning in. "Our interviewing editor is the one who wrote the Jenny Crane piece."

Scott winks as he steps back then quickly busies himself packing up their table. I wander a several paces beyond the table with the ticket pinched between my thumb and index finger, my confidence muffled inside my chest, wanting to break free.

"You're fucking kidding me. You took the last spot?" Theo's disdain penetrates my numbness and I turn slowly to see him walking toward me.

I didn't know you wanted to interview here. It's not my fault I got the last ticket. Do you want me to see if we can go in together?

Instead of words, my mouth falls agape and my body flushes. Theo's eyes bore into me, a mixture of ire and sadness. I can't tell if he's about to shout or cry.

"Unbelievable," he finally utters under his breath, looking to the side and stuffing his hands into his pockets.

He's wearing a gray suit with a crisp white shirt, a deep blue tie cutting down the center of his chest. He looks dapper, as if he's pulled from the pages of a fifty's magazine, when men combed their hair just right and had chiseled chins and swagger.

"I'm sor—"

He holds an open palm up at my face and pulls his cell phone from his other pocket, pressing the screen with his thumb. He morphs his hand-gestured-stop-sign into a fist then brings his hand to the bridge of his nose, pinching it as he turns.

"Hey, Mom. You're not going to believe this . . ."

He begins to walk away, probably to take his conversation about what a bitch I am for stealing more from him away from my ears. Before he makes it more than a few steps, though, something takes over my body and my mouth, and I lunge forward, placing my hand on his arm and wrapping my fingers around his bicep. I can feel his muscle tense, even under the thick fabric of his suit jacket.

"Take mine." I hold the ticket out and he stares at it, his mouth stopping mid-word to his mom on the phone.

"Really. I can go to a different table, a different interview. It's not that important to me, but it is to you. So just . . . take it." I shake the paper, my heart crushing.

It's the most important thing I have left.

Theo's brow draws in.

"I'll call you back, Mom." He ends his call and slips his phone back into his pocket, taking the ticket I'm offering in his other hand.

"Why?" He waves it between us slowly, taunting me.

I shrug.

"Because it's . . . not that important to me."

"Liar," he fires back.

I open my mouth but snap it shut again, wanting to guard my words. I suck my lips in and look to my right, to the shrinking lines of students signing up for their futures. To the remaining tables manned by men in suits.

"Fine, it is. But it's more important to you. I want to do something—"

"Don't say nice," he breaks in.

I swallow hard, this time choking down my building frustration.

Regret seeps into my subconscious, and as I stare at the ticket in his hand, I bite my tongue. I'm about to snatch it back when he pockets it and lifts his chin, drawing my eyes to his stern face.

"You better hurry; the other slots are filling up." He nods toward the dwindling lines, and I follow his view, not even one appealing. By the time I turn back to face him, his back is to me and he's walking away—toward what should have been *my* interview. And the guilt I was trying to ease is still there like an open wound festering in my belly.

Chapter 4

Theo

My pocket buzzes, probably my mom calling back after my quick end to our call. I don't really feel like talking now. I could tell Mom wasn't alone. She's been meeting Neil for coffee more than I'd like her to. She always waves it off as politeness and healthy separation. The only news I'm interested in is a final divorce.

I press the silence button in my pocket and step up on the stage to the far back corner where the red and black banners are hung for *The Affiliate* table. A man and woman are speaking in hushed tones and the woman pauses, holding up a finger to me and mouthing one moment through her smile.

She looks like Anika. Her lips are crimson. Her nose has a small, jeweled stud.

I'm not one to get nervous for things like interviews, but the weight of this seems to be driving my stress up a notch. I feel my pant leg waving against my knee and glance down to catch my leg vibrating with nervous energy. It makes me chuckle to myself and I shift my weight as the woman clears her throat to get my attention.

"No offense, but you don't look like a *Lily*." She arches a brow.

I pull my lips in for a tight, guilty smile before taking the ticket from my pocket and moving forward to lay it on the table.

"Keen observation," I say, putting on my most charming voice. She squints one eye and studies me, less amused than I hoped.

I scratch at my head, mussing up the perfect part I spent way too long on an hour ago. Wincing, I scrunch up my shoulders and come clean . . . *ish*.

"Lily knew I really wanted to interview with you, and she's the kind of person who likes grand gestures of kindness. She rather insisted I take the last spot." I offer a crooked smile and breathe out slowly with relief as the woman across from me seems to ease back in her seat and smile.

"Well, that's awfully kind of her. You know, my colleague texted me to look out for her. He was impressed with their conversation. You must be an important person for her to give up something she seems to have coveted." The woman folds her hands together on top of the notepad as she leans back, and the man sitting next to her smirks, tilting his head to the side as he stares at me.

They think this is about a crush.

"You'd have to ask her what she thinks of me. I wouldn't want to assume." I swallow, unsure whether I successfully danced around that topic. I could not care less what Lily Beachem thinks of me. She owes me this spot. She owes Anika.

"Well, let's get to it, then. Mr.—"

"Rothschild. Theo Rothschild. I'm a four-year varsity tight end, well . . . assuming I make the team this year. I feel confident, though. I have a card with my online portfolio address if you'd like to look at my writing." I slip my wallet from my pocket and slip out two cards. I had these made up over the winter break last year, back when I thought maybe I'd spend my summer interning somewhere instead of guarding my mother's fragile mental state after my sister's funeral.

The woman leans forward with a half-smile and slides the card toward her, eyes darting down to read it briefly before looking back at me.

"Nice to meet you, Theo. I'm Abby Quinlan. I'm one of the editors at *The Affiliate*. And this is Todd Eschland, head of advertising." I reach forward to shake both of their hands.

"Nice to meet you both."

My pulse is finally easing, my body growing more comfortable under the hot lights of the theater stage. The weather in Massachusetts is always too unpredictable this time of year for them to hold this event outside, but why we couldn't do these interviews in classrooms beats me. Maybe there's something behind the glare of the lights, a type of interview technique meant to weed out the weak. Seems unfair to those of us wearing full suits and ties cinched around our necks.

"So, you're more interested in the editorial side of the house, I take it?" Abby says, glancing to her right and making eye contact with Todd.

"I think that's where my strengths are, yes. I have some experience reporting on student government and winter sports here at Welles. And I'm sure every member of the writing department would—"

"It's just that you have a certain something," Todd interrupts.

My mouth snaps shut, and my stomach twinges. I don't

really want to be a salesman, but if this is my only way in, I won't turn it town.

"Like an X-factor?" I joke.

They both laugh.

"In a way, I suppose. What I mean, Theo, is I like your confidence. And our side of the house isn't so different from the editorial side. Sure, we must be guarded about how we spin things, but we get to help brands shape their stories through campaigns. I have a feeling you might be good at this. I'd love to have you come down to the offices next week and maybe we could explore it more?" Todd is holding the card I gave him sideways, tapping the edge on the table, and I can tell in a quick scan of their faces that this is the path I'm getting. It happened so fast, but it's better than nothing, and ad reps make a lot of money.

"I'd love to. Thank you," I say, reaching for his hand again. We both shake and stand at the same time, and my heart is thrumming behind my ribs with a touch of excitement, even if there's some fear of the unknown thrown into the mix.

"Lily! Come on over!" A voice behind me breaks through the whirlwind I've been tossing around in, and I turn to see the man who was at the main table out front waving a hand toward the girl I just sold as kind-hearted to my interviewers. My mouth could not be dryer.

Lily is hovering around some information technology company's table, and as much as I shouldn't care how out of place she looks there, it's impossible to ignore the nagging voice telling me to be the better person.

Plastering on my best fake grin, I hold up a hand in a wave of peace. It will be a temporary truce, long enough for her to get her shot at this table. Being aggressive and outgoing are not in Lily's makeup. There's a reason I didn't know much about her until Anika forced us to talk. I have my doubts that she'll be able to relax for this interview. Still, the thought that she and I could be spending an entire semester interning at the same building in downtown Boston has my leg twitching again.

"Here's my card, Theo. Give me a call tomorrow and we'll set something up. I have a good feeling about you," Todd says, urging my attention back to him. I take the card and tuck it in my wallet then fight every urge not to stare Lily in the eyes and warn her off my territory. I can feel her nearness somehow without even looking.

"You must be the one Scott texted me about," Abby says, standing and reaching out for Lily's hand.

"I should go—" I turn abruptly, maybe a part of me wanting to run from the scene, but instead of making a smooth exit, I elbow Lily in the ribs. Hard. My bone sinks in, and I have a feeling I knocked the wind out of her.

Confirmed by the way she's coughing. Or rather, wheezing.

"Oh, my God! Lily, are you okay?" Abby rushes around the table to help Lily stay on her feet. Her shoes seem to have fallen off amid our collision, and tissues poke out from the insides. I bet she borrowed those.

"Are you okay?"

Todd is squatting and holding her shoulders, staring into her eyes while she nods and makes this god-awful sound like a vacuum with a sock stuck in the hose.

"I nailed her in the ribs, not the head," I say, not really thinking my words through before blurting them out. I can read the asshole-meter on high in the faces suddenly staring back at me.

I wince and shake my head.

"I only meant we need to get her arms up, open her lungs.

She lost her wind. Not gonna get much out of her pupils to help with that." My hard stare catches Todd's and I realize my big opportunity may have gotten smaller just now thanks to my inability to not correct my future boss.

"I'm good," Lily chokes out. She scrambles to her feet and folds her hands behind her neck, drawing in air as her eyes pass over me.

Sorry. I really didn't mean that.

My thoughts never make it to my mouth, and we instead exchange what amounts mostly to sneers.

"I hope your sales skills don't include physical altercations," Abby tosses over her shoulder as she moves back to the interview table. She's trying to lighten the mood, so I play along.

"Only if we need to close the deal and the client is being stubborn." I glance Todd's way. He only squints one eye and purses his lips.

"And I also bring humor to my skillset, ha ha *ha . . .*"

My self-deprecation does more to melt the ice forming around my chances for a future with *The Affiliate*, and when everyone—even Lily—lets out an easy laugh, I relax my spine from the Boy Scout knot it was twisting into.

"Oh, my shoes—"

Lily's eyes dart around, searching for them, and before *The Affiliate* people see the scrunched-up tissues about to blow toward their feet, I snatch them and tuck them in my pocket.

"Seems I knocked you out of them. Here," I say, scooping them up and setting them on the ground by her bare feet. Her big toenails are sky blue, and the others are painted white. Nice that she seems able to ease her mind enough for trivial things like that.

"Thank you," she says, reaching toward me but letting

her hand fall back to her side.

"Least I can do," I say through a tight grin. Our gazes tangle for a long pause but I break the hold before anyone else catches on that Lily and I have a painful, messy history.

I manage to shake Todd's hand one more time to make sure we part on good terms, and I run my finger along the sharp edge of his card in my pocket all the way back to my dorm. Cameron has started to make himself comfortable, his bed pushed under the window, which is cracked as he smokes a blunt and fills our room with a stench so obvious I wonder how he hasn't been expelled this morning. Then I think about the facts—he's willing to room with the guy whose sister died months ago, the guy who's probably going to get straight A's without even trying because who's going to fail the guy with the dead sister? Nobody's going to say shit to us. I'm our free pass. For everything.

"Give me a drag," I snap in his direction, and he hands over the blunt. I suck in one draw, holding it long enough to feel the smoke scratch at my throat and beg to be coughed out. I hand it back without giving him the satisfaction of showing off his smug grin. I don't get high often. Rather, I didn't—before. But after the day I've had, and the semester ahead of me, being high seems a lot more reasonable.

I head toward the door, not high yet but buzzed on the anticipation.

"You just got back. Where are you going? We've got practice in an hour." He coughs through his words, and I wonder if he's going to feel the hits he's about to take out on that field. Full pads only dull so much.

"I've got something I need to do. I'll meet you there."

I let the door slam closed behind me, then continue down the hall and stairs before crossing the lawn on my way to Hayden Hall to get Cinderella a real pair of fucking shoes.

Chapter 5

Lily

I'm officially the last student in the auditorium. I wasted the first twenty minutes of my interview—well the first twenty after getting my lungs punched out by Theo's elbow—gushing over Abby Quinlan *in front* of Abby Quinlan.

Then, once she put together my name with my obsession with swimming, it didn't take long for my own story to come to the surface. I'm less able to talk endlessly about that, but ever-the-reporter, Abby kept digging. I said more than I wanted to, but I still managed to hold my memories close to the vest.

There are some things I don't know that I will ever be able to talk about with anyone other than the therapist my mom put me in touch with the first week I was home after the accident. And even with Dr. Tom Brown—whose name I'm deeply skeptical of since our sessions are always online and via text—I tend to gloss over details. I say I'm feeling better even when I'm not. And my text-bot therapist asks me to rate my depression on a scale of one to ten. I've found that saying I'm a three is like magic. Messed up enough to not be lying, but not dire enough to need any true intervention. And thanks to my mom's epic apathy toward me in general, I don't have to talk about adjusting my meds. Nothing on my menu of emotional tools meets my needs, but none of it works against me, so I simply maintain at whatever fucked up place I'm in.

"I really hope you get a lot out of your time with us this semester, Lily." Abby reaches across the table for my hand, and I give her my shaking one.

"Wait. Does this mean—"

They want me?

I got the internship?

What about Theo?

"If you think you can manage your swimming and studies along with the rigorous deadlines we have, we'd love to have you on staff this fall. It won't be glamorous, but—"

"Yes!" She could offer me a job cleaning toilets and I would take it. I stand and shake her hand with more vigor. "Oh, my God, yes! I can manage. I'll manage anything for this."

I might not even swim this year.

"Great. We'll call you this week to get things set up. Oh, and maybe you two can talk about carpooling or taking the train together?" She glances over my shoulder, and I mentally prep myself for Theo's face. I had a feeling this was too good to be void of pitfalls.

"Carpool . . . right . . ." Theo is staring at the ground, his jacket gone but a familiar pair of gym shoes in his right hand.

He looks up with a sloppy smile lifting one cheek higher than the other. He salutes them both, which feels a little cavalier, but I guess he is a few dozen feet away. I turn back to thank them one more time then slide in Morgan's shoes across the stage to the ramp so I don't have to pick my feet up at all.

"Why are you here?" I whisper once I'm close enough for Theo to hear.

"Princess needs her shoes," he says, chuckling to himself.

What the fuck is that? Princess?

"Were you in my closet? Did Morgan let you in?" I snatch my shoes from his grip, and he stumbles back as if I've offended him. He lifts his arm briefly and I catch a wafting scent that clears up why he's being so nice. "Are you . . . high?"

He holds up his hand and pinches the air to signal a little.

"Awesome. You get that way before or after you punched me in the ribs?" I can feel a bruise forming where he elbowed me.

Theo isn't high enough to avoid rolling his eyes at me.

"I was trying to be nice. You make it so fucking hard, you know?" He leans against the last row of seats in the auditorium and crosses his arms while his eyes rake over me. After a full two seconds, he spits out a short laugh.

"What?" I step out of Morgan's shoes and stuff my feet into my Nikes.

"You make it hard. I mean, that's not wrong. You *do* make it hard." His arched brow is waiting along with his stare when I flip my hair back and look him in the eyes. My brain instantly tells me to look at his crotch, but I manage to ignore that reflex.

"Christ, Theo." I look away, focusing instead on gathering up my things and tucking Morgan's shoes in my bag. My cheeks burn from his words, and I'm sure I'm nine shades of pink and red.

"Look, all I'm saying is I'm not always an asshole. I am

capable of doing nice things." He steps forward and pushes the heavy door open for me to walk out. I eye him as I pass, acting as if I worry he'll slam the door on me. Really, though? I'm thinking about Theo Rothschild being hard, about *me* making him that way. I erase the thoughts almost as quickly as they enter my mind.

We walk in sync and in silence until we reach the place where the pathway diverges toward his dorm and mine, and because I'm weak, *maybe,* I utter a quick thanks as we part.

"It's grief."

I pause my steps but keep my back to him for a breath before turning. When I finally do, his eyes seem suddenly clearer.

"I don't know how to do . . . *this.*" His hands stretch out at his sides, palms up. We stare at each other, two dozen feet apart—wordless. *Maybe I should try getting high?*

"Did it help?" He knows what I mean.

His body shakes once with a silent laugh and he presses his tongue against the back of his teeth, his mouth smiling on one side only.

"Not really." He shrugs and shakes his head before holding up a hand in a half-hearted farewell. "Sorry about the rib thing. I guess we'll be working together this semester so maybe we can find a way—"

He takes a step backward and looks up at the sky with another silent laugh.

"To get along?" I finish for him.

He drops his chin and any trace of amusement or regret, or effort, is gone. His stare is blank, eyes cold, and mouth a perfectly straight line.

"To avoid each other."

He blinks twice before turning and walking toward his

dorm. I hug my roommate's shoes to my chest along with my portfolio bag. My ribs feel sore to the touch as I squeeze my arms tighter, and I mentally picture a deep blue bruise on my skin.

I wonder what Anika would think . . . of everything.

Chapter 6

Theo

Football practice did what I hoped.

For two hours, I thought of nothing other than my route, how many more pushups and up-downs I had, or miles left in our run. I still don't love it like some of these guys do, but I'm grateful for it. And I'm good.

If I could extend the distraction of practice for another hour or two, I would. But I don't think James would be up for that. His dad wasn't kidding when he said he doesn't play favorites or make life easy for his son. He had expectations for him that were levels beyond my game. I get the impression that James might be a bit of a phenom.

I'm lost in my thoughts, still not fully dressed, when someone throws a towel at my head.

"Hey!" I snap.

Cameron holds up two palms in apology. His eyes are so red. He smoked most of the day away before practice. I'm shocked he didn't simply curl up on the forty-yard line and nap. He's a functioning stoner, I guess.

"You were off somewhere. We getting dinner or what?"

He flings his locker door open, and the sharp bang is irritating.

"I could eat," James says from behind us.

The two of them spend a minute tapping knuckles and congratulating each other on a great first practice while I manage to get my ass off the bench and my feet into my shoes. I slip back into my own universe while they shore up plans for dinner at the main hall, and by the time I'm aware of life again, we're almost there. Just in time to enter one side of the room while Lily and her friends come through the other set of doors.

"Shit," I mumble under my breath.

Morgan's eyes meet mine before I can look away. I'm sunk. That girl, as much as she doesn't want to be like her parents, she can't help the socialite gene that seems to flare at the sight of anyone she knows. She's practically sprinting my direction.

"Theo, who's your friend?" Morgan's arm slides behind my neck, her body nestled next to me. That happened fast.

Naturally. She's spotted James.

"Morgan Bentley, meet the new Welles QB."

Her arm leaves me on cue and her hand juts out toward James as he introduces himself.

"James Fuentes, and I don't have the job quite yet." He's being modest. Even if he wasn't coach's kid he'd still be the best arm to pass through this posh-ass place in years.

I quirk a brow and lean into Morgan so only she can hear me.

"His dad's the coach."

Her head swivels and her eyes flash at that mention, her throat moving with the pride I think she may have just swallowed. There was a lot of talk about Morgan and our last coach. I don't think anything serious ever happened, but I wouldn't be surprised if some lines were crossed. Morgan is a little fucked up thanks to being made part of her parents' dynasty and brand the moment she was born. The country club both of our families belong to in the city tends to breed troublemakers. A lot of Morgan's bad decisions have been driven by her craving for attention. At least, that's what Anika used to say.

"James, nice to meet you. You boys come sit with us. Lily's holding the big table near the windows."

My gaze follows Morgan's directions on instinct, and I'm met with Lily's worried stare.

"We'd love to." The words come out of my mouth before my mind catches up to the consequences of them. I'm supposed to be avoiding Lily, yet all I seem to do is get myself involved with her. She's like this itch I'm compelled to scratch, as if torturing her a little every day keeps me connected to my sister. At this pace, we'll be roommates by Friday.

We move through the food line and finish with full trays. I grab two apples, noticing nobody's getting anything for Lily, and fully aware it's something I can use to needle her. Her gaze follows me from the register all the way to the table, where I take a seat directly across from her. I pick up an apple and roll it in my palm a few times before setting it down in front of her.

"You should eat." I lift a brow and grab my apple, taking a bite and exaggerating the crunch. She pushes the fruit toward me until it rolls.

"I'm not hungry."

"Yeah, seems *someone* punched her in the ribs," Brooklyn pipes in from the end of the table. Ah, the perfect one of this newly formed trio. As similar as Morgan and I have always been, Brooklyn has always acted better than us. Her father is an ambassador or some shit. She's . . . *worldly.* She's fucking annoying, is what she is. I had to explain why I needed Lily's gym shoes this morning, and Brooklyn was the only one there.

"It was an accident." I roll my eyes and take another bite of my apple before pushing the abandoned one back toward Lily. She lets it roll off the end of the table and into her lap, her stare locked on my face the entire time. I chew my bite and feel the anger brewing in my stomach.

"Fine. Starve." I blink my focus to the other end of the table and remind myself that I'm supposed to be avoiding her, not engaging her. A task I'm failing at miserably.

James leans into me after a few seconds of willing myself to pretend Lily is invisible and I catch her eyes on him from my periphery.

"Hey, let's compare schedules." James pulls a folded paper from his back pocket and works it open on the tabletop with one hand, a slice of pizza held to his mouth in his other.

"Dude, our schedules look nothing alike. Is that . . . pottery?" I hold my finger on his third hour as I smirk.

"It was the only fine art still open when I registered. What? Is pottery not cool?" He scans the table, and we all remain silent until Cameron finally chortles. Eventually the entire table cracks up, everyone laughing except Lily. She leans across the table and taps her hand on top of the paper until James looks her way. Their eyes meet for a little longer than a second. It's . . . odd.

"It's a good class. They're just laughing because mostly first years take it." Lily finishes with a crooked smile, a show of sympathy. Why does she have to be so fucking . . . I don't know . . . *nice?*

"Great, so I'll be like—"

"Like their babysitter? Yeah," Brooklyn teases. I snicker

under my breath and Lily shoots me a hard look. Suddenly, she's a lot less nice.

"I'll make you a hot chocolate mug," James says, ignoring the mocking completely and smiling at Lily.

She glances at me briefly, her mouth pinched in the corners in a little F-U as if I'm jealous she's been promised a piece of crap coffee cup.

"Let me see your schedule," she says, moving her complete attention to James. He stands to push his schedule across the table, and I do my best not to give a shit about their budding friendship.

"Oh, you have comparative lit with Sharpe. That's a great class. I had it last form," she says. I was supposed to have that class but decided the work would be too much to handle. People in that class don't spend time at parties.

"You're going to want to change that," I pipe in. I bite the inside of my cheek to punish myself for getting involved.

"Why?" James cranes his neck back to look at me.

Crap.

"It's intense, from what I hear, is all. Might be tough during the season."

"It's nothing you can't handle," Lily says, her words practically overlapping mine. Our eyes meet and James does a quick shift from left to right, probably wondering why *Mom and Dad are fighting.*

"I mean, if you have absolutely no social game, then sure. It's easy to spend your life in a book." I take another bite of my apple and shoot Lily a smug look. She simply blinks in return, and I can sense the rest of the table taking her side. That's fine. I'd rather her think I'm a giant asshole. We'll be less likely to cross paths that way and I won't have to think about how badly my sister wanted us to meet, and how angry I am that Lily let her fucking drown.

"Maybe I should see if I can take a different class?" James pulls his schedule back across the table and sinks into his seat. I feel guilty for stressing him out, but I'm not going to fill his head with false ease, either. It's a hard class. And unless he has a personal tutor—

"I'll help you. It'll be easy," Lily says, as if she's reading my thoughts for clues on ways to torture me.

I take one last bite of my apple and toss it on my tray, no longer interested in the rest of my dinner or this conversation.

"I've got shit to do. I'll see you back at our room later, Cam." I jet from our table and return my tray and toss my food in the trash without looking back once. I'm sure Morgan stood and tried to hug me or some shit to make sure I'm okay. She thinks we're closer than we are, and she likes to play good guy.

Now that I've bailed, I'm not sure where to go. I used to love this time on campus. Early enough in the year for the sun to still be up enough to color things orange, but dark enough to thin out the population. I decide to walk through the yards between the classroom buildings, the grass still green and cushioned under my foot. In a few months, these blankets of green will turn to dry, sharp, dead blades that will soon be blanketed by snow. During one of our wandering late-night walk-and-talks last year, Anika and I discovered an overgrown but never locked door into the basement of the Welles library. On a whim, I decide to see if it's still open. The familiar path here floods me with memories of my sister, how many times she would tell me she was doing fine during our time together. I never pushed for more. I didn't want to know, but I should have. She would never say it out loud—that he hit her, or worse—but there was enough unsaid. I remember when she was in a coma. I remember the first seizures she experienced after her supposed "fall" down the stairs back home. I know in my heart she didn't slip while my mom and I were out buying a Father's Day gift for the man Anika and I hated most.

I reach the door before my mind spirals into the darkest places I try to keep buried. As I tug the handle, I feel it give a millimeter or two, a season of vine growth the only thing holding it shut. I rip away some of the thickest areas and pull with both hands until it gives completely. The musty odor of old books and abandoned desks greets me. I lift the collar of my shirt to cover my nose but head inside the dark room in search of the light switch. Anika and I came in here a few times, but never stayed long. She was afraid of finding rats, which I'm surprised I haven't encountered yet myself.

I make it to the far end and run my hand along the wall adjacent to the stairs, flicking the switches as my palm passes over them. The fluorescent bulbs buzz to life, some of them blinking a few times until fully settling to glow. Everything in here is covered in dust. I blow at a stack of books closest to me and immediately regret the choice as a cloud of what's probably spores clouds in front of me.

Scoping out the rows of shelves and deserted file cabinets, I make my way to another door and twist the handle expecting this one to be locked. It isn't, though, so I step into what looks like an archive of old but well-cared-for books. Shelves run from floor to ceiling and the wood accents in the room more closely mirror the look of the library upstairs.

I feel around for more lights, finding one near what looks like a small office to the right. Illuminated, the space is vast. It's clearly used, the layers of dust plaguing the other area spared in here. Enormous scanning stations sit in the center of the room, one layered with what appear to be maps. This must be where they digitize things that are donated. The

Welles historical archives are better than those of some nearby universities.

I kick out a rolling chair from an enormous mahogany desk and step into the space. Flattening my palms on the desktop, I flex my fingers and scan the room to make sure it's truly empty. My head tilted, I let out a growling scream, my body tingling from the boiled over emotions finally escaping my body. It leaves me panting, but also somehow better.

Reaching back, I find the arm of the chair and I pull it in to sit. I lean back in the leather and lift my legs, resting my feet on the desk as I thread my fingers behind my neck. I like the way it feels, sitting in a chair behind a desk like this. I think this place is just what I need. In here, I will rule.

Chapter 7

Lily

I suspect Morgan thinks I have a thing for James. She asked about a thousand questions on our walk back to the dorm room after dinner last night, each probing my intentions from a different angle. I didn't want to tell her the truth—that I want to tutor him so he'll do well in the class, despite what Theo says. Instead, I've stuck with a much better reason, even if it's not the real one: that I could use the distraction.

I have no idea why I'm so bent on proving Theo wrong over something so ridiculous. I don't even know James, though he seems nice. I'd like to think I'm the type of person who wants everyone to succeed, but I'd be overselling myself. I don't root for people to fail, exactly. I'm just too tired to invest in deep, meaningful relationships in which I may need to be a support system. And the accident didn't make me that way. I was broken long before I met Anika.

By some miracle, I don't have a single course with any of my *friends*. The only person I was truly worried about running into today was Theo, and we crossed paths—literally—several times. I started to wonder if he made sure the registrar kept us out of sync. More than once, he was in a class the hour after me or the hour before. If we were on better terms, we could share notes and tips on tests. We're not, though. And I'm not interested in helping people succeed for noble reasons. On the contrary, I'm a little hopeful Theo will fail and be forced to leave Welles completely.

I'll get my first taste of forced proximity next week, when our internships officially begin and take up our Tuesdays and Thursdays. It's probably extreme wishful thinking—and naivete—to think he'll be fed up with anything so quickly. I have a feeling he's as bullish as me in some ways.

Survivors.

I'm stuck on that thought, on that word, when the devil himself pushes through a nearly hidden door on the back side of the Welles library across from the bench I'm sitting at. He doesn't see me at first, his attention on making sure the door he shut isn't fully locked for some reason. I find myself staring at him the way I do movies I've seen a dozen times. Invested, but not fully engaged. I pull my water bottle to my chin and wrap my lips around the straw without shifting my gaze away from him.

He glances to his left then right as he seems to be pulling vines back over the door, as though he's covering it up. He appears satisfied with his work until he spins around and claps the dust from his hands just before his eyes find me. He stops his steps as soon as they begin and his head tilts to one side.

"What, are you following me or something?"

Huh?

I twist my face up rather than speak.

"I see. Whatever. Fine . . . *stalker.*" He mumbles that last word as he begins to walk around me. I laugh out loud once, a single, snarky punch. He stops a few steps beyond me and backtracks, pausing near the end of my bench where he puts one foot on the seat. Leaning in, he moves his tie to one side before folding his hands together and leaning his elbows on his knee.

"Am I wrong?"

I'm struck by how much he looks like Anika right now. It's not only his eyes—pools of blue-like concrete that always seem to be trying to hide under squinted eyelids—but the slight angle of his head as he stares at me, and the relaxed way his body commands the space. He has that same confidence about him. It's what I found so attractive in both him and his sister to begin with.

"I'm not following you around, Theo. If anything, I'm trying my hardest not to." Truthfully, I'm not necessarily disappointed when I get glimpses of him. As much as the sight of him scratches at fresh scars, I'm also curious. I do want him to find peace. I want peace, too.

"Why did you paint your toes?"

I jar a bit at his strange question, then remember how he knocked me out of Morgan's shoes yesterday. I curl my toes inside my black pumps, as if he could see through them right now.

"I . . ."

I shrug and offer nothing. I did it a few nights before we moved in because I was alone in my room back home. I'm better when I'm busy. My mom wasn't speaking to me much, either because she doesn't like to or because she no longer knows how. Painting my toes is something my therapist suggested after my parents divorced. Busying my hands with something other than the small cuts they wanted to make. I can produce almost any color in the world in nail polish at this point. I only brought a dozen of my favorite colors with me.

"What's in there?" I turn the tables on him, gesturing to the door he seemed so intent on hiding. He shifts his weight and drops his foot from the bench, straightening his spine and dropping his hands in his pockets before meeting my gaze. The tip of his tongue wets the center of his lips as his mouth hints at a smile.

"Just somewhere you're not invited." He holds me captive with his stare for a long second before blinking once.

I shake my head slightly and breathe out a faint laugh.

"What's new?" If he means to make me feel excluded, he's a little late. I did that to myself when I got here. I've learned it's easier to beat other people to the punch.

"So tell me, Lily. Are you planning on tutoring the new quarterback in his room when his parents aren't home? Or maybe playing coy at the library over your favorite piles of books? I'm sure he'll melt when he sees how fucking hard that class is you talked him into keeping." He rolls his eyes, but I sense something else in his tone. *Is Theo jealous?*

"I guess that's up to him and whatever he needs." I form a tight line with my mouth, staving off the buzzing sensation tickling my skin. I say stupid things when I get angry, and I don't want to spend my year sparring with Theo. I want to unknow him. I want to *not* think about him. I want to quit feeling guilty, to quit wishing for his forgiveness though I did nothing wrong. I want—

"Oh, such a heroic thing to say. *Whatever he needs.* Lily to the rescue." His eyes deaden as I stare into them. My chest collapses and the air in my lungs burns.

"I don't think I'm a hero," I croak. I pull my backpack to my lap and zip it closed before slinging it over my shoulder as I stand. I leave before he has a chance to utter another word, and even if he does, I refuse to acknowledge it. I can feel the tears prickling at the corners of my eyes, and I can't let those gates open. Once I start to fall down that rabbit hole of guilt and shame, it will take me hours to crawl back out. I've worn mental pathways to those dark places. It's too easy for my mind to travel them.

Instead of leaning into my weaknesses, I let my body go on autopilot, my feet marching me toward the fieldhouse. My coach texted me the locker combination when I arrived on campus, along with a note to feel no pressure. Maybe I won't be able to do it again, but for whatever reason, I want to try right now.

I fumble through my phone until I find the text and pull up the string of numbers as I slip into the locker room. The locker reserved for me is on the end, out of the way. In case it never gets used. It takes me two attempts to get the combination right. When I finally yank the lock free and open the red metal door, I'm hit by my past all at once. I never took my suits, swim cap, goggles, or slide shoes home after last year. The contents of this locker weren't even a blip in my mind. Coach Forbes took care of my things for me, storing them here, out of the way. *I wonder if he even thinks I'll make it to the water.*

With a deep breath, I close my eyes and toe off my shoes. *You got this.*

When I open my eyes again, I'm doing this. All the way.

I breathe in through my nose and hold it, my neck muscles flexed and jaw rigid. My hands pull my blouse from the waistband of my skirt and feel around my hips for the zipper. I drag it down until the fabric falls down my hips and pools at my feet. I shimmy out of my black tights next, then concentrate on undoing the buttons on my shirt. When I'm somewhere halfway up my chest, I let my eyes open wide and

I stare at the bright red suit I wore like a second skin since I was old enough to compete at Welles.

The butterflies tickle inside my chest and my hands start to quake.

No. You're doing this.

I finish stripping down and unfurl my suit, shaking it out to free the dust. I step into it and pull it taut up my body, slipping my hands through the straps and letting them snap against my skin. I allow another deep breath and it burns, the sensation of water rushing my lungs flirting with my memory.

No. Stop that.

I continue my routine, taking the things I'll need out of my locker and dropping my school bag and clothes inside. I let the goggles rest against my forehead as I snap the lock back in place, my phone the only other thing I kept out. I don't trust myself to remember this combination. There's too much noise trying to break into my thoughts.

The cold water from the shower makes me shiver, and it masks the nerves that wrestle with my body as I ready myself for the lanes.

One lap. You can do one lap.

I used to glide through dozens every day, yet this one single trip from one side of the pool to the other and back again feels like an Olympic feat. It feels impossible. I can't let it win.

Nobody is in the pool yet. That's why I must do this now. In an hour, the team will begin to trickle in and get their workouts done. I'm not sure whether any of them really miss me. I've always been quiet and kept to myself, even during events. But I'm not just a wallflower anymore—I'm a story.

Hero.

I grab a towel from the rack near the entrance and make my way to the far lane. Lane 8. *My lane.*

My feet slip out from my sandals methodically, and I nudge them in alignment with the pool's gutter, feeling better that they're turned and ready to go right back on my feet. I'm already planning my escape.

I drop the rolled towel next to them and pull my goggles down from my forehead to cover my eyes. The suction feels strange. It's been a while, longer than I've gone in years for this sensation. My pulse jets with panic.

Just breathe.

I breathe.

Shaking my arms and legs out, I bend forward and stretch my spine, rolling back up to stand slowly. Maybe I'll pull a muscle and not be able to do this.

You looking for an excuse?

With one final glance around the fieldhouse, I resolve myself to moving forward. I have to do this, if only to know what my new limits are, to know if I can. I don't have to do it well.

I kneel, then swivel to sit on my ass and drop my feet into the water. It's not freezing, the water always kept tepid for training. I swirl my legs in figure eights until the sensation of water on my skin doesn't feel like fire and claws. I'm not sure the panic has left, but maybe I've numbed to it after a few minutes. Propping my weight up on my arms, I lower myself into the pool, air leaving my lungs as I sink in. I didn't bother with a cap today. My hair is tied back in a tight bun at the base of my neck and as my head sinks below the surface I feel each individual hair follicle react. My skin is screaming for air—pleading. I force myself to stay under a little longer.

One lap.

When I pop up for air, my mouth opens wide and I gasp. The air is there.

I turn and hold the edge of the pool with both hands,

pulling my feet up until my arches flex against the wall beneath the waterline. I sense it all swirling around my body —the fear, the memories, the phantom sounds of heartbeats, screams and metal bending to water.

The lights are on.

I'm indoors.

This isn't a river.

There is no current.

There is nothing to fear.

I can see the bottom of the pool. It's clear and safe, and I can walk the entire way underneath the surface if I need to. I can push up.

With two clearing breaths that are loud enough to echo off the bleacher seats and walls around me, I commit, pushing off and twisting in the water with my hands stretched out in front and my body and aligned like an arrow. It almost feels natural, like home. My body remembers what it's like to glide and let the current work with me. It isn't quiet underneath, though. The noise in my head follows me everywhere, and the pool is no different. With one stroke, what seemed like warm water is suddenly freezing cold.

My right arm feels for the pool's floor, the smooth ground playing tricks on me. Where are the rocks? The soaked limbs from fallen trees? Where are the pockets of air bursting into a million tiny beads as they travel from the car up to the surface? I feel them. They're on my body, as if I'm swimming in carbonation.

I draw my legs in and try to remember where the surface is.

Seek the floor. Feel the floor.

Water rushes in my mouth and I swipe at my goggles that have become tangled in my hair that has quickly unraveled. I'm failing.

I can't do this.

My body jolts at the sensation of two hands forcing their way under my arms, wrapping around my shoulders as someone pushes up from the pool's floor with my body braced against theirs. My instinct is to fight back, then I quickly shift to fighting *with* my rescuer. An arm moves around my chest, holding me tighter. Legs kick along with mine, the pace manic, and when the surface breaks, I gasp. I cough up water and choke as my hands furiously feel for the pool's edge.

I tear the goggles away from my hair at the side of my face and toss them on the cool deck before lifting enough to rest my forehead on my hands as I pant and fight to see clearly. Everything is bright, flashes darting in from the edges of my vision. A hand is on my back. It isn't moving, but it's steady— warm. Assuring.

It's . . . Theo's.

My head rolls to the side, my cheek resting on the back of my hand as I still fight to get more air, coughing . . . blinking.

Theo's hand falls away.

He's fully clothed from what I can tell. His polo shirt clings to his body, his hair slicked with water and dripping in his face before he runs his hand through it then over his face to clear water from his eyes. His eyes bore into me. It's all I can do to focus on the shape of his face.

I wasn't ready.

Theo turns so his body faces the wall and he folds his arms over the edge, dropping his forehead on his knuckles. His breathing is ragged, almost angry.

I'm sorry.

My mouth fights to form the words. I can't speak, though. I'm too lost.

Theo saved me. I was being stupid, swimming alone.

Swimming at all.

"Fuck," he utters.

I blink away the water drying on my eyelashes. My hands are frozen on the edge of the pool. My body is as taut as a stick. My lungs hurt.

"Thank you." My voice is a rough whisper, but it's audible. At least, I think it was. Theo must have heard me. He turns his head and our eyes meet.

More air fills my lungs and my vision clears.

I'm so sorry. For everything.

Several seconds pass, wordless ones, until Theo abruptly lifts himself from the pool, his pants clinging to his legs, his feet in socks but no shoes. I scan the pool deck and see them tossed off to the side. A second later Theo picks them up along with his backpack. He turns to walk backward a few steps toward the exit. His body shivering, his clothes ruined, his eyes full of anguish and fury—it should have been him who was there that night. He would have saved everyone. He would not have failed.

His mouth opens and I brace myself to be scolded, but instead of speaking, he merely tightens his jaw and pulls his lips in tight before looking down at his feet and the puddle forming around him. Then he turns around and pushes through the doors to leave me alone once again.

Chapter 8

Theo

What was she thinking?

I'm shivering through the hallway, dripping my way around people as I try to ignore the weight of their stares. Cam is leaning in our doorway talking to the guys who live across the hall. They're younger, but that's Cam's thing; he wants everyone to like him. It's half the reason he does so much obnoxiously dangerous shit—he loves it when people give him attention. I tried digging into that last year, what makes him tick, or rather, what makes him practically *boom!* He was about to open up when some of last year's sixth forms dragged him out to smoke. Two puffs and his walls went right back up. The daredevil came out. Pot doesn't make Cam honest; it makes him stupid.

I suppose that's what Anika always liked about him. They never dated, but that edge was always there when we all hung out. I think if I weren't in the picture, meaning the brother's best friend thing wasn't a thing, they'd probably have been a couple. They were close, though. Sometimes, I wonder if they were closer than me and Anika were. She had secrets, and secret *deep* friendships wouldn't surprise me.

"Hey, Theo, *wha—*?" Cameron pulls my sleeve away from my arm as it practically suctions to my skin. "Is it raining, dude?"

"No." I glance up at him, then shift my gaze to the two idiots still standing across the hallway from us. "Go inside."

The bigger of the two—*I think his name's Cooper?*—he snorts out a laugh, but I lunge at him once, hard, and he stumbles backward through his doorway. His roommate, Bryan, rolls his eyes at me but pushes his friend the rest of the way into their room then shuts the door. Bryan should hang out with cooler people than Cooper. I can't stand Cooper's bleached blonde hair that I'm pretty sure is permed. *Why is it always crunchy? And perfectly sculpted?*

"I fucking hate those guys," I mutter as I drag Cameron into our room, closing the door behind him.

"Yeah, *they're* the problem," he says, punching out a laugh. I give him a sideways glance that he meets with defiance.

"What? Tell me I'm wrong?."

I can't. He's not.

My hands work the buttons of my shirt as I toe my way out of my shoes. I'm going to need to throw this crap in the dryer, otherwise our whole room is going to smell like my mom's mudroom after a heavy snow. Cam flings himself onto his back on his bed and folds his arms behind his neck while I strip down and pile my wet shit into a basket.

"We gonna talk about why you're soaking wet? Or should we start with your foul-ass mood?"

I pull a pair of sweats up and side-eye him.

"So, mood it is, then, huh?" He's poking the bear. I flip him off.

"How about I take a stab at things?"

"How about you don't." I throw my Welles sweatshirt on and push my feet into my slides before grabbing the basket of wet clothes from the floor.

"This—" He circles his finger in the air in my direction. "It's because of Lily, isn't it?"

"No."

He laughs at my immediate response. I probably could have sold that better, but he's pissing me off, and I'm already at an eleven.

"Dude, you need to work through whatever it is you have with that girl. Because if you keep it up at this rate, she is *never* going to give you a shot."

I stop at the door, letting my hand slip from the knob before turning around.

"I don't want a fucking shot, Cameron. I don't want Lily in my business. Ha! I don't want Lily at this school!"

"Uh huh." His smug smirk makes my stomach twist. I could punch him right now.

I open my mouth to lay out all the reasons for my case, but the thoughts get jumbled in my head the second I start to speak, leaving me with no words at all. Instead of getting into it with my roommate, I scowl and leave him with a heavy sigh. The hallways are less busy on my way out. It seems everyone's made their way to the break room in the basement, and because my luck is basically shit, all six dryers are in use.

I wade my way through a few fake conversations, giving knuckles to a few guys from the team and pleasant *what's up* nods on my way back to the stairs. My clothes are still soaked, and the front of my sweatshirt is wet from where they've dripped through the basket. I'm tempted to just head to my car and lay everything out on the hood to dry, but it's too cold out for that to do any good.

"Hey, Theo!"

I turn to follow the voice calling out for me and spot James walking across the main lawn, and Lily is walking away from him. Her hair is twisted in a towel, and shorts are pulled over her swimsuit. I instantly assume James saw us and let my bad mood take over, answering with a scowl and a nod.

He jogs closer and I train my eyes on him, away from the girl heading up the steps to Hayden Hall. The girl I just pulled from the bottom of the Welles pool. The girl who let my sister drown. The girl I couldn't let go in that building alone.

Because I had a feeling . . .

"Taking your laundry for a spin or what?" He chuckles.

"Huh?" My face wrinkles and my lip sneers, then I look down and remember what I'm doing out here. "Oh, yeah. Spilled something and the dorm laundry room is packed."

I struggle to make direct eye contact because I'm waiting for him to call bullshit and ask me about diving into the pool with Lily.

"Just use ours. Come on." He steps around me and gestures me to follow, unfazed by my lie. My shoulders relax as I sense he didn't see *shit* in the fieldhouse. I don't know James that well, but I don't think he's a spectacular bluffer. Just a hunch.

I follow him inside and glimpse his dad and a woman I assume is his mother laughing while cooking in the tight kitchen space. My chest tightens at the vision. There's this photo Anika stole from one of our mom's old albums. It's of her and our real dad, laughing just the way these two are. Happy. For a little while, we were all so happy. And then our dad died, and nobody was ever truly happy again.

"Theo needs the laundry. I said it was okay," James says,

leading me through the living room and past the dining table where we first met.

His dad pops his head around a corner.

"Don't get used to days off, Theo. We hit the field for full pads practice tomorrow at three." There's a seriousness in his expression. Coach is invested in winning, which means he'll be running a tight ship. I like that. Less room for my mind to wander. Between school, my internship, and football, I may just make it through this semester.

If I could somehow get rid of Lily Beachem . . .

"You serious about letting Lily tutor you?" My scheming takes over on instinct as I shovel my wet clothes into the dryer. Hopefully the chlorine smell will fade.

"Heck, yeah. She seems smart, and my dad would kick my ass if I switched out a class just because I thought it was too hard. He's big on perseverance. You know her, right? Is she as smart as I'm assuming?"

My back to him, I push my tongue in my cheek and consider the many ways I could take this. I shake my head and go with the first idea that forms on my tongue.

"I mean, she's average. She took that class, I guess." I'm not technically lying. I know from that night when we talked that Lily isn't in the top of our class. She's smart, but I wouldn't say she's brainy. She's not really lazy, either. She's . . . like me. *Indifferent.*

"She was in that accident, huh?" His voice goes quiet, and I know that's his way of being *delicate.* There's no gentle way to bring up my sister's death, and I want to punch him a little for thinking there is.

"Uh, yeah." I keep my focus on the dryer, twisting the simple knob around as if I don't understand it. *Fuck! It's a basic dryer.* I don't want to talk about this.

"Sorry, man. I know it's probably a lot. I'm sorry I didn't know more before we met."

"It's fine," I clip, pressing the button to start the cycle and flipping around, leaning my weight on the dryer and dropping my hands in my sweatpants pockets instead of folding my arms around myself defiantly. My heart is pounding under my arms, behind my ribs.

James leans against the counter opposite me, his family's laundry folded into perfect piles. Everything in his life is in order. He has no clue how quickly that can change.

"So, your sister . . ."

My stomach squeezes more.

"What was she like?"

I breathe in, a slow draw of air that coats my internal pain. I actually like when people ask about Anika, about who she was. Those are the things I enjoy talking about. It's hard to get to that stuff lately. All anyone sees when they look at me is her death, the tragedy—and Lily. *The hero.*

I chuckle at a brief thought of Anika pulling her gum from her mouth mid bubble and sticking it to my ass when we were in the mall two summers ago.

"Anika was all the good stuff." A smile settles onto my lips and my rigid muscles relax as my eyes move up to meet James'.

"Let me guess; you were the troublemaker and Anika was the goody-two-shoes."

"Ha! Hardly! The opposite. She was just good at never getting caught. She was good at throwing *me* under the bus. Like when we were kids, it was always Anika's idea to pull off the candy heist when our parents weren't looking. And when we first got our licenses, she was the one who figured out how to back the car out of the garage without the engine on and get us down the street, out of earshot."

"She sounds like a blast," James says, and I blink at his reaction, suddenly very present, the past gone.

"She was that, but she had layers. She was my best friend, but *fuck*, you know?" I shrug, masking the shivers gripping my body as ache tackles my heart. "She had a lot to her that even I didn't know. And now I never will."

My eyes flutter shut, partly out of self-hatred for letting such dark words come out of my mouth. I don't want to be like that here. I want to escape it.

"I'm really sorry, Theo."

My eyes draw in and my mouth clenches as I breathe out through my nose and nod at the ground. I can't meet his gaze.

"Lily . . . she's probably going through a lot, too, huh?"

"Fuck if I know," I fire back.

I don't have to look at James to know my hostile response caught him off guard. Before he can dissect my response and probe any more, I step out of the laundry room and change the subject.

"Got a few minutes? I wanna show you something."

I glance back to see if he's following me, and he is. He gives a quick nod.

"We can grab dinner after, unless you're eating here?" His apartment smells of homemade pasta sauce and garlic. My mouth waters at the scent.

"I probably should. Hey, you wanna stay and eat?"

I do.

I turn to walk backward toward the door, taking in the view of his family—the table set for three.

"I'm good. Thanks. We'll just be a minute." I open the door before his mom has a chance to work me over, convincing me to stay. I'm not sure I'm up for being *that* immersed in a real family life tonight.

"Okay, but your loss. Hey, Dad . . . be right back." James'

dad lifts a hand to wave us off, his eyes concentrating on the boiling water and spoon in his other hand.

I pick up the pace as soon as we're out the door, the air starting to chill. The lights that glow along the walkways of Welles flicker on. It's not even close to dark yet, but those days are coming soon. Summer is fading fast, fall is here, and winter is on its heels. I'll be finishing up football practice under moonlight in a month or two. Less time for my mind to wander, more time to sleep.

I guide James to the back door behind the library and glance around to make sure nobody is watching us. Satisfied we're alone, I usher him to get close and I pull it open enough for both of us to slip inside.

"Dude, I don't think we're supposed to be in here."

"Oh, Coach's kid, I've got work to do with you," I say through a devious laugh.

"Yeah?" He sounds skeptical and a bit concerned.

I shut the door behind him and flip the lights on, the room exactly as it was when I left it a few hours ago.

"I did some investigating, and nobody is using this area right now. It's for archives, and they finished documenting the most recent donations and collections. It's almost totally sealed off from the main building. In fact, nobody gets in here without a key. And since I have that key—"

My brows rise slowly and James' face flushes. He's panicked. He's going to need convincing.

"You stole the key to this place?" He hugs himself and moves closer to the door I just closed.

I shrug.

"You say stole. I say borrowed. I'll put it back before we leave." It was too easy to take. I found it in the main desk drawer, labeled with a plastic tag.

"And this door?" He puts his hand on the knob. I step close enough to grab his arm and urge him to let go.

"Relax, dude. We're in a library, not a speakeasy." *Of course, I do think this is the perfect place to party.*

James lets his arms relax and he turns slowly to take in the place, perhaps finally letting his mind imagine the possibilities.

"That lock is busted. I have some thoughts on putting up a deadbolt or a temporary lock, just for when we're in here. But we'll see."

A hint of a smile tugs on his mouth as he starts to wander.

"You're seeing it now, aren't you?" Maybe I'm more like Anika than I said I was.

"I might be seeing things, yeah. What's the sound-proofing like in here?" He pushes one of the chairs away from a desk, making room to sit. He stretches back nearly the same way I did and scans the room and the offices off to the side.

"I doubt you hear much. Hang on, let's test it." I hold up a finger and move to the door. "As soon as I shut it, scream as loud as you can. They're gone upstairs. It's just us."

James nods. I step outside and back away a few paces, waiting several seconds and hearing nothing at all. When I come back in, James is still singing "Don't Stop Believing" as loud as he can. He stops mid lyric and his eyebrows lift. I shake my head.

"Nothing."

Our mouths mirror each other, our smiles a reflection of plans.

"Party?" James suggests. That was my plan all along, only with a caveat.

I hold up a palm.

"Exclusive party. Me, you, and Cameron—we say who can come, and who needs to go."

James chuckles.

"I like it. Yeah," he says.

He leans back again and spins slowly in the chair. When our eyes meet again, he sucks in his bottom lip.

"Lily. You cool if I invite Lily?" His eyes squint as he studies me, waiting for a reaction.

I laugh through closed lips.

"Sure. Whatever." My inner-voice curses, the words in my head so loud I wonder if James can somehow hear them.

Fuck! Fuck! Fuck!

"Nice. So, this weekend, yeah?" If I'm going to have to share this place with my least favorite person in the world, I may as well start making her feel unwelcome right away.

James stands and reaches out his hand. I take it and we pull in for a bro hug.

"As long as you really think this place is on lockdown." He levels me with a look that feels like a contract waiting to be signed. He's awfully anxious to break rules for a guy who's so worried about getting caught.

"Key's up in my dorm room. Deadbolt will be ordered online tonight. Now it's just a matter of booze."

"I know someone who can help with that," he responds.

Look at James, full of surprises.

We make our way out the door, and he helps me cover it with the overgrowth again once we get it shut. I follow him back to his apartment to check on my clothes, and despite every fiber of my will begging me to let it drop, my mouth betrays me as soon as we're back in his laundry room.

"Lily, huh?" I laugh it out, the way a father would teasing his son over a crush. My eyes are dead, however, since my back is to James.

"I don't know. She's . . . interesting."

I close my eyes and feel my clothes, ticked when I find they're still super damp.

"You think I can just grab these tomorrow or something?" I have to get out of this place. Right now.

"Yeah. I'll bring them to practice. No problem."

"Thanks." I shut the dryer door and let the cycle continue.

She's interesting.

"We'll talk more tomorrow, about . . . ya know." His voice is a whisper at my shoulder as he walks me back through his living room and to the door.

"Yep," I respond, giving his dad another wave and smile.

"Better be studying tonight, Rothschild. I'm a stickler for grade checks."

I salute him.

"Of course, sir."

When his attention drifts, I make wide eyes at James who simply nods with a closed, smug grin. It's the first day. There is literally nothing to study.

"Hard-ass," he mouths.

I laugh and pound his knuckles with my fist before heading back to my dorm. I should have stayed and dealt with Cameron. I should have waited out the dozen people in line to use the dryer in our laundry room. I should have transferred to another fucking school for my final year.

I should have been in that car to save my sister.

And that's what this is really all about.

Being here, that's my punishment.

Lily Beachem? She isn't interesting.

She's my curse.

Chapter 9

Lily

Nobody saw anything, except James.

And I lied to him.

The crippling weight of that moment when he caught me leaving the fieldhouse with wet hair and my team suit has worn a hole in my gut for the last three days. Morgan and Brooklyn were gone when I came in. The only person who needs to know I dove and failed is Theo, and I'm sure he isn't going to say a word to anyone. He'll have to admit to saving me, to seeing me—to following me there because . . . *because why?*

He won't do that.

But James knows. James knows a different story. In his version, I was putting in laps and am about to start back with the team. He "couldn't imagine how strong I was after all I'd been through." I swallow hard at his reaction because I'm not brave at all. I'm terrified. I'm fake. I'm not even here in so many ways. I'm lost.

The relief I felt when he spotted Theo was temporary because there were suddenly three of us, and no matter how fast I darted back to my dorm, there was no way to make him unsee me and James together, all the obvious signs that I was "swimming." Two very different stories. One painful truth.

I can't do any of this.

I've lived with the fear of this moment for three days, and the intensity of my anxiety is greater than I could have fathomed. It's lunch, and I should be sitting at a table with Brooklyn and Morgan and the many girls who clammer to sit at our table just to be near them—maybe near *us.* Instead, I'm at one end and Theo is at the other, his eyes fixed on me and James as we talk. I haven't heard a word James has said, other than asking if I was serious about helping him with comparative lit and could we start tomorrow.

I think I said yes. Did I respond?

James is still talking and showing me his syllabus, so I must have.

I prop my head on my fist, bent elbow resting on the tabletop as my hair falls forward and shades my face from the penetrating glare about six feet away from me.

Focus on the words, Lily. Just read the damn words.

This class was easy for me, and the syllabus is the same. I should be able to help James without much effort, but if I were smart, I'd tell him to seek out help from Angela. She'd tutor him just to brag about being able to do something I couldn't. *Weird, competitive freak.* Despite the imaginary warning buzzers in my head, I press on. I'm too far in to back out now.

"The hardest part is going to be keeping up with the reading," I say, flipping through the stapled pages.

James slides back in his chair and his arms slump at his sides. I fake a laugh. That's what a normal person would do right now, a person not hiding from Theo Rothschild's judgement. It feels like it's working until he laughs with me. Not really *at* me. It's clear, though, that this laugh is mocking me. It's purposeful, and the mood at the table instantly shifts. James shakes his head at me and rolls his eyes, then shifts his attention to Theo.

"Sorry we aren't all speed readers like you, Theo." He thinks he's mocking him for not liking to read. It's sweet. I know that contempt is one hundred percent for me, though.

Theo pulls a single chip from his bag and makes a presentation about placing it on his tongue, his eyes lazily sweeping my face as his lips close in an almost sensual way just before his teeth gnash down and break the chip into a million harsh bits.

"It's easy to fly through things like *See Spot Run*," Morgan says, coming to my defense. Uneasy laughter titters from everyone's mouths but mine and Theo's. We remain locked in this staring contest, unspoken truths bouncing between us, until finally—

"How was the pool this week, Lily?" Theo's lip ticks up with satisfaction. *Fucking prick.*

"You swam? Lily! That's amazing!" Morgan shifts in her seat to face me directly and lays her hand over my arm. I want to collapse in defeat on the tabletop, but there's a tiny fire in me that refuses to go out. Anika would hate me being weak. She'd hate the way her brother is treating me. I feel it in my gut.

My eyes close as my gaze moves from Theo to my roommate, and I decide to live the lie I spun with James. That will be the new truth, and whatever happened with Theo in that pool will die there, in the past.

"Yeah, it felt . . . good." I smile even though my stomach twists. The feel of the water engulfing me, cutting off sound and blurring sight, is sharp in my memory.

"That's great," Theo says, his tongue sharp, words crisp.

I'm too weak not to look at him, and he rewards my focus by eating another chip, just as slowly until his shark-like teeth crunch down. I flinch. I hate that I flinch.

"Do you think you'll be ready to compete in the first meet? You know we'll all come." Morgan's hand taps on my arm and I fight Theo's draw to return to her. I nod because that's what the lie would expect of me, and my throat starts to close. I'll never be able to get in that pool and compete again, let alone in two weeks.

"I'll tell my dad to check the schedule. At our old school, he was big on teams supporting other teams. I know he'll want us to be there as a team. It really does foster community," James says.

"You have to be fucking kidding me." Theo's words are mumbled, but they're clear enough for us all to hear. He gathers his trash, smooshing half his sandwich into a napkin as he wraps it up.

"Dude, what's your problem?" James demands.

Theo's body suddenly feels twice the size of anyone else in the room. He laughs to himself silently, his eyes still down on the table as he stands. He looks at me first, and I'm too weak to will my eyes to plead with him to stop. I'm frozen in place. Maybe I want to feel the discomfort, to take it in as punishment for failing him and his family.

He blinks his attention to James next and forms a conciliatory tight-lipped smile.

"You're right. I'm in a mood is all. Got hit with a ton of studies I wasn't expecting this semester. I'm sorry; I was out of line." He holds a fist toward James, who stares at it for a few uncomfortable seconds before knocking against it with his own.

"It's fine. I get it." I can tell James isn't being sincere, but this is what one is supposed to do in a situation like this. He's being civil. Look at us all—playing parts we're no good for.

"Oh, hey. We should tell them all about tomorrow night, yeah?" Nobody else may notice, but I spot the way James looks at Theo as he throws this hook out into the depths. There's a bit of a chess game happening, and I don't fully understand it. I do recognize it, though.

"Sure." Theo lifts his chin a touch and holds his tight smile in place.

"What's tomorrow night?" Brooklyn asks.

"Party or some shit. Theo found this place. It's like his *secret lair.*" These are the first words Cameron has spoken to us in days, and he's so unfazed by the tension drowning me, it manages to ease its grip on my throat a little. He's also high, which I guess lets him glide through awkward moments on a cloud.

"Do tell," Morgan spurs Theo on.

"Midnight. Just be out in the common lawn, away from the paths and lights. I'll show you where to go from there," James says. Theo's weight shifts, and I'd swear there's a power move happening.

"I'll be waiting. You know, in my *fucking lair,*" Theo adds, glancing down at Cameron and lightly slapping the back of his neck before leaving our table in his wake.

Cameron laughs it off and picks up Theo's abandoned chip bag, digging in to eat the crumbs his friend left behind while I sift through the figurative ones he left for me alone.

James types his number into my phone and saves it as a contact so we can get together tomorrow morning, and I try to seem distant about it because I feel Morgan's eyes on me. I don't want any of this. I didn't want to be a failed hero, I didn't want to be part of the *in* crowd, and I am not interested in James for anything other than pleasant conversation to pass the minutes I have left at Welles.

"We can study at our place. My dad makes a mean omelet. Come hungry," he says, pointing at me and smiling crooked and cute as he backs away from our table, taking Cameron with him.

It takes approximately seven seconds for Morgan and Brooklyn to pounce.

"What was that about?" Brooklyn breaks into things first, probably because her concern is more about me, and the way Theo is treating me rather than the thing Morgan is interested in—James.

"He's struggling. I get it. And if he has to take it out on me sometimes, it's okay." I push my mostly uneaten sandwich away and tuck the unopened chips into my backpack for a snack later.

"Uh, no. It's not okay. We were there, Lily. I know we haven't talked about it since we've been back, and we're probably all sick of talking about it from before summer, but what we went through was a real fucking nightmare. He wasn't there to see the things we saw, and Morgan and me? We didn't see the things you saw alone, Lily. So, no. it's not okay. He doesn't get to take things out on you." Brooklyn's right, but she's also wrong.

"Yes, he does," I relent. My friend growls in frustration and pushes her chair away from the table, the feet squealing against the linoleum floor just before she stands and walks to the opposite side of the table.

"Brooklyn, let it go. She just got shit on. Maybe let her recover before you give her a lesson?" Morgan's hand slides to the side on the table toward Brooklyn and their eyes meet for some silent bargaining. They've been close for so long they can do this, have these conversations in silence that I'll never quite understand. I envy it yet in a way I'm glad to be on the outside.

Brooklyn takes a deep breath then lets her eyes close, her nostrils flaring as she breathes out. She nods then opens her eyes on me.

"Morgan's right. I'm sorry, Lily. I just can't let him treat you that way. He has no idea what you did for me. For Morgan. What you tried to do for—"

"It's fine," I interrupt, cutting her off before she utters Anika's name.

"And thank you," I add. I push my mouth into a soft smile, but inside, I'm fighting tears. If today is any indication of how the rest of this semester is going to go, I'll never survive.

Chapter 10

Theo

There's a chapel on campus. Welles cut ties with its Presbyterian affiliation decades ago. It became an issue for one of the major donors to the school, a former graduate who had strayed far from God.

A politician.

Since those days, mandatory chapel has turned into optional, and more recently, into rare. Religion has never been much of a thing in the Rothschild family. We claim to be Christians, or our mother does because her mother was, but I can count on one hand the number of times I've been in a church. That number would be zero if it weren't for a wedding and two funerals, including our father's.

I barely remember burying my dad. We were eight, and Anika always carried more of the memories than I did. Call it ADHD or simply being a boy with idle time, I was often too busy in my own messy worlds to focus on the present, even that day in the church. I cried, but more over the fact my fishing buddy was gone. I didn't get it—*my dad died*. I didn't get it until our mom started dating Neil, and then it became abundantly apparent how different he was from the man I lost.

We were ten when Neil moved in. I can't remember much of my dad's funeral, but I fucking remember every second of Neil taking over our house.

There's a layer of dust on the pews in the Welles chapel, a sign of apathy. I drag my finger along one of the arms then step into the row, taking a seat. They still bother to keep the lights on in here. It's a pleasant dim glow. It's quiet. In here, I can think. Alone.

I've spent the entire day avoiding the obvious—I can't stand that Lily spent the morning with James. Acid has been crawling up my esophagus all day, the root cause clearly stress. James is *my* friend. I staked a claim to him first, and she and I cannot share more people—*or places*—in common. It feels like my world keeps getting smaller here. My internship, my circle of friends, and now my apparent *secret lair!* She's like a Goddamned invader. *Sorry, can I think that word in this place?*

I pull one of the hymnals from the back of the pew in front of me and flip through the pages. Someone drew a naked woman on the very first page and the sight makes me chuckle. We're all a bunch of heathens in this place. I drop the book back into place and pull my phone from my pocket to check the time. My mom has called a few times today and I haven't picked up. I worry about her constantly. My sister's death changed her, as if she died with Anika and left a carbon copy behind that was programmed differently. She's gotten into volunteering for ridiculous non-profits, like this one group made up of women who want to preserve the old light posts on our street in Charlestown.

Anika would have made fun of that. My sister was passionate about actual causes, like world hunger and health care for impoverished countries. She wanted to join Green-peace and take some gap time before college. Maybe she just wanted to run away, like me. Her way always sounded more noble, though.

My thumb slides to call my mom and I stand to pace, already pinching my brow and preparing myself for her.

"Oh, hi," she answers, mid-giggle. She must be out with the streetlamp ladies.

"Hi, Ma. Sorry I missed your calls."

"Shhh, stop." She's muffled the phone.

"If it's not a good time, Mom—"

"I'll be right back." She's still covering the phone, but that voice she's trying to block out cuts through and it's unmis-takable.

"Hi, Theo." She's putting on the sing-songy voice, hoping I don't lose my shit. I'm going to lose my shit.

"Why is Neil with you?" I pace faster. I may wear a path in the aged carpet in this place if I keep this up.

"What?"

She's still trying to evade and pretend.

"Ma, I heard him. Please don't pretend."

Her heavy sigh vibrates in my ear, and I pull my phone away from my head and place her on speaker. I set the phone down on the altar and rest my palms on either side, leaning into it and staring at the photo of my mom that comes up when we talk on the phone. That's Neil's body I cropped out of that photo. That's his arm draped around her possessively. Those are his chubby fingers.

"He was simply checking in, Theodore." She uses my full name when she wants to exact her authority. It's infuriating.

"He said he'd be right back. Where is he coming back to? Are you out somewhere? Is he coming back to our house?" I'm in a mental spiral picturing him moving things around to suit his tastes, making himself comfortable, worming his way back into my mom's life. She finally got him out, though she wouldn't file actual divorce papers.

"Theodore. Relax. He came by to visit and help with a few things around the house."

"Oh, I bet he did. Like rearranging your pantry to his stupid obsessions or maybe pulling his man-cave shit out of the basement." My head is pounding suddenly, and my hands have formed fists without me even realizing it.

"He lost her, too, you know."

My mouth drops open at her words and I stand only to fall back a few steps. I can feel the heat climbing up my ribs and down my spine. My teeth clench and my jaw pops. She may as well have pummeled me with a heavy fist.

"He's grieving, Theodore. Just like we are."

I inhale, a beast growing in my chest.

"No. He's not." I grab my phone from the altar, and before my mom can utter more bullshit that is only going to send me into a bigger rage, I end our call and storm out of the peaceful chapel into the brisk late afternoon air.

I've been giving Ma endless amounts of slack, but this feels too far. Inviting Neil back into her life after the damage he did to our family—to my sister—is unacceptable. It's as if she has completely wiped her mind of the day she threw him out. Anika was in tears at the kitchen table, and it was the first time I'd ever seen our mother stand up to someone as she piled Neil's belongings at the front door. It seemed to take hours for her to convince him she was serious about him leaving the house. Time wasted now that she's invited him right back in.

This is usually the time Cameron heads down to the riverwalk to smoke. I start in that direction in hopes of joining him to take the edge off so I'm not completely wound for tonight, but my path is cut off by the only person I want to talk to less than my ma. Lily is walking across the main lawn, and I know she sees me. I know the exact moment she spotted me because she picked up the pace and shifted the towel on her shoulder to block her face from my view.

Good. If she can pretend not to see me, I can do the same. We both know the reality, but it seems we've come to a silent agreement on what's best to make it through this. Maybe she'll ignore James' invite to the archive room tonight too. Probably not since they spent most of the morning together, but her reaction right now gives me hope.

I make it to the other end of the lawn before chancing a glance over my shoulder. She's still motoring away from me, toward the fieldhouse. I know what she's doing, but I can't make it my business. If she wants to torture herself—if she wants to drown—it's none of my business.

Except now it's all I can focus on.

Pausing just before the pathway breaks into the river-walk, I squeeze my eyes shut tight for a second and twist my body to look her direction one last time. I can still see her, barely. She isn't slowing or turning around, rather she seems committed to whatever the hell she has planned.

I know what that is. I practically pushed her into this.

A low growl emanates from my throat, and I turn slowly, part of me hoping to spot Cameron nearby, wishing he'll see me and call me over. It still won't erase the nagging voice growing louder in the back of my mind, screaming at me to be responsible.

"Damn it," I mutter, shoving my hands in my pockets and trudging my way in Lily's direction. I'm going to make sure she understands this is a final-time deal. I'm not her babysitter; I don't care what I did to push her into swimming again.

It's a stupid pissing contest. She isn't supposed to actually go right back to the goddamn pool.

The campus is eerily empty, most everyone else in the dining hall or back in their rooms getting ready for tonight's social plans. Welles keeps a busy calendar, always offering entertainment on the weekends. Sometimes it's movies on the main lawn, other times it's karaoke in the rec room. I think it's a sock hop tonight. The rec room will be filled with first and second years teeming with pre-teen energy. *Annoying.* Those of us who have been here long enough know the real fun happens off campus, in the woods or the abandoned barn. At least, it used to. Getting off campus got a lot harder after the accident, as if that's what caused my sister's wreck. The student parking lot is monitored and gated, and the punishment when caught went from a first offense to possible expulsion. Which makes the library hideout, and any invites inside, even more coveted.

I peek through the small window in the fieldhouse door before I enter. Nobody is in the main breezeway, just the ghosts of trophies from decades ago, the last time Welles was a champion at anything—*besides swimming, of course.* That's probably why Lily came to this school. Anika said she was a strong swimmer. *Not strong enough.*

I pull the door gently, trying not to announce my entrance in case Lily is in here alone. There are a few guys playing pick-up basketball in the gym, but the weight room is empty as I pass by. The air gets thick with chlorine the closer I get to the pool, and I pause at the double doors that lead into the main deck, pushing them open a hint so I can peek inside. Lily is pacing, goggles covering her eyes as she marches ten feet in one direction then the other as she pounds her fists against her thighs. She's trying to psych herself into doing this. It's pointless.

I push the door open wide, ready to stomp toward her and tell her to quit being stupid. Before I make it more than a full step inside, she dives into the water and sinks to the bottom, gliding with her hands stretched out as they run along the tiled lines on the floor. With a single move, she has contained the angry fire that was brewing in my chest. It's still there, but not as raging. The urgency I felt to reprimand her, to lecture her on what her actions do to me, how she interrupts my life, is instantly replaced by curiosity.

Before she comes up to breathe, I back out of the door and duck as I pass the windows on my way to the stairwell. I take the steps two at a time, my inner voice urging me to hurry. I'm not sure whether I want to have eyes on her because I want to see if she's really that good at swimming or because I want to make sure she doesn't get herself in trouble again. Maybe it's a little of both.

I peer around the wall to catch a view of her just as she breaks through the surface and flips her head up from the water. Her hair is slick along her neck and shoulders, the ends spread around her body like a blooming flower. She treads in the middle of the pool, her back to me, for several long seconds. Her arms draw slow circles in the water, sending ripples away from her body, like an echo of herself. A part of me wants to slink back down the stairs and leave her alone. This feels private. Yet something has me anchored here. I'm not sure, but I think it's my need for information. I wasn't there when it happened, the accident. I never got to see what Lily did. I'm hungry for details, as much as I also want to avoid them.

Without catching her attention or making a sound, I manage to slip into the back row of seats and slink low enough to peer through the space between the seats in front of me. Almost a minute passes of her in the middle of the pool, treading. There's a sadness to her movement, as if the water is as thick as mud and she's fighting her for life. Or maybe that's just how I see it.

In a smooth motion, Lily transitions to her back and her arms windmill, pulling her body toward the edge, closer to me. She isn't swimming for speed. Her strokes are more leisurely, those of someone who's still learning or someone whose body is no longer meant for speed. It's a jarring juxtaposition. Her legs are better toned than half of the guys on our football team, and her shoulders are broad, biceps defined, and arms long and powerful. Her fingers stretch behind her, reaching for the wall, gripping it at first touch. She spins around so her feet are against the pool wall, her body poised to push off, eyes focused on her flexed hands. I hold my breath in anticipation. She finally pushes and twists along the water's surface, her arms digging in for commanding strokes that propel her to the center of the pool in seconds.

She is good.

I stretch my neck to get a better view, careful not to get too comfortable like this. I don't want to stick out. I don't want her to see me. I don't want to have to talk to her, to answer the questions she's likely to have. *Did I follow her? Why?* I can only answer one of those, the obvious one.

She's three quarters across the pool, and my jaw tightens with the suspense. I can't deny that I want to see her make it the entire length, just once. I'm not sure whether that will make me feel better or worse about her. Her effort somehow feels tied to me. We will either both keep failing, or . . . not.

Without warning, Lily stops hard about twenty feet from the opposite edge of the pool. A wave catches up to her as her arms sink to her sides while she buoys in the water, as if everything she worked so hard to build these last few seconds simply slipped through her fingers and passed her by.

She let it.

And then she screams.

Her voice breaks several seconds into the raw pain tearing its way from her throat, but she pushes through her vocal cords' betrayal, the sound curdling. It's not a fearful noise she makes. She isn't afraid of anything. She's angry. Her body rises and falls in the water from the exertion as the sound finally dies from her lips. Her arms raise and flap down into the water like anchors. Without context, anyone seeing this would think she's a petulant teenager not getting her way.

That isn't what she is at all.

"Fuuuck!" Her own damning word echoes right back into her face, and this time she pushes a wave of water at the wall she failed to reach.

I sink lower, still unable to leave. Lily kicks her legs out and floats on her back, growling into the empty room before windmilling her arms as her legs punish the water to take her back to where she started. I can see the top half of her body when she lifts herself out of the pool, and I grip the arms of my seat to ready for my escape. Before I slide out of the chair, though, Lily dives in the water, her speed urgent, her arms determined as she rushes across the pool yet again.

She isn't giving up.

She stops in the same place as before. She screams again, this time adding to her words, reprimanding herself with a loud, strung-out "Fuck you, Lily!"

I should smirk at her unraveling. If I were a better person, I'd leave her to go through this alone. But I'm not. I'm not reveling in her self-hatred. I do, however, appreciate it. Suddenly, I feel a lot less alone.

Chapter 11

Lily

A party is hardly the place I want to be. It feels . . . inappropriate. If we hadn't gone off campus that night, into the woods, Anika never would have gotten the idea to take that car for a joyride. She'd still be here, rooming with us. Truth is, she'd still probably be prodding me to get ready for a party. She made it her personal mission to ruin my introvert status.

"James didn't give you any details on whatever this place is we're going?" Morgan is on her fourth outfit. She looks amazing in everything she wears, but it doesn't matter how many times Brooklyn or I tell her that. She has a crush. She also wants to be mad at me for spending the morning with James, but she's astute enough to know how immature that would be. Or maybe she's biting her tongue until she can't stand it anymore.

"We talked about Willa Cather," I say with a shrug.

"Willa who?" Morgan holds the red dress she discarded two outfits ago up to her chest.

"That's his first reading assignment. And Morgan, you

look amazing in what you have on now." She's wearing knee-high black boots and a deep green tunic dress with a neckline that opens to the jeweled stud on the center of her black bra. All the time in the world under the most talented hands and I could never look like her.

She chews at her lip and glances to me then back to her reflection, still holding the red dress. Brooklyn and I make eye contact and she nods toward Morgan, I think urging me to put her worries to rest.

I toss my laptop on my pillow and slide to the edge of my bed, stopping just short of standing. Anika was always the best at these types of things—those mini pep talks that seemed to be filled with whatever magic words a person needed at that time. That's what I need to do here. I need to say something Anika would say.

"I don't like James. Like *that*, I mean."

Morgan's hands stop fidgeting and her eyes widen slightly as she looks at herself. Brooklyn turns around, and I wish I could turn around too because this feels so awkward, but I know it's what a real friend would do. That's what Anika wanted for us all—real friendships. She'd also tell me to get off my ass and go to Morgan.

I walk over to stand behind her and rest my hand on her shoulder, my chin on my hand so we're looking at each other in the mirror. She drops the dress to the floor and meets my reflected gaze.

"Do you think he'll like this outfit?" She finishes with a crooked smile, and it's the only thing on her face that is not perfectly symmetrical.

I step back and take her hand, stretching her arm out as I evaluate her curves, the boots, then back up to her waves of cinnamon-colored hair and lashes that are real and thick and long over blue eyes.

"If he doesn't make a move on you tonight, I will."

Morgan's smile straightens, her blood-red lips coming together and stretching into the confident grin that suits her best.

"I'll fight you for her," Brooklyn adds, throwing the one-liner over her shoulder.

"You guys . . ." Morgan fakes modesty, but it's not annoying. She's embarrassed and trying to shift the attention. I get that. I *so* get that.

I should do that now, before it's too la—

"You're not seriously wearing your school uniform, are you?" Morgan has quickly shifted into project mode again. My shoulders fall and I back up until the backs of my legs hit my mattress, and I flop down in my skirt that's too big.

"You said I couldn't wear my shorts or my joggers," I protest.

Brooklyn picks the abandoned gray pair they forced me out of up from the floor and holds them out in front of her.

"Honey, these are sweatpants. You can't call them joggers." She proceeds to toss them into my clothes basket, and I stand to retrieve them.

"Hey, those are clean."

Morgan nudges my shoulder, pushing me back down to sit.

"Does it really matter?" She's right. They're sweats. They don't really need to be in a drawer, I guess.

"Are you at least going to wear a cute top?" Morgan kneels in front of me and unscrunches my socks, stretching them up my calves to wear the same way she does.

"I was thinking my Welles hoodie?" I glance to where it rests on the foot of my bed. Brooklyn quickly snatches it and tosses it on top of my joggers . . . I mean sweatpants.

"I have a black tie-top that will look cute. You can borrow

it." Brooklyn moves to her closet section as Morgan snaps at me to pull my white polo shirt off. She's nice enough not to cringe at my basic white bra. I figure out why as soon as she and Brooklyn start "styling" me in the black shirt.

The two of them spend five minutes wrapping these long strips of fabric around my midriff and under my boobs, literally lifting my tits up in their palms and forcing them as close together as they'll go. By the end, they've somehow made my bra tighter because I know my breasts sure didn't get bigger. The edge of my bra lines the top curves of my breasts, held in place by the tight wrapping of the black shirt that is tied just below the only cleavage I've ever had. Morgan talks me into trading my skirt for one of hers, the shortest one she owns, and the only chip I won by bargaining is being allowed to wear my white Vans.

I manage to snag my hoodie from the pile on our way out the door and I hug it to my chest as Brooklyn threatens to burn it if I put it on before we get to this party, wherever it is. We're all playing a part tonight. Whether we say it aloud or not. I crave to feel normal, and my roommates *must* feel it too. It tugs at me from the pit of my stomach.

Anika. Tonight would make her so happy.

"Ladies, this way." Cameron rolls his hand in front of him before bowing. He's already drunk, or high. Or maybe this is just the way he is. It's hard to get a read on him. He's continually mellow, which is even odder because of the extreme stunts he pulls off. During fourth form, he leapt from the roof of the admin building using a parachute he won by sending in energy drink can tabs. He sailed three hundred yards before getting hung up in a tree.

We follow him along the main path until we join a few more people who seem to have earned this special invite. I recognize them all, though I don't truly know them. They presume to know me, though. Everyone at Welles does since the accident. What a strange and tragic way for me to become popular.

"Voices down, guys," James says in a rather loud whisper. He waves us all over to the door behind the library, the one I watched Theo come out of the other day.

"Behold," he says, opening the door and waving us all inside a dimly lit room as he scans the area around us. The night patrol guards drive the same loop every night from eleven p.m. to sunup. You can hear the hum of the golf cart when it's close, which is what made sneaking off campus so easy in years past.

"I guess technically we aren't off campus," I mutter to Morgan.

"Good point," she says, relaxing her arms. She repeats my observation to Brooklyn, who seems to destress as well. Maybe the two of them will enjoy themselves tonight. Since James closed the heavy door behind us and locked it with a deadbolt, I've only gotten more anxious.

"I mean, fire hazard," I say under my breath.

"That's what I said," Cameron says at my shoulder. Our eyes meet and he rolls his before moving ahead of me. He leaves a sweet scent in his wake, and I smile to myself. *Yeah. He's high.*

"Welcome, everyone. No beer tonight, but we do have this lovely bottle of Jack and half a bottle of gin. Plus, whatever weird shit Cameron brought," Theo says, holding the two bottles of liquor up for us all to view.

His gaze passes right over everyone, landing directly on me in a matter of seconds. He tips the whiskey bottle in his right hand and lifts a brow. I shake my head and look down.

I'm not drinking. I think I'd have a panic attack before I brought the glass to my lips. Besides, this way Morgan and

Brooklyn can if they want, and I'll be able to make sure we get back to our room.

"I didn't even know this place was here." Brooklyn runs her hand along one of the huge scanning machines. I've been in this very room before. I helped our head librarian two years ago when Welles received a major collection of foreign documents. I didn't realize this is where the door lead when I saw Theo exit the other day. I'm terrible with directions and orientation. It took me years to learn how to make straight lines in the water when I swim.

I see the appeal now. Nobody uses this space except for those rare times, and on the occasion that a visiting student from one of the universities needs to gather research. Our archives are better than some post-secondaries.

"You're getting a lot of looks, Lily. The good kind," Morgan says, winking at me and nodding to a small group of football players, probably friends of Theo's. Rather than looking away when I gaze at them, they smile and one of them holds up a small glass of whiskey. I brace myself for them to utter something I can't quite hear then laugh, but it never happens.

"They're looking at me because of—"

"No. They're not," Brooklyn cuts me off. I turn to my side to meet her stern expression. "Tonight, you are a hot Welles girl."

"No, she's one of the girls from Hayden Hall," Morgan corrects, throwing her arms around both of our necks and shoulders.

My lip ticks up.

I've always wanted to be in this place. With them, like this. They're the girls from Hayden Hall, and I sold my soul to be one of them.

"Lily."

I shake my head at the sound of my name, jolting from my daydream. Theo is leaning against a large wood desk in the far corner of the space, the sleeves of his white shirt rolled up just below his elbows as he braces himself with a hand on either side of him atop the desk. He crosses his feet, maybe to appear disarming, and lifts his chin as he flashes me a faint smile.

"Look, an olive branch. Go talk to him." Morgan releases me from her arm and gives me a not-so-gentle shove. I stumble a few steps forward, glad that at least I'm wearing sensible shoes for this occasion. *For being bullied into making small talk with the guy who hates me, for reasons I totally understand.*

"I didn't realize you were straight-edge." He reaches to his left and slides a glass of whiskey closer to him, his fingers toying with the rim of the glass. I can't help but watch their movement. He's wearing the thick gold ring stamped with his initials on his pinky. He wore that the night it all happened too. He taps it against the glass and my eyes dart to his face instead.

"I'm not. I just don't feel like it tonight. And I don't really drink much." I shrug one shoulder as my hands kneed the hoodie I'm clinging to, desperate to slip it on.

"Me, neither," Theo says, cupping the glass and bringing it to his lips for a long, slow sip. "But tonight I am."

He holds the rim of the glass to his bottom lip as he studies me. I can hear the chatter around us, the dozen other students who were deemed worthy to be in here laughing and comparing stories about their first week. Yet they're muted in my ears. It's as if Theo and I are trapped in a room made of glass.

"How was your first week?" I hug my hoodie tighter and Theo's gaze dips to my folded arms before rising to my breasts. This blouse suddenly feels even tighter, which is impossible because I can barely breathe. It may as well be a corset.

"Eh," he finally says, shrugging one shoulder and taking a smaller sip before putting his drink down on the desk. He folds his arms over his chest, matching my posture, and my eyes are drawn to the way his forearms flex. *Of all the boys in Welles to have a crush on, why did I have to choose him?* I can't help my girlish affection. It's still there. Only now there's a whole lot of other feelings mixed in, some of them incredibly sour, others deeply sad.

"Mine too," I say. I barely remember details from my classes. The only moments that have truly stuck with me were in the pool. Probably because those felt like torture.

"How did the first tutoring session go?" Theo shifts his weight when he asks, and his eyes scan the room. I follow the path they take, and we both end up looking at James. I smirk and turn back to face Theo.

"A success, I'd say. In two hours, I managed to convince him that comp lit is his favorite class." That may be a stretch. I did help him write his talking points for his first reading, and he said he felt a lot more prepared thanks to me.

"Mmm. Two hours, huh?" He lifts a brow.

"It's Willa Cather," I respond, as if that somehow makes sense to him. Her work is kind of complex, and really, it's unfair that the teacher is starting them with that.

"When the season starts, he's not going to have two hours to give up on the weekends." His mouth settles into a straight line, and I sense that he's leveling me with some sort of challenge, as if he thinks James will fail because I won't be able to tutor him on a Saturday.

"I guess we'll work during the week. Some people study

at night, you know," I snark, leaning in to whisper my retort. His eyes dim and the corners of his mouth turn down.

"Or you could convince him to switch to something a lot easier and worth the same amount of credit."

"And teach him it's okay to quit? I don't think so," I answer.

I meet his stare and fill my lungs with a long, slow draw of air through my nose. It feels as if I'm smirking, and I partly hope I am. The sense of victory lasts for several seconds, until it dawns on me that Theo's faint frown has only hardened. I retrace my words in my mind, and I find the source of his reaction quickly.

Theo thinks I'm a quitter. He thinks I quit on his sister.

So do I. It's all I think. All the time. Every day.

"I'm looking forward to starting our internship," he says, surprisingly still willing and seemingly wanting to talk.

Morgan moves to a group of chairs to the right of us with Brooklyn and James, and she motions her hand for me to drop my hoodie. I don't think she gets how naked I feel without it. I know she'll march over and steal it if I don't do something soon, though, so I set it down on a nearby chair. When I look up, I catch Theo's eyes on my bare stomach and instantly have no idea what to do with my arms or hands. I end up leaning awkwardly with one hand on the wooden back of the chair and the other on my hip. I feel utterly ridiculous.

Theo spurts out a laugh, which he tries to cover with a fist, but fails. I snag my sweatshirt again and stand up straight, hugging it to my chest and wanting to crawl inside it, wishing it were the size of a sack.

"I'm sorry," he says, his voice still wobbling from stifled laughter. "It was how you were standing. Not . . . not the way you look."

He clears his throat and glances to the side, his eyes squinting as he swallows. His laughter stops, and his mouth straightens.

"I'm not wearing my own clothes. This is Brooklyn's and it's Morgan's skirt, and I feel stupid—"

"You shouldn't," he cuts in, his gaze back on me.

He shifts his weight and stands tall, leaving the edge of the desk. His eyes dip from my face down to where my hands work the fabric of my hoodie into a stress ball. He reaches forward with one hand, hooks a finger in the material, and tugs it toward him. On instinct, I clutch it harder. His hand flinches a little, but he doesn't let go. His eyes flit up to mine and his lips form a crooked smile that normally I would say is to mock me. But something between us right now feels . . . different.

I give in and let him pull my sweatshirt into his hands, and he tosses it back to the chair, rolling his shoulders as he straightens and drops his hands in his pockets.

"Damn."

The word spills from his lips slow and thick, and my skin burns under his glare. I fight my urge to wrap myself up again. His gaze returns to mine after a slow blink.

"You look . . ." A soft laugh puffs out and he runs his palm over his jawline, glancing to his side for a moment. He almost seems embarrassed, which tugs at my lips, tempting me to grin. His focus comes back to my face, and for the first time since the night we talked at that party—since *the* night—his eyes are clear, and blue, and full of kindness. "You shouldn't hide yourself, Lily. You're very pretty."

My lips buzz from his attention. I know I'm blushing. My cheeks tighten and my legs feel wobbly.

Theo's stare hovers on my face for several seconds, and it's the first time since I've been back that his expression when looking at me isn't tinged with some sort of disgust. Maybe that's not the right word. I've been repelling him, and I understand why. I don't have to, though. We really could help each other. To heal.

Almost as if he caught himself staring too long, his mouth quirks up on one side, and he bites the edge of his tongue in a guilty way. He twists and takes the glass back in his hand, bringing it to his lips and tilting it back, swallowing every last drop. He runs his forearm along his mouth and releases an *ah* while his eyes roam about the room.

"I should probably make sure everyone here understands that this place is to be kept in total secret. A part of me is sorry I ever shared it." He shuffles his feet and adjusts his sleeves, which have crept up his muscular forearms, and though his words were probably just some afterthought, they stab at my chest.

He means me. He shouldn't have shared this place with me.

I turn slowly in place as he walks past me. He stops with his back to me, and I swallow my breath. His head falls forward and my eyes move to his hand, his finger tapping on the rim of his empty glass, the way my stepfather does when he's considering how to say something just right to my mom.

Twisting his neck, he looks back over his shoulder, and I glance up in time to catch him taking one more glance at my chest before flitting his gaze up to my eyes.

"We should head into the city together. On Tuesday?"

"Okay," I respond. "I can . . . drive?"

"We'll take the train," he says, our eyes locked for a beat before he nods. "The T has a stop a block from their building. And parking is a bitch."

"R-r-right. We'll take the T." I've taken the train twice since I've been at Welles, and both of those trips were under

Anika's guidance. I like the control of having my car, of leaving places when I want to and at least having a way to drive around lost on my own.

Theo smirks at my attempt to sound like a local, like he does. He doesn't exploit it to make fun of me, though. And there's a touch of warmth to his gaze that passes over me one last time before he turns and strides across the room.

Maybe he's all right letting me into his secret space, for just a little while.

Chapter 12

Theo

"Y**ou're riding** the train together for convenience, and it has nothing to do with you wanting to spend extra time with Lily?"

I'm not having the greatest day, and Cameron is pushing things by questioning me and staring at me with that smug look on his face.

"You do realize I'm tying silk around your neck right now, right?" I thread the long end of his tie through the loop and slip the knot tight against his throat, maybe a little too tight. He's lucky his windpipe has room.

He coughs and steps back, laughing as he sticks a finger in the collar of his shirt to loosen my work.

"Yeah, but I can't help it. I like to poke the bear."

I roll my eyes. Truthfully, Cameron would get off on poking an *actual* bear. He likes to step into confrontation. It feeds an insatiable adrenaline rush for him.

"What am I supposed to do for an entire semester? Sprint away from her while we go to the same building in downtown Boston twice a week? Leave on the fuckin' four-thirty train and get there three hours too damn early so I can avoid her?" I go to work on my own tie.

"You could always drive your car," he says.

My hands drop to my sides and I tilt my head to the side, glaring at him. I don't have to respond with words. I shared that car with Anika, even though she never drove it. I took her anywhere she needed to be. Time spent in that sedan is filled with memories of time spent with her. If it were up to me, I would have left it back home. My mom insisted I might need it, though, and I am all about keeping Mom happy.

"I'm being civil. I believe that's what everyone wants me to be."

"Not me. I like it when you're uncivil. Makes me seem like I've got my shit together." He grins, satisfied with his comeback, then drops his hands in his pockets. I blink slowly and do my best to not react . . . *at all*.

I tug on my Windsor knot, forcing it straight. It kind of pisses me off that Cameron's turned out better.

"Maybe I'm coming to terms with the fact that what happened was an accident, and not Lily's fault." My mouth waters just saying those words out loud. I think maybe I realize they're true, and that leaves everything rawer and more open-ended somehow. Lily was at least an answer to the impossible *why*. If she's not to blame then really, all that's left is life being cruel and fleeting.

"Imagine how she feels," Cameron says.

I pause my hands and blink his direction again. My instinct is to tell him to fuck off and quit talking about it, but he's already slipped into his jacket and headed to our door.

"Well, unlike you, I'll be riding into the city in a van with five people who probably can't stand me." Cameron is interning with a law firm run by one of the legacy parents from Welles. One of the other interns is the daughter of the head of the firm, McKenna Lowell . . . *his ex*. The other four people in their group happen to be her best friends. McKenna's dad, however, took a liking to Cameron and could not care less that he broke his daughter's heart.

"You could have interned anywhere, dumbass." I smack him on the back of the neck as I pull our door open and step through.

"Yeah, but what fun is that? This is a challenge." He pops a stick of gum in his mouth as if that's somehow going to make him smell less like he's been hotboxing in his car all morning. Somehow, I think he's still going to come out of this with a glowing recommendation and prospects while I will be looking at state school and a burger flipping gig.

We fly down the stairs. Cameron spins when we hit the front steps to our dorm and salutes me as he heads out to the main parking lot where our school's political science teacher is waiting with a van. I check the time on my phone and do my best to breathe and relax my neck and shoulders. I told Morgan to let Lily know I'd wait for her outside Hayden Hall, but she was distracted by James and his wet hair because it was after football practice. Who knows if that message made it all the way to the target?

I walk around the main lawn, sticking to the walkway rather than cutting through the grass so I don't get wet clippings on the bottom of my pants. It rained last night, and the air is still moist. I'm nearly to the Hayden entrance when Lily steps out. She stops with one foot out the door, and when our eyes meet, her face instantly pales. I don't know how I sense it, but she's about to run. Her hand lets go of the door and she leans back just as I grasp her arm, my fingers sliding along her skin until I cuff her wrist. She freezes at my touch, and my focus jets to the cool chain I feel under my palm. I peel two of my fingers from her arm and uncover the bracelet my sister wore almost every day since I gave it to her for her sixteenth birthday.

"Where'd you get this?" My words come out harsh. Lily jerks her arm free and covers the silver bracelet with her other hand.

"She gave it to me. I thought . . . maybe it would make me confident. It's stupid. Here—"

"No, it's fine. Keep it." I take a step back and put my hands in my back pockets to keep them from ripping the thin chain from Lily's wrist. Of course Anika gave it to her. My sister was the queen of generosity. I don't know if there's a single thing she owned that she didn't also share with someone else.

Lily twists the bracelet around her wrist as she chews at her lip. Her lashes are heavy, blinking as she forces her gaze back up to me. I barked at her, so I get it. I take another step back and turn to the side, encouraging her to leave the safety of the door frame by easing my overbearing presence.

"Better hurry. We'll be late."

My gaze flits to her then back down to the concrete steps. A tiny part of me hopes she'll sprint back inside and quit. It's the worst part of me, but I won't deny it's there, boiling in my belly. Festering.

She leaves the door behind and takes to the steps to join me, and soon we're in step. She's wearing her uniform with the addition of a tailored jacket. Even her shoes are the plain black loafers most of the girls wear every day—even the pre-teens.

"Good thing *The Affiliate* isn't a fashion rag," I tease. When I glance to my side, though, I catch her hands fisting the edges of her jacket and my chest squeezes with guilt.

"Hey," I say, nudging her elbow with my own. "I was joking."

She forces a tight-lipped smile that lasts maybe a second, then blinks her focus forward.

The train is pulling in just as we get to the platform. There are more students here waiting than I anticipated, maybe fifteen or so, and the T is usually packed with regular business traffic. I hope we're able to get a seat. It's only a thirty-minute ride, but that's a long time to spend on our feet. On instinct, I lurch forward when the doors open, but Lily gets lost in the shuffle of people filing in behind me.

"Lily!" I call, gaining her attention and waving her toward the front of the train where a few seats remain.

She raises up on her toes and nods at me, doing her best to swim through the chaos, but by the time we connect, there's only a single seat left.

"Take it," I insist, grabbing a tight hold on the bar to the right of the seat.

"Are you sure?"

I nod and she slips into the space, hugging her small leather bag against her chest and drawing her legs in tight. My eyes scan the car to see who's heading into the city with us and I nod and smile at a few guys from the team. Two girls sitting directly across from Lily are whispering in each other's ears, and I catch them glaring at me right before they turn away and hide behind their portfolio books. I gnash my teeth and draw in a deep breath with my lips closed tight. I wonder when the gossip and posturing about how I'm getting on is going to stop.

The train jerks forward and I steady my feet, my body swinging back on the jolt. Lily shifts to her right in her seat, and at first, I assume she just isn't used to the lurch of the train. But as my eyes trail from her lap to the man sitting in the sit to her left, I notice how much of her space his leg is taking.

"Theo, hey! I didn't know you were in the city, too." It's Elias, one of the linemen on the team, and maybe one of the few truly nice guys at Welles. His dad is one of the younger form teachers. In fact, he was my very first teacher at Welles.

"They managed to squeeze me in at *The Affiliate*. I mean, sales, for now, but we'll see." Elias and I have both talked about the magazine in the past. He's a huge reader, too.

"Oh, man, that's awesome. Are you . . . both working there?" He points toward Lily, whose eyes are trained straight ahead without focus, her knees locked and hands clutching her bag for dear life.

"Yeah. It wasn't planned or anything, just a fluke." I don't know why I feel I need to say that. It's not as if interning at the same place somehow makes us a *thing*. We're already enough of a thing because of . . . *well*.

"Right. Still, that's awesome. Good luck, dude. I'm at Duckworth for accounting. I'm good at math, I guess." Elias shrugs then holds up a fist. I tap it with mine then he shifts to return to the conversation behind him.

Our conversation lasted maybe thirty seconds, and in that time, Lily's jaw has gotten vice-grip tight because the asshole sitting next to her has encroached even more. I let my eyes linger on his thigh, his wallet and keys probably stuffed in his tight pants, causing him to protrude even more. Taking up space is one thing, but this guy, he's trying to get his fucking rocks off. His knee is practically knocking into hers with every sway of the train, and his hand has miraculously found its way to the side of his thigh, his spindly, hairy-ass pinky finger flirting with the hem of her skirt.

My eyes shift their attention to his face, and I couldn't give two shits if he catches me staring at him right now. His eyes are fixed on his phone, propped up on his other thigh all cool and casual. His hair is slicked back to cover the thinning spots on top. He's probably in his thirties, and I don't see a ring so I'm guessing his moves haven't worked on anyone. He's flipping through some social media shit, never stopping on one image long enough to really look at it. He's acting on this side of his body while his other side gives our gender a bad name. My right hand is in the pocket of my jacket, balling tight. I'm *this close* to knocking his teeth out of alignment.

I glance back to Lily, her eyes still fixed ahead, unblinking. *Come on, Lily. Look up at me. Give me the go sign.*

She's too trapped to be able. She's terrified, and uncomfortable. *She looks like Anika did sometimes when Neil sat next to her on the couch.*

I've traveled this route a hundred, maybe two hundred times. I know every bump and hitch along the way, and this next stop crosses over a pretty old intersection in need of some serious street repair. I time it just right, falling forward and slamming my hand down on this asshole's thigh as I fake falling forward. My fingers dig in, giving him a hard squeeze, and when I pop my head up our eyes meet. At first, he looks pissed, but after a beat he must see the rage in my eyes. My jaw flexes and I glance to his right, where Lily has taken this opportunity to create more room. When I return my glare to him, I arch a brow and keep my mouth in a hard line. If I open it, about a million different insults are going to fly at his face along with my fist. His Adam's apple dips with a hard swallow and my lip ticks up on one side. As more people file into the train, he gets up and moves to the other end and I take the seat next to Lily.

The stop lasts about a minute, the T filling every remaining spot. We'll lose people at the stops ahead as we enter the financial district. Lily and I will probably be the last two to get off. I plan on stalking Mr. Touchy Feely until he departs, and if I didn't have somewhere to be, I might get off with him and follow him to work to let his employer know the kind of man he is.

I'm not sure when Lily started staring at me. I only feel it now and turn my head enough to meet her waiting eyes. For a second, she looks the way she did in the pool after I scooped her up from the bottom, tired and confused, but color is starting to touch her stark cheeks again. She blinks, and my heart kicks so hard in my chest that it feels like a stab wound from the inside.

"Thank you," she whispers.

I glance down to her mouth in time to see it form the faintest of smiles. My eyes flit back up to meet hers, the weight of what happened evident in their glossiness and slope. I nod and loosen my jaw enough to soften my mouth and try to smile.

We both look away at the same time. That's not the kind of thing I want to say *you're welcome* for. I shouldn't have had to do it at all. What I really feel the need to do is apologize.

The whole thing made this morning feel more stressful somehow. I feel it, my blood on a constant simmer and my pulse finding it hard to slow. I'm sure Lily is rattled. She's been twisting my sister's bracelet around her wrist nonstop since I sat next to her. She's loosened her death grip on her bag, though, and she no longer looks as though she's about to faint.

Our train stops at Copley, and I stand. Lily follows, but I don't want to lose her in the crowd again so I hold my arm out to keep her from passing me while the rest of the train's passengers file out. Once the crowd thins, I lead us through the station and up to the street level. Maybe I should have let her drive. Perhaps next time. I'm not sure either of us can handle another morning like this.

"It's only a block south. We're even early." I turn to face her, dropping both hands in my pockets. It's warmed up since we left Welles, the crispness gone from the air. Another month and this trip will be colored with fall leaves. That was always Anika's favorite.

"Come on," I say, returning some lightness to the mood between us. Funny how I wanted to build nothing but walls and tension between us only a week ago.

We make it to the building with fifteen minutes to spare. I'm about to ask Lily if she wants to grab a bite on the corner before we head in when her body slams into mine and her arms surround my entire body. My hands are stunned still in my pockets as she squeezes me. For some reason, I laugh. Not in a cruel way, but more surprised. I almost sound happy, and when Lily steps back, her cheeks are apple red but she's smiling, too, and avoiding direct eye contact.

She scans around us, then points to the double glass doors painted with *The Affiliate* logo. She skips up the few steps that lead to them and I trail behind, a strange numbness traveling around my body and arms. I don't mind the feeling, and as I draw in a full breath I realize how tight I've been tethering myself inside. I let the door close between us before I catch up to her, and in that moment I mutter, "You're welcome."

That hug? That was her saying thank you again. Not for taking care of that jerk on the train, either. But for finally being fucking human.

Chapter 13

Lily

I feel like I stepped off the Gravitron ride from our state fair after spinning in it for thirty minutes straight. I wouldn't say I'm completely dizzy, but I'm definitely buzzing with some strange energy.

In the span of a thirty-minute train ride, I went from feeling smothered and afraid to having my lungs drunk with oxygen and my heart skipping with life. Not because Theo stepped in to defend my honor or anything like that. I was about ten seconds from throwing my elbow and hitting that dick dead center in the chest when Theo stepped in and basically did it for me. It's that Theo saved me from making a scene. I wasn't afraid to defend myself. I was dreading the heat of everyone's glare—the confrontation and ensuing attention. The probable applause that would only increase the chatter about how strong I am.

The hero status has gone quiet in the last few days. I want it to go quiet. Less talk about the river and me and my roommates. Theo saved me from the Welles gossip storm.

But it was more than that. He also shed some of that

armor for me, giving me a glimpse of the guy I was really falling for before our world tilted its axis.

Of course, now that I hugged him like a third grader hugs an amusement park character, I feel completely awkward standing here next to him in *The Affiliate* conference room. It doesn't help that I'm wearing a schoolgirl uniform while he's dressed like he belongs here. I can't stop fidgeting, and I'm rocking on my feet nervously, something I don't think I've ever done before, which would be fine except that the strap for my bag jingles every time I sway.

"Relax," Theo says, leaning into me. He's so close, and all I can think about is hugging him downstairs on the street. Like he's Santa.

"Lily," he breathes my name. I flinch and blink to look to my side and meet his eyes.

"Huh?"

My eyes feel like they're bugging out. Theo is trying to hold in a laugh. He's cute this way—*kind?*

Are we over guilt and grudges? Am I allowed to go back to thinking he's the cutest boy I've ever seen? Would Anika be okay with that?

"Breathe," he says, finally letting a quiet chuckle slip from his mouth and coaxing nervous laughter from my lips, too.

"Sorry, I feel a little . . . out of place." I give him a crooked smile and pull my skirt out to one side as I glance down.

"It's not as bad as you think it is."

"Not *as* bad? Meaning a *little* bad?" My brow pulls in and the panic tingles in my stomach and legs again. I feel the urge to sway.

Theo laughs.

And then his hand is on my wrist again. A light touch, but one that freezes me in place and stops my heart completely. His fingers curl in and he pulls his hand away, quickly stuffing both in his pockets.

"You look fine, I mean. But maybe . . . a shopping trip to expand the wardrobe a little?" He lifts one brow and looks down at my feet. I follow his gaze as he kicks lightly at my toe. "Your roommates have big feet."

I shake and spit out a quick laugh at the memory of me fumbling out of Morgan's shoes. That's when Theo went to get my shoes, even though he supposedly didn't want anything to do with me.

"Fair point," I say as Abby and Todd walk into the room, the same duo from our interviews.

"So, are you guys ready to immerse yourselves in *The Affiliate* world?" Abby is three-cups-of-coffee amped. It's a bit jarring.

"Let's do this," Theo says, somehow mirroring her enthusiasm and energy level. *Chameleon.*

I was thinking maybe his response spoke for the both of us, but as Todd and Abby's focus drips to me and their smiles go stale, I realize they're waiting for me to say something too.

"Yeah!" I fist pump, which is something I've never actually done once in my whole life. It's obvious, to everyone, but at least it gets a laugh. My face burns and the smile I'm trying hard to push outward tingles with the urge to cringe.

"All right, all right," Abby says, nodding and moving in to shake our hands. "Theo, you'll be going through orientation with Todd. He'll introduce you to our advertising team and the sales manager. It's a great group. I think you're going to like them. And Lily . . . you're with me."

Her eyes lock on me again, and the only thing I can think of doing is a repeat of the fist pump, which, shocker, did not get any better over the span of four seconds.

Abby shakes her head and laughs, then motions for me to

follow her down a long hallway to the row of offices in the back. I glance over my shoulder before we dip inside her office and manage to catch Theo before he's swallowed up by a group of people all dressed exactly like him. It's hard to say from this far away, but I think he winks. I've come to my senses enough to not try and wink back, *thank God!* I've shared enough of my nonverbal communication skills today.

"Have a seat," Abby says, motioning to the set of chairs in front of her desk. Her office is modest, room enough for a small table in the corner that's covered with tear sheets and a wall decked with framed covers of some of their biggest name interviews. I get caught up looking at the names as she sits down across from me.

Labron. Pedro Martinez. Phelps.

"He let me race him at the training center for that interview," she says, snapping me out of my daze.

My gaze jets to her and I know my mouth is agape. But Phelps . . . in a pool? Wow.

"He lapped me. Twice," she says, leaning back in her chair and holding up two fingers.

I chuckle.

"He'd probably get me three times," I respond.

"Oh, I bet it would be closer than that. You're quite the swimmer, I hear." She pulls her hands in, folding them at her lap as she swivels in her chair and smiles at me with admiration. It's a nice compliment. I don't really want to talk about my swimming, though.

"Doubtful, but thanks," I say, brushing the topic off.

Her stare lingers on me for a few seconds, and my anxiety claws at my stomach and chest again. I slide my feet under me and pull my bag in tighter to my chest.

"I had the team pull the last six months of issues together for you. I'm hoping to start you off with an easy but important project. If you want to look at one of the issues . . ." She shifts the stack of magazines from her side of the desk toward me and I scoot forward, glad to have something to do with my nervous hands—*and edgy focus*. "Flip to the back. Where you see those briefs?"

I head toward the back to the regional stories, the pages where I always found the most interesting features about athletes my age. I wonder if I'll get to report on some of these. That would be amazing.

"Like most magazines have already, *The Affiliate* is going completely digital."

"Oh," I say, glancing up with a frown.

"Yeah, I'm with you. There's something about turning pages that I'm going to really miss. But paper is expensive. And digital ads are endless. It's a bottom-line thing, and if it means we get to do more storytelling, then I'm willing to let go of some ink . . . I guess."

I'm warming to her.

"Makes sense," I say.

"I'm glad you get it. We're transitioning things slowly. Our events calendar has been digital for years, and we've done a lot of spot video and highlights on our website and app. Our next section to really embrace the digital space is this one. When we launch, we'd like to have some video stories already in place. You know, to make the section look bigger, have some depth."

"Sure, yeah." I curl my hand in my lap to keep myself from fist pumping again. It's becoming a problem.

"How would you feel about interviewing some of our past subjects? Sort of a where are they now video, kind of an update after their season, or a look ahead or whatever? We were brainstorming and thought it would be cool to get those stories about high school athletes told from someone on their level. And given that you're a competitor yourself . . ."

My mouth goes dry at her mention of me competing again, but I'm too jazzed about the opportunity to let panic settle in.

"Awesome," I say.

She tilts her head to the side and squints over her smile.

"Yeah? I was afraid it would be too much to start with, but I feel like you, of all people, can handle it."

I swallow. I'm not sure what she means by that, and I may be overreacting that she's talking about my surviving an accident last spring and saving two of my friends. *Not three.*

"It's not too much. I'd love to do it." I let go of my ego enough to bring my fist up for one last pump—a small one, clearly in jest.

Abby laughs.

"Great. Well, maybe spend the morning looking through these issues and come up with your list of potential angles and questions and then this afternoon we can narrow down which five you'll work on. We have a photographer, so don't worry about the video part. You'll be doing the interviewing. But Ken can teach you how to edit if you're interested after you guys get the interviews in."

I'm giddy again. Maybe even more than I was after the train when I tackle hugged Theo. I'm working toward something—a dream, or a goal or whatever. I feel like I'm finally turning a new page.

Abby sets me up at a cubicle near the other staff writers, all names I recognize from stories I've read. Tony, the guy who covers most of the men's college sports stories, hooks me up with a coffee, and I dive into the magazines. I'm so engrossed that I don't realize when three hours have gone by, not until someone pulls my wheely chair back fast and spins it around.

"What the—"

Theo stops the spinning by grabbing the chair arm, along with half of my hand. My fingers grab hold at the touch, almost out of instinct. It's probably the adrenaline rush that causes it, but the few extra seconds he leaves his hand awkwardly tangled with mine and we simply hold on are because of something else. Something neither of us seems to want to acknowledge, even though I feel it.

All the awful things that have happened haven't removed that pull we have. It was so easy to bond with him that night at the party, before the accident. It was as if we were old friends who simply picked up a conversation where we'd left off. Along with lots of lingering looks, the kind of stares that stick for way too long and feel both good and terrifying.

Electricity.

Theo backs away and shoves his hands into those protective pockets he seems to store them in whenever we're together. I stand and straighten my skirt, then mark the article I was reading with a sticky note and stack my magazines.

"There's a grilled cheese truck on the corner. Come on, lunch is on me."

My stomach has been growling for the last hour, and the mere mention of cheese makes it roll over and echo cries of emptiness.

"Okay, but I get to buy on Thursday," I offer, slinging my bag over my shoulder and pushing in my chair.

Theo holds out a fist and I stare at it for a moment before huffing out a laugh. I eventually tap it with my fist. We've gone from sparks to bro-taps, I guess.

"What do they have you doing? Filing?" he asks as we head down the main hall back out toward the street.

"No! It's amazing. They're letting me do some video interviews for a new digital launch, and—" I cover my mouth when I realize Theo wanted this gig, too. He took the sales offer, but I know he really wanted to work in editorial.

"Lily, it's fine. I'm glad they're letting you do things. I'm making cold calls. It's, well, it might be the fourth level of hell. I've found it. And it's pretty fucking terrible."

"Circle," I say, back pressed against the main door to hold it open. Theo stops in his tracks and glares at me.

"Are you serious? That's what you get out of my story? That I didn't quote Dante correctly in my analogy of advertising work?" He shoots me a wry smile and I'm not sure whether he's kidding or not. My gut knots up with guilt either way.

"I'm messing with you," he laughs out, brushing the back of his hand into my arm as he walks by. I note the way his jaw ticks after he passes, though, and I don't think he was joking as much as he tried to make me believe he was.

I decide to tone down my excitement a little and change the subject to something I know we can both agree on—Morgan's family. I don't know her nearly as well as Theo does, but she and I are close enough for me to have a pretty good understanding of the messed-up power dynamics in her family.

"You've known Morgan for a while, right?"

"Yeah, since we were kids. Like, before Welles," he says.

We both step up to the truck window and Theo orders two lunch specials. He pays with a card, and I notice the He-Man design. Before he can slip it back in his wallet, I snap it from his hand and dash away.

"Hey! Okay, I know what you're going to say." His face is

legitimately red right now and he flattens a palm over it, shaking his head.

"Theodore D. Rothschild. What's the D stand for? *Destined to become He-Man one day?*"

"Ha ha. Give it back." He lunges at me, and I pull his card into my body, hugging it against my chest while I whirl around, swinging my bag like it's a mace in an attempt to ward him off.

In seconds, his arms are around me from behind, his chin on my shoulder and his hands working to unfasten my grip on his He-Man card. I'm giggling, and this is most definitely flirting. His arms are warm and he's the perfect height against me, and I could play this stupid game of keep away for the rest of the afternoon if I could.

"Shows what you know. There's only one He-Man. Clearly, I can't become him." His serious tone makes me laugh harder. Eventually, he holds me tight enough to lift my feet from the ground and his card slips from my hands. He sets me on my feet and scurries to grab it before I can. I didn't have a chance. I'm too drunk on whatever just happened.

"Theo! Your order's ready," the man shouts from the truck.

"You mean He-Man," I holler, getting some snickers from a few people waiting in line. Theo rolls his eyes at me and steps up to the window to get our food.

He takes the two bags and walks to an empty bench nearby. I sit facing him, curling one leg up and tucking my skirt under my thighs. I hold my hands out and he eyes me sideways before setting the second lunch bag on the other side of him.

"You really think you deserve lunch after that scene?" He's playing, and it's so nice to see this side of him come to life. It's also stirring butterflies in my chest. And here I thought I was empty.

"I'm sorry. But it was hard to resist. You must admit, He-Man is a bit of a kid's thing."

He grimaces, but a smirk breaks through after a few seconds and he tosses me my bag.

"The guy only had one cold pop, so we're gonna have to share. Maybe." He bends the tab back and takes a long sip, eying me the entire time before pulling his lips away with an *ahhh*. He hands it over, dropping the charade finally, and I hold the can to my lips, embarrassed that the first thought in my head is how this is almost like kissing. His mouth was just right here.

Who's immature now, Lily?

"I kept losing my card. Like, it happened at least once a month. Anyhow, it pissed my mom and stepdad off, and my stepdad, Neil, is kind of a prick. He got a little *too* mad about it my freshman year and he threw one of his whiskey tumblers at my head. Cut me right here." He dips his head slightly and points to a faint scar that cuts across his right eyebrow. When he looks back up, our eyes meet, and that playful connection has suddenly morphed into something deeper. Lately, this is when we pull away—when glances last too long and drudge up painful memories. For whatever reason, I pledge to myself to hold on this time, to not look away. And Theo hangs right in with me.

"Anika lightened the mood, teasing that I should have to carry a kid's card until I learn how to be responsible. We were freshmen, and I never lost my card again after that. But I keep getting the same card anyhow because . . . she picked it."

He unfolds his wallet again and pulls the card back out, running his thumb over it. As my focus blurs around his knuckle, a strange wave of calmness cools me.

"We're twins," I say, drawing his attention to the skin above my right brow. I run my finger along the familiar line etched with seven stitches. "Rolling pin."

Without pause, Theo reaches up and runs his thumb over my long-healed wound. I haven't felt the scar in years, but his touch makes the skin feel soft and lovely again. My mom was enraged. My father sent me a Christmas gift, and she waited for me to come home and see it wrapped on the kitchen counter before she promptly threw it in the trash and picked up the closest object she could strike me with. In her head, it's always been my fault he left us.

The worst part was at the ER after, when I thought she was racked with guilt only to find out she was terrified I was going to tell someone what happened. I don't know how I knew to lie, that that's what she wanted. But the words came out, and I kept repeating them to every person we saw.

"I ran into a tree limb."

"I was running and didn't see it."

"I guess I turned around too late."

Nobody batted an eye. My story held up. Mom hugged me while they sewed me up. And the minute we left the hospital, she let me go and we didn't speak again for an entire week.

"Dean," Theo says.

I quirk my brow under his thumb. He chuckles, and unfortunately pulls his hand away.

"The D. My middle name. It's Dean."

I give him a half-hearted, crooked smile.

"I like He-Man better."

Theo rocks back with a laugh that scares away the few birds that were creeping closer to us. It's the purist laugh I've ever heard, and my cheeks hurt from the smile it causes on my face. I did that to him. I made him laugh.

I made him feel.

* * *

My stomach full and my heart oddly happy for once, I fly through the rest of the articles and finish writing up my questions before the workday is done. I print them out and bring the copy to Abby's office, where she's talking with an older, heavyset man in a suit and tie. I can tell somehow that he's a step above the sales manager, so when Abby waves me in, I tug on my jacket and straighten my skirt, wishing like I hell I was wearing anything else so I look like a grownup.

"Lily, I wanted to introduce you to Michael St. James."

My eyes stretch wide. I feel it, and I can't help that it happens. Michael is the founder of *The Affiliate*. He started the magazine after selling his stake in a very popular New England football team.

"Sir, it's so nice to meet you." I'm fawning, and it must amuse the man because he chuckles and takes my hand in two of his, patting the top the way I always pictured a grandfather would to his favorite granddaughter. I was never anyone's favorite anything.

"Lily, nice to meet you. Abby's been catching me up on you, says you're our intern for the next three months. Hope we don't turn you off sports journalism by working you too hard."

"Impossible," I say.

"Good to hear. Sign her up!" He holds a finger in the air and moves toward Abby's door. "Let me know, Abby, about that thing we talked about."

He pats the door frame on his way out, and my body is completely buzzing from the day.

"Are those your questions already?" Abby brings me back

down to earth, and I switch gears, shifting into overachiever mode. As much as I've coasted through my classes at Welles, I can't let that happen here. I may not want to shine academically, but this is about my career. In this building, I want to be the best intern they've ever had. That way when I head to college in the fall, I might find my way back here again and again. Until they hire me for real.

"Yeah, I got super inspired. I know I have too many, but I thought you could strike the ones you don't like, or I can ask them all and we can trim. If Ken shows me how to edit, I can help—"

"Okay, whoa. Slow down, Lily," she says through light laughter. She leans back and scans my document. I try to read her reaction on her face, picking out what question she's on by the way her lips move silently. "These are great," she says, spinning slowly in her chair.

I slip into a chair when her back is too me, mostly so my knees can bounce out of her view. By the time she rotates toward me again, she's done. She lays the pages down in front of me and taps them with her finger.

"This is good work. If you're game to learn editing, I say do them all."

I slide them into my hands while my legs jackrabbit with energy behind her desk.

"Really? I'm glad. Okay, yeah. I'll . . . I guess, meet with Ken next?" If it were up to me I would sprint to his office right now and drag him down the street, take the T, and head to whatever school is closest to nail our first interview.

"Yeah. He should be set on Thursday, and he can walk you through some things. Today was a full day. How did you like it?" She leans back and pulls a cap from one of her pens, twirling it in her hand like a mini baton.

"I don't want to leave," I joke. *It's only a half joke.*

Her smile broadens.

"Good. I think you're going to do great here."

I nod and smile back. Her eyes linger on me for a few seconds, and she shifts in her chair then chews on the cap she was just twirling.

"Before you go, I did want to run something by you." Her head wobbles slightly as her mouth pulls in tight. My mom does that when she's about to sell me on bad news, like the way she told me Drew's son was moving in with us, and that he'd be more suited to my room. I could have the one over the garage.

"It's bigger," she said. *It's freezing.*

"Sure," I say, trying my best confident voice on for size. *It's not very confident sounding. And that was a tiny word I uttered.*

"How would you feel about documenting your journey . . . back to the water?"

Her question lingers in the air. My mouth hangs open. I'm not sure how many seconds pass since she's asked it, but I know it's been a few. I can read the hesitation on her face, the slight wince. If I look hard enough, every little tick in her eyes, gnaw at her cheek, and attempt to speak is a signal she's reworking her approach.

I feel sick.

"I mean, of course you'll still do the interviews for the regional section. I was just thinking, you know, because you're so unique . . . it might be a great format for you to tell your own story, in your own words. As part of this, almost like a soft launch for it."

For a moment, her lips move but I hear nothing. The issue is on my end. I'm near fainting. I always lose my hearing right before I pass out. Sweat streams down my sides from my armpits and my hands have crinkled the papers in my fists.

"Lily? Do you have any thoughts?"

I'm pretty sure she's repeating herself. I left this planet for a blip there. I'm not sure how I got back, and I sort of wish my body could have evaporated out of this situation too, not just my mind.

"Or if you have another idea of a way it might work? I could interview you, too. But I'd really love to see you get the credit for your own story. It only seems right that way."

It only . . . seems . . . right.

"Can I, uh, can I . . . think about it?" *Why didn't I just say no? Do it now, Lily. Say no. No!*

"Of course. We'll circle back next week. And I'll think about some ideas for it too. We can really brainstorm." She puts her entire gut into that word—*brainstorm.* That means talking about *me,* with other people, and thinking about *me,* and *my story.* Putting words to it all—to Anika, my room-mates, my failures.

Theo.

I leave Abby's office in a daze, the energy that fueled me most of the day now on a drip line, barely holding me up. Theo is waiting for me at my cubicle, leaning against my desk while he scrolls through his phone. It was such a good day. It was a good day for *us.*

I swallow down the bile climbing up my esophagus and squeeze my eyes shut. I can do this. I can erase the last ten minutes from my mind for a little while, to continue this amazing day.

When I open my eyes, Theo has moved to stand. He's impossibly handsome. His tie is loosened, but I'm shocked it lasted around his neck all day. At school, he usually has it wriggled loose by second hour. He's been doing that since our first year. Some boys just don't wear ties well. Not that he doesn't look incredible dressed in a crisp designer suit tailored to him perfectly. He does, indeed. But I've seen him in sweatpants, and in T-shirts and swim trunks. I've seen him with his shirt off after football practice. All those times when he barely knew I existed, I was watching. *Truthfully, I was crushing.*

"I'm pretty sure today calls for a happy hour. You in?" He steps aside so I can close out my computer and gather my things.

"It's obvious I'm not twenty-one. I'm dressed like a four-teen-year-old," I respond through nervous laughter.

"First, you do not look like a child. Far from it. And two, of course we're not going to a bar. Why would we when we have the world's best speakeasy in the middle of campus?" He holds up the key he had made to keep the prying eyes of faculty out of the archives room.

I chuckle. Maybe a happy hour would do me some good tonight.

"All right. I can message Brooklyn and Morgan on the T."

"Already done," he brags, holding up his phone and showcasing a new group chat he created. I squint to see it, mostly because I'm looking for my name.

"You can see the messages on your own phone, silly." He must know that's what I was looking for.

"Oh, yeah. Duh." My face fires, and it only gets hotter as he leans into me. Shoulder to shoulder, arm to arm. I'm over-come with the urge to hug him again.

"We'll have to do eleven tonight. Some of us have an early morning. New coach wants us to lift at six a.m." He grimaces.

"I'll think of you, ya know, when I roll over and go back to sleep." I smirk and he glares at me with a shocked, open mouth.

"You're terrible. I'll remember that. Paybacks and all." He

laughs softly as he leads the way down the corridor toward the sidewalk outside. I avoid looking in the direction of Abby's office, though the glow of her light spills into the hall-way. I refuse to burst my bubble.

It can't be happy hour if nobody is happy.

Chapter 14

Theo

I hate sales.

Not only do I *hate* sales, but sales hates me right back.

My mouth hurts from all the forced smiles I contorted my cheeks and lips into today. Every client who stopped in—smile. Every new sales rep I met—smile. Even when I was on the phone, going down a sheet of cold calls and often getting my ass chewed out—smile.

I appreciate that Todd got me into this company and trusted me with this gig, but I'm not cut out for this. I don't know how people take the constant rejection. I don't get the fake interest that fills you with hope just so someone can ultimately say they aren't interested. Like, I spent fourteen minutes talking about the Kentucky Derby with some guy today to build a report, only to have him call me *sport* and say his budget is spent for the year.

Professionally, today was a zero.

Personally, though? Today was a good day. A damn good day, despite the way it started with the creeper on the T.

I haven't talked and joked with anyone like that since . . . well, since I talked and joked with Lily the night of the accident. I let go today. Maybe it was the guy moving in on her space that pushed me over the edge, or perhaps it was her hug that did it. I kinda think I just missed her. Missed that *what if* feeling we were nurturing months ago.

Practice was hard today, and it didn't even faze me. We ran. A lot. And I had plenty in the reserves. At one point, I turned and ran backwards, mocking James. I think it pissed him off a little. It felt great, though. And he got over it by the time we changed out in the locker room. Good thing, too, because I needed to talk him into snagging some more liquor for tonight.

It feels good to slide into jeans for once. Even when it's a casual thing, I usually play the part of the perfect Welles man. There's a standard that goes with this school, one that's pushed by people like my mom and Morgan's parents. They fought like hell to keep the zero-tolerance dress code in place, which meant a student was either in an approved Welles outfit or their fucking PJs. The board didn't relax the rules to allow for casual wear on weekends and after hours until my fourth form. Anika led the debate for change.

Tonight, I wear these jeans to celebrate the bad-assness of my sister.

"You're giddy. Why?" Cameron asks with what sounds like chips in his mouth.

Shit. Am I? Damn, I think I am.

"Or maybe you're just high," I respond over my shoulder. I button up my flannel and spray a dash of Gucci at my chest. I'm pretty much ready. Meanwhile, Cameron is in gray sweatpants and a long-sleeve metal band T-shirt with a slice across the center. And there's a cheese stain on it. He's been licking the bottom of that damn nacho bowl for the last ten minutes, shoving every crumb in his mouth. "Dude, that cheese drip looks like vomit. Can you at least change shirts?"

Cameron sits up straight, a rarity for him, and levels me with a very serious expression as he tosses his nacho tray to the side, missing the garbage can by a foot, then grabs a hoodie from the space where his bed meets the wall.

"Is that even clean?" Cameron is the reason we had a severe dress code, and right now, he's making me regret it relaxed.

"There's no cheese on it, so . . . yeah, it's clean." He pulls the hood up over his wild hair and stands, sliding his socked feet into a pair of Birkenstocks. Sometimes, the dude drives me nuts. But I think one of the reasons I love him so much is his overly relaxed persona. He's a walking, breathing treatment for my anxiety. Just being in a room with him has a mellowing effect. Or maybe it's a contact high.

"Let's go. People are probably waiting for me to open up the place."

Cameron slides his feet down the hall and even loses one of his sandals on the stairs during our trip down. I feel like he's purposely dragging ass to piss me off, but it simply amuses me instead. We slip outside through the back door and head toward the library where, surprisingly, nobody is waiting.

"Small gathering, I presume," Cameron teases through a cough.

I purse my lips and glare at him just outside the hidden library door.

"Maybe ease up on the smoking?" I chastise.

His only response is to make a hand puppet at me and say, "Blah, blah, blah."

I shift the vines to make room for the door and give it a tug. When it doesn't even budge, I back up and glance around as if I somehow came to the wrong secret library door. As if there's more than one.

"What's up?" Cameron rests his chin on my shoulder and looks on at the knob as I twist and pull again.

"It's stuck or something." My brow pinches. This door was loose the other times I came in here. There isn't a lock on it, which is the reason I discovered it in the first place. Of course, I *did* add a deadbolt inside.

"What the fuck?" I pull again, irritation growing with my suspicion. I pound with my fist then press my ear against the door to listen.

"They're in there," I huff, backing away enough to give me space to kick the door. "Open the door, assholes!"

"Dude, relax. It's not like you own the joint," Cameron says. I glare at him until he backs away a few steps and raises his palms at his sides. "Fine. Whatever. Someone will open it."

Cameron wanders over to the bench across the walkway and I pull my phone out to text our group. I understand what Cameron means, but seriously—I'm the one who planned tonight. I'm the one who found this room, who had the idea of using it to kick back and maybe party a little. I never should have shared it with James.

I start to pace, waiting for someone to respond to my message.

"Just sit down, Theo. They'll get to us when they get to us." Cameron's voice oozes chill, and normally that winds me down. Tonight, though, it has the opposite result. My pulse has ratcheted *way* up.

I flip through my contacts, mad that I only have Lily on the student messenger app. I should have made sure I got her number today. I wonder if she's in there. Probably is, with James . . . *studying.*

My thumb stops at James' contact info. I press CALL and promptly begin pacing back and forth in front of the door while I keep him on speaker. He doesn't answer the first time, but the second time I call he decides to answer in person, unlatching the door and swinging it open wide.

"Hey, there he is! Man of the hour." His laugh is sloppy. He's been drinking for a while, it seems.

I step in close, my chin just under his. I hate that he's taller than me, and my chest automatically inflates to match his size.

"What's up, man? Oh . . . the door!" He slaps his forehead and the whole thing feels like a performance. "Sorry, I wasn't even thinking. Really. Habit, I guess."

I hover in his space for a long second, then back away into the archive room. Music is playing in the back, soft enough to not be heard outside. I catch the sound of Lily's laugh, too, and the mixture with the music diffuses the tension in my chest.

I leave James to relock the door—now that we are *all* here —and head toward the sound of Lily's laughter. I find her sitting on a desktop next to Morgan, wearing a long-sleeved cropped shirt that shows off half her stomach and a pair of plaid pajama pants. Cameron slides up next to me and immediately points out the hypocrisy.

"And you gave me a hard time over the hoodie. Girl's wearing PJs, bruh." He leans forward and tugs at one of the pant legs, drawing a giggle from Lily.

"First of all, I'm pretty sure nothing Lily is wearing is covered in processed cheese sauce," I retort, leveling him with a hard-lined mouth. "And second, Lily looks absolutely nothing like you. You look like a bum. Lily, is . . ."

Shit. I was about to say hot.

"Go on, Theo. Tell us. What *is* Lily?" Cameron slings his

arm around my neck because he's an asshole and part of me wonders if he baited me into this trap from the very beginning. His mind works that way. He's a genius, legitimately. It's just hard to tell by his ridiculous exterior.

"Lily's fucking gorgeous, that's what Lily is," James cuts in as he slips into the space between me and the girls.

Lily's eyebrows jet up to her hairline and her lips part. Her cheeks blush too. She turns to her roommates, but only Brooklyn sticks around to help her with this situation. Morgan, who I'm pretty sure has a thing for James, excuses herself to refill her drink. I decide to join her because if I don't, my mouth is going to get me in all kinds of trouble, and probably the kind that includes my fists.

I step up next to Morgan and she gives me a slight eyeroll as she glances at me.

"I'm fine. I don't need your pep talk, Theodore."

"Wow! I mean, first of all, *Theodore?* And second, since when have I ever given anyone a pep talk."

She sets the liquor bottle down on the desk and screws the cap back in place, then takes her glass in both hands and turns to face me.

"We were twelve, and you told me to suck it up and run faster." She arches a brow and brings the tumbler to her lips, taking a sip and offering a cocky smirk.

"Ha! That's right. The three-legged race. I really wanted our team to get free pizza." I was a super competitive junior high kid. Sometimes I miss first and second form.

"Your legs were twice the length of mine!" she protests.

"We won, though, didn't we?" I lean back against the cabinets across from her and fold my arms, just to be smug. "Okay, so four years ago I gave you a pep talk. I claim statute of limitations."

"Maybe you should be interning with Cameron. You'd make a great lawyer," she says.

"A better lawyer than salesman." I wince remembering my day of cold calls.

"That bad, huh?"

I shrug in response.

Morgan taps her nails against the glass a few times then clicks her teeth.

"How are things . . . with . . ." She leans her head toward the group we recently abandoned. James is talking with Cameron, and Lily is nursing her drink while she listens to Brooklyn talk about something that requires her to be very animated with her hands. I must admit I'm glad to see that she's not talking with James.

"Surprisingly . . . good. Like, *really* good." My gaze lingers on Lily for a few seconds. I'm kind of hoping she'll glance my way and catch me, give me an excuse to call her over. I stop staring when Morgan kicks me lightly in the shin.

"Really good, huh?" Her lips quirk up in this suggestive smirk that's really fucking annoying.

"Yeah, I mean. It's been weird between us, just trying to be friendly without constantly thinking about . . . *it*." Today was mostly void of weirdness. And we weren't friendly, we were *friends*. And something . . . else.

"Well, you've been a dick. So I'm glad you've moved past that phase."

"Oooo-kayyy." I chuckle. Morgan has always had a way with words, meaning she's blunt as fuck. "And on that note."

I reach behind her and take the bottle in my hand, pulling out a clean glass from the desk drawer. We've gathered a decent collection for our makeshift bar, mostly stolen from the ambassador dining room, which is where the Welles board and headmaster butter up the wealthy families a few times a year to squeeze them for more money.

I fill my tumbler halfway with whiskey, then clink my glass against Morgan's before heading back to Lily—*and James*. They're talking again, or rather, James is talking, and Lily is listening. But she's smiling. She's engaged. It's hard to watch James be so . . . flirty.

"Friday, then? Our first game is Saturday." I catch the end of whatever James is planning as I step up.

"Are we talking about pre-game? Tailgate or going out? There's a great place two stops from here on the T—" I stop talking when I notice James' head shaking.

"Nah, man. Lily said she needs a shopping partner, and I've gotta get a few things at the mall, so we were thinking of going Friday since practice will be short," James says.

I stare at him with a blank face for a second, then shift my gaze to Lily. She smiles with tight lips, her face colored pink with the awkward feeling building around us.

"I see." I tuck my top lip under my bottom teeth as a precaution, to keep the irrational shit I want to say from spilling out. So what if they go shopping. Lily and I talked about it, but we didn't really make plans.

"You could come too, if you want." Lily throws me a bone of an invite. I know that tone, the pity tone. It's a verbal Band-Aid. I would rather field another sheet of cold calls before playing third wheel to these two.

"Ah, that's okay. I'm sure James has things handled. You two have fun." I hold up my whiskey as if I'm toasting this bullshit, then down it completely before slamming the glass on the desk right between her and James. It was an obvious tantrum, and the only thing helping me save face as I turn and walk toward the door is that Morgan didn't see it.

"Yo, you leaving?" Cameron is licking the paper for his joint and he looks up at me mid-tongue-to-paper.

"Try not to burn this place down, huh?" I flick his joint with my finger, ruining it, and I don't really feel bad about it.

"Hey! You're a real dick sometimes, you know that, Theo?" He flips me off and I press my back against the exit.

"So I've heard." My mouth stops in a hard line and I look past my roommate to Lily. Naturally, *now* she's looking at me. This is what she sees. Well, fine. Maybe that's the side of me she should have gotten all along. I don't know why I thought letting my guard down would do anyone any good.

Chapter 15

Lily

I'm not a big shopper. I don't enjoy it. Probably because things never seem to fit me right, and unlike my friends, I don't exactly have a no-limit credit card to go all willy-nilly with. I have to be choosy, which is code for clearance rack. It's rare that I find a bargain that is also in my size and stretches around my curves but also hugs my waist. Things are either skintight at the hips and arms or baggy around the neck and waist.

My dad always says I should embrace my muscles. It's easier to do when he's guilt-buying me things from the active wear websites. I can't exactly parlay active wear into office attire, though *The Affiliate* is rather sporty.

Dad buys me a lot of things out of guilt. He bought my time at Welles. It used to make me sad, but by now, I'm fine with the good education and occasional sports bra in the mail. I gave up trying to have a relationship with him, even though my mom likes to call me "daddy's favorite." I quit arguing with her. If I were his favorite, I'd get more than one-word answers to the texts I send when I need something.

Nothing stings quite like getting left on *read* by your own father.

I need to get out of this shopping trip with James. It's upsetting Morgan, which it shouldn't because James spent the rest of the night after Theo stormed out prodding me to invite Morgan to come along with us. I get the feeling he's flirting with me to get her attention, which . . . I don't like. She won't, either. Hell, maybe I should let the two of them go and pick out a wardrobe for me. It would help if they picked up the tab too.

I'll have that talk with James tomorrow, when we study. I do *like* studying with him. He listens to me, and I think he's maybe getting something out of the lit course. We've set up standing dates on Thursday nights after their practice and on Sundays.

If I could just get myself to make the same commitment to my time in the pool maybe I'd be ready to tell Coach to add me to the roster. I have yet to make it through a full lap.

That's the goal tonight. One lap. Nothing more required, but nothing less acceptable. Or so I keep repeating to myself mentally as I near the fieldhouse.

I have everything with me tonight. My bag is filled as if I were going to a real practice—energy packet, water bottle, cap and goggles, chafing stick, earplugs. My thought is, if I treat this like the real thing, then just maybe I'll make it.

My sweatpants hang low on my hips over my suit as I shuffle in my slides the remaining distance to the doors. I drop my bag before getting out my key and removing my hoodie to stuff into my gym bag. It will be warm by the pool, warmer than out here. Humid. I miss the smell.

I knot my hair in a tight bun and stand up straight, key in hand and poised to unlock, only it's unnecessary. James and Theo are staring at me from the other side of the door. I slink back a step and sigh before nodding at the door, which James opens. Theo stays back a few steps, his eyes slits as he studies me. I'm not sure what his judgement is for. Is it because I'm swimming again after he had to save me? Or is it because he doubts my success? The latter seems most probable, and I don't blame him. I scared him.

I scared me.

"Hey, you're back at it! Want company?" James' enthusiasm is a bit off-putting. My confidence isn't steady to begin with; it's definitely not audience-ready.

"Oh, yeah. No." I laugh out of one side of my mouth, then grit my teeth behind an awkward smile. "I'm more into solo swimming right now. But . . . thanks?"

"Sure. Yeah, I get it. Competitive mindset and all," James says, tapping his finger to his temple. They're both sweaty, shirts soaked to their skin, leaving little to imagine when it comes to their pecs and abs. I'm guessing they put in some extra lifting after practice today. Or based on the way Theo left yesterday, maybe they went a few rounds on the wrestling mat. I'm tempted to tease about it, but there's something in Theo's expression that warns me not to. His eyes have somehow hazed more, and I think maybe his jaw is flexing. Either that or he's chewing on bolts.

"I should get to it," I say, pointing to the hallway beyond James, away from Theo.

James steps to the side and I chance a quick look in Theo's direction. He's wiping sweat from his forehead with the hem of his shirt, exposing his washboard abs. The sight makes my mouth water a little, which causes instant blush, and as I turn my attention back to my destination, I smack right into the wall.

"Ow!" I blurt out, my palm flying to my brow. It stings where I touch, and I have a feeling I skinned myself on the rough surface of the wall. Maybe I'll get a nice knot to go along with it.

"Oh, geez, you okay?" James is at my side in a blink, his hand over mine, pulling it from my forehead so he can inspect my wound. Theo, however, is tittering, and doing a poor job at hiding it. I let my hand drop completely and shake James' attention off so I can glare at Theo. I thought we were making progress. I thought . . . well, what I thought was wrong, I guess, so it doesn't matter.

"What? It was funny, you have to admit," he defends.

I purse my lips as James scolds him with a "Hey!"

"Oh, come on. And *you!*" He punches out a laugh and holds his sides as he looks at James then waggles his finger. "Oh, geez. Who says that? Who are you?"

"I'm a decent human who doesn't think it's okay when someone gets hurt," James says, puffing up his chest a little. This is clearly about something more than this moment, and it feels offensive that I'm in the middle of it.

I roll my eyes and pivot to head down the hall without a word, but before I get to the door for the pool, Theo catches up to me. He slips past me and leans with one palm flat against the wall and his feet near the other side, like a human blockade.

"Hold up. You're not seriously going to do this again, alone." His glare meets mine and we war through a long, silent breath.

"It's not a big deal. Besides, you're the one who told everyone I was swimming again, remember?" I shoot him a tight smile and fold my arms over my chest, my bag dangling from my shoulder.

Theo straightens and pinches the bridge of his nose, letting out a heavy sigh. When his hand falls away, I'm left looking at a lost boy. I worry that we're suddenly taking a massive step back, and my heart hurts.

"I'll be fine, Theo. I promise," I say with a nod, encouraging him to leave with James. I don't really want him seeing this. I failed a lot last time, and it's easier to keep at it if nobody is watching me punish myself in the water. I'm not an impressive sight.

I'm weak.

Theo leans to the side, glancing toward James, then his eyes come back to me and hold on for several quiet seconds. The longer we stand like this, the harder it is to feel my feet—to breathe. Anika is here, in our thoughts, tangled up with the idea of me getting in the pool. No matter what we do, there will always be a shared misery between us.

"I promise," I repeat, allowing my hand to reach forward and tug at the front of his shirt, the cotton cool with sweat. It's a bold move, one that causes his chin to drop to his chest and his eyes to stare at the imaginary line I left behind.

"We're still on for Friday, yeah?"

I'm not prepared for James' question. And when Theo's eyes pop up expectantly, searing into me as he awaits an answer, I stumble.

"Oh, uh—"

"Cuz I really need some new lifting shoes if I'm going to keep up with this guy," he says, clearly meaning Theo, who hasn't taken his eyes off me since James uttered that question.

"Sure . . . I guess." Those last two words come out in a gravelly whisper. They were meant for Theo, a small sign to let him know I'm not really looking forward to going, well, anywhere with James.

It's you. It's always you. I hate shopping but I'll go with you.

My chest caves in and my breath goes short with instant

panic when his eyes dim. He eventually looks down, shaking his head.

"Have a good swim," he says, pushing off from the wall and skirting around me, wider than necessary, as if I'm toxic to touch. As if we shouldn't share the same air.

What just happened? I lost something. Something I wasn't even sure I had.

I look over my shoulder in time to see Theo push the door open wide as the two of them leave. Nobody softens its closure, and it slams shut, metal clanking against metal. The sound startles me even though I knew it was coming.

My eyes blink closed, and I draw in a long breath through my nose.

Somehow, I find my resolve and head to the pool. Theo's hot and cold personality, which I can almost forgive because I understand his pain better than most, isn't going to help me conquer my own demons. The trouble is I've started to feel things, and whatever I was feeling for Theo was growing greater than the guilt that's been residing in my head and heart for months. I don't want to stop those feelings, maybe even if they're one-sided. Unrequited beats tormented.

By the time I'm at the pool's edge, I've morphed everything that just happened with Theo into fuel. I kick my slides off and shimmy out of my sweatpants, then kneel to pull my goggles, earplugs, and cap from my bag. The entire time, I'm having imaginary arguments with Theo, conversations I will likely never really have. My textual therapist encourages these delusions, so why not indulge them now, when I'm alone.

"You know what? Fuck you, Theo Rothschild. Yeah. That's right. Fuck you," I mutter through gritted teeth, pointing at the air.

"Glad I came back for that."

Shit.

I spin to find him standing a dozen feet from me. *How is he so silent?* My brow pulls in so tight I bet I could hold a penny in the crease above the bridge of my nose. I'm both sad and angry. He wasn't supposed to *actually* hear me. But also, he deserves to.

"You pissed me off." I fold my arms over my chest, my goggles dangling from my wrist and my earplugs and cap gripped in my fist.

"Good. You pissed me off." His arms cross his chest, his hands tucked under his biceps that completely fill the sleeves of his gray Welles T-shirt. It's distracting and I blink my eyes free of the visual, forcing myself to—*shit*—stare into his incredible eyes.

"You can't just copy what I say and make that your argument. This is stupid." I shake my head and turn my body so I'm not directly facing him as I do my best to pretend I'm blocking him from my mind. He's all over my mind, though. He's in my head, and he's stealing my oxygen. Now, he's poisoned the pool.

"You and James." That's all he says. I get the gist, even if my low self-esteem denies it. This is about jealousy. I can't believe it's truly about him liking me. It can't be. It has to be more about staking a claim.

"*You* and James. There!" I growl. He flinches a touch and his brows pinch. "I'm repeating things, just like you're doing. It's frustrating, isn't it?"

My cap isn't opening the way I want it to, probably because my hands are trembling.

"Gah!" I throw it down on top of my bag. My earplugs are still nestled in my palm, and if I were truly bold, I'd put them in my ears right now and mock him. The visual in my head amuses me, and it must show on my lips.

"What's funny?"

I laugh under my breath at his question and shake the plugs in my hand as if they're dice.

"Nothing is funny, Theo. That's the point. *This?*" I point between me and the pool then do the same to the space between me and him. "It's so far from funny. It's torture. I don't know how to do any of it, and for a while, only a few months ago, I thought I did. I was becoming a better version of me, and now—"

"I don't know what to do about the way I feel."

My eyes jet to his the second his confession hits the air. His arms fall limp at his sides. His eyes slope with the weight of stress, with pain, and with something else. It's that something else that has my heart bruising the insides of my body. He almost looks . . . lovesick. My skin is numb. My lips . . . numb. I don't know how to respond to him.

"Are you hurting?" I relax my muscles and tilt my head, holding his gaze and trying not to blink.

He chuckles at my question.

"Yeah, Lily. I'm hurting. All the fucking time. But that's not what I meant. Or maybe it is."

"I don't know what you mean," I shout, shaking my hands out at my sides.

He sucks in his lower lip and shuts his eyes.

"I can't stand the idea of someone else touching you." His lashes lift enough to shed light on his blue-diamond eyes. The beam. I'm pierced by them.

"Nobody is touching me, Theo." My voice is raspy, and quivers with my nerves.

"He is. In here," Theo says, pointing to his head.

"James?" I ask.

Theo nods slowly, his eyes steady on mine. His finger slides from his temple and he takes a cautious step forward.

My knees threaten to give out, and the idea of leaping into the pool and swimming away from him passes through my mind. Perhaps I'd make it the entire distance to avoid this threat. To avoid really giving in and allowing myself to want, to have.

"I hate shopping."

Theo's lip ticks up slightly on one side.

"Yeah?"

I nod.

My body is buzzing and my breath hitches, and for a moment, it's that night again. Not the awful part, but the hours before. The air between us crackles with hope and anticipation. All the while, Theo inches closer to me.

"I lifted *way* more than I normally do tonight. Probably going to have some injuries to nurse from it. Had to pile more on than James because—"

"Because in your head he was touching me?" My face and neck warm at the words I just spoke, but when Theo licks his lips and nods slowly, the gamble was worth it.

"He's not, though. Not really." As if I need make that clear.

Theo shakes his head and closes the remaining distance between us. His thumb presses into my bottom lip while his fingers gently lift my chin. My mouth parts with a quiet gasp. I can feel my nipples harden against my swimsuit.

"I watched you swim last time," he says, and my mouth contorts into a slight frown.

"Why?" I cry. I'm embarrassed. More than that, I'm a little ashamed. "You shouldn't have watched."

His thumb runs across my lips.

"I was afraid to leave you alone." He swallows hard. His eyes probe mine, and the mortification I felt a second ago fuses with a new drug making its way through my body. My chest grows warm, my stomach echoing with my beating heart. It's as if he's given me a dose of dopamine.

"Why?" I utter.

On the surface, I know why. Because he saved me once. And even if I don't accept that I needed him to, the reality is I probably did. I don't think I would have blacked out and drowned. I can't say I would have gotten in the pool ever again, though. And my next move probably would have been to the enrollment office to demand a withdrawal. I would have quit—everything. I would have crawled back to a family that doesn't really want me in it, to a life that would lead to average and unfulfilling. And the damage in my heart would only gather more scars until the burden was so heavy it would turn me into a copy of the girl I was supposed to be. And pieces would be missing.

"I don't know what to do about the way I feel," he repeats. His gaze caresses my mouth and cheeks, my nose, my eyes. His thumb moves along my jawline, making room for his other hand so he can cradle my face in his palms.

"But you feel . . . something," I croak.

He nods and his eyes close as his forehead falls forward to rest on mine. My hands quake at my sides and I flex my fingers to wake them from shock before grabbing hold of his wrists. I do it partly to anchor myself, but also maybe a bit to hold him still—to keep him from leaving.

His lashes tickle against my own, and the sensation coaxes my lips to curl until my smile brushes against his. With a tiny shift of his head, his bottom lip brushes against mine. Every nerve in my face is going wild. I feel nothing and everything all at once. And then his lip passes over mine again, this time his mouth stopping long enough to nip at my bottom lip.

"I feel like I need to kiss you," he whispers against me.

"Aren't you?" I whisper in nervous laughter. He nuzzles his nose to mine.

"I want you to *feel* it." He nips at my bottom lip again, first with his own lips, then with his teeth. The razor's edge is initially a graze, then his teeth hold on tighter, pulling my lip into his mouth as he suckles. His tongue passes over my mouth, and my nerves lessen enough that I taste him, too.

I don't want to interrupt to tell him I've felt everything all along, from the moment his eyes hit me and leveled me with the truth. From the moment we ran into each other on move-in day. And every time he tried to push me away—to hate me. Whether it's our pain, Anika's felt presence, or a million other things, something in each of us completes the other. When I'm with him, even when we're fighting, I am whole.

Lifting myself up on the tips of my toes, I step into him to deepen our kiss. My hands slide down his arms until my fingers cling to the sides of his shirt, gathering the sweat-damp material into my fists. We kiss as if our bodies need the touch to survive, as if it gives us oxygen and life. And when we finally part, breaths ragged, I feel like the girl who jumped into that dark river without hesitation. I feel mighty, and strong.

I tug on his shirt where my hand still holds on tight.

"Stay. While I swim. I want you to stay." I look up into his eyes and he runs his thumb along my cheek.

"I was never planning on leaving."

I step up to kiss him once more, my lips pressing to his out of gratitude, out of relief. I feel like this seal that's been binding us has finally been broken.

When I break away, I don't bother with my routine. My earplugs fell away the moment I exchanged them for a better hold on Theo. And if I spend time looking for them, I'll grow cold—*scared.*

Theo backs off a few feet and crosses his arms over his chest, giving me a nod. I smile faintly and turn my attention to the water, scooting to the edge, my toes on the precipice. If I'm going to do this, I need to be able to dive in head first. Bending down, I tap my fingertips on my toes and bend my knees slightly. Before my mind has a chance to catch up to my actions and fill my body with doubt, I slip in like an arrow, and by the time my fingers touch the other side, I'm crying.

Chapter 16

Theo

I walked her to her room. Not simply to her dorm, but all the way up the damn stairs. To. Her. Room.

And then I heard her roommates on the other side of the door.

I left.

Maybe she could excuse that. Panic in the moment. This all happening so fast, being *real*. It's the truth, but that's not why I ran. I bolted because of the exact words I said.

I don't know what to do about the way I feel.

"I know the polite thing to do would be to look away and not intently stare at whatever's on your phone screen, but I'm a rude motherfucker and I always snoop on your shit. Why are you hovering on the text screen with Lily's number? Which begs the question—you have Lily's number? And did you get that yourself like a big boy or did you simply piece it out of the group chat for parties? And—"

Before Cameron can utter another annoying fucking word I throw a half-empty water bottle at him, nicking him in the chin.

"Dude, what?"

I don't grace him with a look in his direction. Instead, I let my hand make the *Cameron puppet,* something I started doing to him last year when I realized it was effective.

"Dude, what?" I mock his voice while my hand forms a mouth.

"You're just pissed that—"

"You're just pissed that—" I keep up with him.

"You're an asshole."

"You're an asshole," I echo. Or rather, the Cameron puppet echoes.

Swinging his body around, his feet hit the floor with a heavy thud as he rises from his bed, half-dressed, and slaps my hand puppet, *aka my hand,* then gives me the middle finger.

"I'm hitting the shower. Have a nice day in sales." Our door slams behind him and I flip him off in return, mostly because I fucking hate sales.

That's not why I want to call in sick today, though. If I could take my sales penance from home, I'd make cold calls all day to avoid a face-to-face with Lily this morning. That's what this is about. I've lost my ability to make good decisions. My head and guts and heart are all twisted into this grotesque knot. I barely slept. All I keep doing is replaying yesterday's events. Every step of the way, I made choices that were wrong.

James asked me to stick around and spot him. I did, not because I wanted to be a friend but because I wanted to flirt with the idea of letting the bar fall on his teeth. Of course, I wouldn't let that happen. But it was clear we both have thoughts on some unsaid shit. He packed on more weight, so I packed on more weight, and that futile routine went on and on. He only brought Lily up once.

"You and her, are you close?"

I met his stare as he looked up at me from the bench and a million different answers stirred in my head.

We're tied.

We're acquaintances.

We're friends.

I hate her.

She pisses me off.

She's cute.

We talked a little last year.

She and my sister were good friends.

We . . . *almost* . . .

"Nah." That was my response. His pupils widened and his jaw ticked, and I knew that meant he called my bullshit.

And then we ran into her. All those other variables went away. Or maybe, rather, they morphed together into my actual feelings. It hit my stomach like an iron fist, and the only thing I could think of was self-preservation.

But I couldn't let her swim alone.

My phone buzzes in my hand, startling me.

LILY: *You coming? I brought you something.*

My eyes flutter shut with guilt, and I swing my limp body around until my feet are on the floor and I'm standing. My shirt is wrinkled but there isn't time to switch it out, so I stuff the ends into my pants and keep it pulled taut to manually stretch it into shape. I snag my jacket from the back of my chair and drop my phone and keys in my pocket, spinning my way through the door and out into the empty dorm hallway. Lily and I are going to have to haul ass to get to the station in time, but third through fifth forms are already in class so I (we?) don't have to contend with people watching us until we get to the platform. My pulse is racing as my mind plays out the possibilities.

And then there she is. Clearly she's borrowed from her friends' closets again, wearing tight black pants and a red sweater that hugs her body as if it were knitted as she wore it. Her hair is curled into waves and draped over both shoulders. She still shifts her feet, as if uncomfortable, but she doesn't look out of place at all. She looks perfect.

"Red's a good color on you," I say as she steps forward and hands me a foam cup with a glorious stream of steam emanating from it.

"You don't have to be nice. I would have given you the coffee anyway," she says. My hand brushes against hers as we exchange the cup and my heart beats with a heavy thump, the kind I get when a roller coaster drops.

"I would have fought you for this coffee," I say, winking before taking a sip. I leave my gaze on her, noting the redness creeping into her cheeks as they round, her mouth dimpling the corners with her tight, bashful smile.

"And the compliment was genuine," I add. I expect her to hide her face from the attention. That seems to be her usual reaction. But she doesn't. Instead, her lashes kiss her checks gently with the slowest bat and her lips part as her smile grows a little more.

She leans her head to the right, toward the pathway, and we head to our train. We're later than last time, and the platform is more crowded, so as the train approaches I take her hand to keep her close. I didn't think before I acted, but now that her hand is flush to mine, my fingers wrapped around hers, I am doing nothing *but* thinking about what this is and what it means.

I maneuver us to an open set of seats and our hands break the second we sit down. I notice she doesn't have a coffee, so I offer her mine. She shakes her head and leans into me.

"No, that was a gift," she says.

My eyes drop to her mouth, briefly, and her tongue makes a short swipe across her bottom lip before she sucks it in and looks down at her lap, her leather bag flat under her palms.

I feel the eyes on us. She must, too, though she seems intent on keeping her focus on her lap and the leather strap her thumb keeps rubbing obsessively.

I give in and scan the train, catching a few whispers between fellow students to our left, and knowing smirks on the faces of a few girls to our right. My phone becomes my refuge as I pull it from my pocket to scroll through social media. It's a good distraction until a photo of my sister fills my screen. I blacken the screen immediately and put my phone away, having seen too much already.

The posts have gotten less regular, but they still happen. Usually, it's girls from the younger forms who have turned my sister into this sort of icon. They lament her passing and talk about how Welles isn't the same without her walking its halls. They're right, too. It's not. But they didn't truly know her. They like the attention, and that's what squeezes my insides. They aren't even photos they've taken themselves. They're the ones Anika shared on her page.

I haven't visited her profile in a few weeks. Morgan offered to take it down after the services, since she had Anika's passwords. My mom wanted her to leave it up, though, as if that somehow lets my sister live on. Maybe it does. Or maybe it just keeps the door open enough to prevent closure. It isn't worth the fight for me, not if it means that much to our mom.

There's a different kind of heaviness in my chest now that I've seen my sister's eyes. She would tell me I'm being a jerk right now. As I glance back to Lily's hands, I notice the shimmer of Anika's bracelet and it brings a faint smile to my lips. It's hard not to add these things up. I may have called the mystical crap my sister was into bullshit, but she believed it to her core. "Signs," she would say. "They're everywhere."

I shift my coffee to my other hand as the train slows for the last suburban stop and under the cover of bodies shuffling in. With standing passengers now to shield us from gossip, I stretch my right hand toward Lily's, eventually linking our pinkies. It causes me to chuckle once, silently. A quick glance to Lily's face reveals something in her expression I don't know that I've ever seen—a peaceful confidence. Her smile is barely there, and maybe she's not even aware of it. Maybe it's a hint for me, a gift to let me know I did the right thing just now.

We ride the rest of the way without speaking, and I never once move my hand.

* * *

Whatever balance I struck in my soul on the way to *The Affiliate* was wrecked the moment I made my first cold call this morning. Or what was *supposed* to be a cold call but instead was a direct line to one of the company's biggest ad client CEOs.

It started out harmless enough. Charming banter about me being the new guy and someone was probably pranking me and having me call the "big guns." We hit it off initially. Of course, that was when the conversation was brand new and I was answering the man's questions about my plans after school, what I wanted to study, how I liked working for *The Affiliate*. From there, things . . . *escalated*.

I'd like to argue that it wasn't completely my fault. Though our dad wasn't around, his brothers were, and they made sure that I had a good sense of right and wrong, meaning the Patriots over the Cowboys, the Red Socks rule the Yankees, and real men bleed Celtic green.

"Please tell me you didn't say the word *chump?*" Todd is rubbing his head across the desk from me, head down, phone positioned between his resting elbows.

I wince and he pops his gaze up, brows raised.

My shoulders creep toward my ears.

"I didn't exactly call *him* a chump. It was more a general term, for Yankee fans, and…"

"Theo, the man's license plate is literally THEBABE." Todd's mouth gets slack, like he's gonna vomit, and I shake with nervous laughter.

"Well, that's kind of false advertising. Clearly, *he's* not *the Babe.*" I swallow down my chipper tone when Todd's eyes meet mine again.

I'm so fired.

"Theo, do you know how hard that license plate is to get in New York?" Thankfully, his phone rings before I'm able to answer. I was going to mention that I saw them available in one of those shops in Times Square.

"Cosmo! Hi, thank you for calling me back," Todd begins, pouring on the charm. He waves a hand toward me, I assume to dismiss me, so I get up and push my chair in as he spins his back to me. "Yeah, I mean interns, right? You get what you get and sometimes it's scraping the bottom of the barrel."

Ouch.

I slip through his door and shut it quietly, my stomach burning with stress. My jokes can usually get me out of situations. Anika always said I could be "disarming." I'm starting to think maybe that was not a compliment.

"Theo, have a minute?" Apparently, it's Abby's turn to scold me. Maybe she'll find it more amusing, being on the editorial side.

I follow her to her office and as I take the seat across from her desk she closes the door. My body warms and I straighten my spine. If one is to be fired, they should at least have good posture for it.

"Abby, I'm really sorry about this mess."

"Oh, that?" She bunches her face and waves her hand in the direction of Todd's office as she rounds her desk and takes her seat. "That's a sales problem. Todd will have Cosmo meeting him for drinks during his next visit in no time. Somehow, he'll work this into a bigger account. He's that good."

I smile tightly on one half of my mouth. I didn't quite get that vibe from my last conversation, but okay. She knows Todd better than I do.

"I have a proposal for you." She leans in, hands in the praying position. I rest my palms on my knees and rub them. They're sweating.

"You had your heart set on editorial, and I think it's amazing that you and Lily have found a way to both get your foot in here." It's funny how only a day and a half working in sales has taught me the differences in smiles. Abby is pitching me. Of course, if it gets me out of sales, *well?*

"Like I said before. I'm glad to be in this building." In the spirit of things, I channel my inner Lily and offer an awkward fist pump. Abby laughs.

"Love it! Love the team spirit," she says.

My pulse is thrumming. I want to hit fast-forward on her mouth and get to the point, past the point. I want to be hired in editorial and working on big stories. Hell, I want to be getting coffee for writers working on big stories. Just get me out of sales.

"Tell me what you think about this. And maybe, take the day, or the week."

My shoulders deflate a little at her nonchalant delivery. I

guess it was shooting high to think she'd start begging me to join her writing staff right now, today.

I nod.

"Lily's story, it's really something." Her eyes narrow and her mouth pulls into a serious line. My stomach folds in on itself until it's nothing at all.

Lily's story is also my story.

"Uh huh." My voice croaks and I don't bother to clear my throat or make it sound any less skeptical. She notices. I can tell by the slight tilt of her head.

"You and Lily are . . . close?"

My chest caves.

I suck in my bottom lip and breathe in long and hard through my nose as I sit back in my chair. Eventually, I lift one shoulder, because how do I answer that? I'm still trying to define it. And I'm doing a shit job at navigating our relationship.

"Sure." That's the best I can give.

"I mentioned this to Lily last time you guys were here, so she's thinking about it too. But after she and I talked, I got to thinking—maybe it would be easier for her to tell her story if she was talking to a friend."

I am no longer here. My head is nodding. I'm pursing my lips and trying to push a smile into its edges, but the darkness is closing in at my periphery. My view has narrowed to the dimmest of light around Abby's form as her head moves and her hands gesture with her words that sound like muffled horns.

"What do you think?"

I shake my head from the fog.

"I . . . don't know."

No. The answer is no. I will not interview the girl I have feelings for—feelings I can't get straight—about what it was like the night she failed to save my sister. No.

No. No. No!

But that's not what I say at all. And apparently, not what Lily said either when Abby approached her with the idea.

Chapter 17

Lily

I don't know how to behave with Theo. I'm not even sure what to call us, or if I should tell my roommates that we kissed. If Anika were here, I'd have replayed every word for her. She knew her brother—and me—and would have given the best advice.

I felt like an idiot with the coffee. I needed something to do with my hands.

No.

I needed something to do that would involve my hand and his, a reason for us to interact, a chance to touch. I was about to give up but then the train ride happened. Our touch was chaste and innocent and somehow secretive, but still out in the world, existing. Kissing him is like exploring an ocean. Holding his hand is like finding a pearl at the sea's floor.

My hope that things would pick up where we left them off were dashed when he stayed at his desk for lunch. And now, that same train that was full of hope this morning is stifling and dead inside, filled with zombies—at least two of them—on our trip home.

"You were busy today, huh?" This is my second attempt at small talk.

Theo glances up from his phone. He took the seat across from me, despite the open one beside me.

"Yeah. It's not fun work." His eyes drift back to his screen. He's thumbing through photos, liking the ones of girls at our school. It feels very much like he's putting on a show.

"I was thinking maybe tomorrow we could make a group trip to the mall. I might not hate shopping so bad if it's less about the trying on clothes part and more about hanging out with . . . *friends?*"

His head wobbles and he looks up with an arched brow.

"Since when do you like hanging out with people?" He holds my gaze for a breath, and I wait for the sign in his eyes to indicate he's kidding with me. But his glare remains slightly cold and harsh. His edge is back. That place he lives where it's impossible to tell whether he's being cruel or nice or . . . honest.

I'm so taken aback that my mouth simply opens and snaps shuts. When he looks back to his phone and likes a photo of some girls from the Catholic school two towns over, I laugh to myself and cross my arms over my chest as I slump back in my seat. Tongue held between my molars, the tip pushes the inside of my cheek to quiet the tempest heating my chest.

Like Theo, I pull my phone out for some anger scrolling. It only makes me more annoyed, though, because every picture I pass already has a heart by it from him.

"I wish you never kissed me," I mutter under my breath.

That gets his attention. I don't have to look up to know he's staring at me. I *feel* it. My face warms from his glare. The faint click of his phone screen going to sleep tames my angry blood. The boil is still there, though.

One more tiny push.

Without acknowledging him, I sift through my contacts until I land on James. I wish I had his picture attached to his profile so I could make an even bigger show of what I'm about to do. Lifting my phone up to block my face, I sit up straight and roll my shoulders—for no other reason than the fact that Morgan's sweater makes my boobs look big. A slight shift to the side lets me get a quick glance in, and I smirk when I confirm Theo is watching.

"Are you . . . taking a selfie?" His tone mocks me, but I ignore it, clicking with the filter Morgan always tells me to use in place. *Damn, she's right. Every picture looks good with this thing on.*

"I'm chatting with James. He's on his way back to campus, too." That's a lie. I have no clue where James is, but clearly neither does Theo because his eyes are studying me hard as if scanning for bullshit.

I send my pic to James with a friendly hello, hoping he'll write back quickly. When he sends a photo of him smiling from the passenger seat of some car, I let go of the breath I'm holding and lay my phone flat on my thigh so Theo can see whatever he feels like spying on.

"Why are you doing that?" Theo asks.

I laugh out once as I continue typing to James. I needed to text him to set up our study session anyhow. I'm simply embellishing the process to make a spiteful show out of it.

"Messaging my friend about our study session? Uh, because I'm a free woman and I can chat with whomever I want." I purse my lips and level him with a death stare as my finger hits send on my latest message.

Theo's head tilts slightly and his nostrils flare with his exhale.

"I mean, why are you trying to be, I don't know, mean about it?"

My phone buzzes on my lap with James' return note and I puff out another short laugh.

"I'm not the one being mean, Theo." I hold his stare for several long seconds until the train crawls to the first stop and we lose half of the passengers. The car is empty, minus a handful of students who finished their internships at the same time we did.

It's easier to be emboldened around strangers. The people sharing our space all know too many details. They have their versions of our stories that they like. Whatever's happening between Theo and me right now isn't a part of their world. It's barely a part of ours.

Intimacy doesn't seem to be a barrier for Theo, however. When I look up as the train begins to move, I catch his eyes on me again. Or perhaps he never looked away. Whatever expressions I've made in the last thirty seconds must have amused him, though. His smirk is a stain on his lips.

"What?" I challenge. My voice is louder than I expect, and I look left and right to see whose attention I've drawn. Two girls to our right noticed, but they're pretending not to listen in. I recognize that move—the slight turn of the body while your ear remains to the action, hair tucked carefully behind it as to not obstruct.

"I never said I was a nice guy, Lily. I simply said I didn't know what to do about the way I feel." Theo may as well be putting on a play in Boston Common. His voice fills the car.

My stomach sinks and my neck flares up. I'm sure I'm red. My eyes shift to the girls spying on us and they've sunk lower in their seats, ears still poised as they remain silent. To my left, two guys Theo knows from football and a girl I recognize from my statistics course are staring at me.

When I look back to Theo, he's leaned forward enough to reach my knee with his hand. He doesn't touch me, though. He simply leans in and gazes at my screen, my stupid attempt at making him jealous.

"James says he'll see you at seven. Enjoy your tutoring time." He slides back in his seat and holds my gaze, his face void of any emotion at all. Then, he pulls his phone back out, looks down, and goes about hearting every photo in the world.

He's not even sincerely looking at them.

"Yeah, well, you enjoy thinking about him touching me. At seven." The fact that those words left my mouth shocks my skin numb and makes my mouth water. Theo doesn't look up this time, but his posture sure does change. The repetitive tick in his jaw is rewarding. And I almost don't care that five people from Welles are now steeped in our business.

Almost.

* * *

Back in the comfort of my sweatpants and two-sizes-too-big Welles sweatshirt, I feel more like myself. And oddly less confident than I was a few hours ago on the train.

Kissing Theo has made me stupid. I don't know if it's that I imagined it for so long that I assumed everything that went along with kissing Theo Rothschild would be roses and fairy-tales or what, but now that I'm back on earth, I realize that fairytales are scams and cute boys are grifters. It was silly to believe that was it—*we've kissed and now everything is amazing!* I still represent so much baggage for him I'm basically the luggage claim area of the airport. Thing is, though? He's still Theo Rothschild to me, and while seeing shades of his sister in him hurts some, it also reminds me of how incredible she was. *How incredible he can be, too.*

Bag slung over my shoulder, I step up to James' family apartment and knock. Coach Fuentes opens the door to let me in.

"You come to join the party?" he says, swinging the door wide and revealing James, Cameron, and, *of course,* Theo, all piled on the sofa with video game controllers in their hands and intense scowls denting their foreheads.

"Dude, you shot me!" James shoves Theo in the arm and gets an elbow in return.

"You shot me first," he responds.

I roll my eyes.

"Great. So, not a lot of studying happening tonight," I mumble as I step into the living room for a better view.

"Oh, hey, Lily! I'll be done in ten minutes. The guys are staying for dinner, but they'll be quiet." James is a dreamer.

"Boom!" Cameron's voice echoes as he falls back on the couch as if he were *actually* hit with space shrapnel like his blue character was on the screen.

"Sure," I say, smiling through tight lips. I glance to Theo, but he's still in the ignoring-me mode.

Unlike these guys, I have a paper to work on. I was going to flag some quotes to use from the Gulf War memoir I read, but I'll be lucky if I can scratch a single coherent word on paper in this atmosphere. My old roommate Angela is the teacher's assistant in my recent history class, so I'm sure she'll ask to help grade my paper so she can put it at the bottom of the curve. I'm supposed to proof James' essay for him too. I'm starting to feel overwhelmed.

"They wanted to blow off some steam. I put them through hell this week at practice, and I figured with the game Saturday and all . . ." Coach Fuentes shrugs innocently so I smile with teeth this time to pretend all of this is fine.

"Great. Penny's making enchilada casserole. You'll take a plate, yeah?" he offers.

I nod, because at the very least I should get an excellent meal out of this situation.

I dump my book bag on the table and pull out my notes and the memoir to attempt a jump on things. My note cards fall to the floor, though, scattering in a dozen directions.

"I got this," James says without pause, tossing his controller to Cameron, who can apparently handle playing two at once, and leaping over the back of the sofa to scour the area under the table with me.

"Thanks, but I've got this. Go back to your game," I say through nervous laughter.

James insists on helping, though. In fact, he dives under the table before I can, crawling on his hands and knees. I reorder the cards in my hands, glancing back to the living room out of curiosity. Not even a peek from Theo. Somehow, he seems even more focused on the screen.

"Here, I think that's all of them," James says, handing me a messy pile.

I smile and sit back in the chair to organize the rest of my work. Rather than rejoining the guys, James stays, pulling out the chair next to me and grabbing his backpack that was slung over the arm. He slides the chair over so it's inches from mine and pulls out his comp lit folder. I do my best to stare only at the table and the papers in front of us, but the draw to sneak glances toward Theo is too strong.

"It's not very long, but I think I got my point across well," James says, sliding his paper in front of me.

I clear my throat.

"Let me give it a read." I make it through the first two

sentences before losing interest. The paper is fine. I can tell from his thesis statement. And me pretending to review it will give James the confidence to turn it in. I'm too distracted to give it any actual attention.

Theo shifts his body, scrunching his arms while he works extra hard to grip the controller and lean forward to stare only at the screen. He's pretending, too. I can sense it. Cameron's trash talk lends small clues as he calls Theo out on his shit play. My eyes dart from the page in front of me to the view from under my lashes. The louder and more animated Cameron gets, the more rigid Theo's body becomes, until finally, Cameron stands in the middle of the room with his arms in the air declaring victory.

"Loser!" He points to his friend.

Theo tosses the controller into a large pillow on the floor, and for a slip of a moment, his gaze comes to me. My head lifts a fraction as my breath stops. He breaks our stare in less than a second, standing and stretching his long body, his arms reaching toward the ceiling. It's rare to see him like this— jeans, a T-shirt, his hair tossed in a million directions, socks on his feet. The urge to crawl up in his lap fills my mind, my body warming at the thought of his arms wrapped around me.

I wonder if he could ever be the kind of guy who would stroke my hair and kiss the top of my head while we did nothing but watch reruns of old Disney shows all afternoon.

"Hey, man. Can I borrow your charger in your room for a few?" Theo's attention squares on James, and it's almost as if I'm suddenly invisible as he steps up to the table across from us.

"Sure, it's on my desk." James nods toward the hallway and Theo disappears around the corner.

"It's good. Your paper, I mean." If he fails this assignment, I'm probably fired. He won't, though. I spent enough time in that class to know the buzz words, and his opening lines will get him a solid B at the very least.

"Ah, thanks. That's a relief." He sighs as he slips the paper back in its folder.

"Your restroom . . . is?" I didn't use it the last time I was here. I don't honestly need to now.

"Yeah, down that way. Right past my room before you get to the master. You either end up in there or the laundry room." He sifts through some other folders in his bag as I slip behind him and follow in Theo's footsteps.

James' room is dark, but I can see the glow of Theo's phone inside. I force myself not to look his direction as I pass the doorway and step into the bathroom. I flip the lights on and scan the stark space. Navy blue towels stuffed around a rack, a bottle of men's cologne, some toothpaste, and a brush in a red Solo cup. Coach and his wife must have their own space because this is definitely *all* teenage boy in here. I stand at the sink and chew at my lip, wondering how long I should hang in here with literally nothing to do.

After maybe a full minute, I wash my hands and dry them on the only towel that's semi-folded and flip the lights out before cracking open the door. My sight still not adjusted to the pitch black, I don't see Theo waiting against the wall across from me. And when his body moves into mine, my mouth opens with a loud gasp that's quickly swallowed up by his. He kisses me hard, his hands gripping the sides of my face while my hands fly up to shackle his wrists. My back finds the edge of the doorway and Theo rests his forehead against mine as he breaks our kiss.

"Why are you being so mean?" he whispers at my hear.

I'm out of breath, and suddenly acutely aware of my lack

of bra and the nearness of his hard chest. His body is hot, and he tastes like caramel.

My hands release his arms and flatten against his chest, and I battle between wanting to push him away and wanting to pull him closer. His stance widens, his legs straddling mine as I lean back, caged by him. His body smells of dirt and sweat, and I doubt he showered after practice.

I find the inner strength to gather his shirt in my fists yet keep my head down enough to deflect another kiss, no matter how badly I want it. His breath is hot against my forehead as his mouth opens enough to kiss my hairline. My eyelids shut and my heart flutters, but I shake my fists against his chest.

"Why are you treating me like a secret?" I grit the words through my teeth, and I utter them right into the center of his heart before giving him a push. He relents easily, taking a half step back, giving me enough space to escape.

There's no way I can keep this up. I can't make it through a meal with him, especially at a table in front of people we know. Who knows what passive aggressive quips he'll make? I'm done with that Theo, no matter how fucking badly I want to feel his hands rush over me.

"I'm so sorry, but I don't think I can stay for dinner. I have this paper to work on, and I'm super stressed about it, so I'm going to go study on my own. Another time, maybe?" I can barely hold eye contact with Mr. Fuentes, and I'm sure I seem flustered. My cheeks are heated, and I can smell Theo all over me, like a wild animal who marks his prey.

"You're welcome anytime, Lily," James' dad says. It's the kind of statement one makes to try and fix an uncomfortable situation. It's the type of thing my stepdad Drew says when my mom hurls backhanded insults at me.

"I'll text you after dinner. Maybe I can help you for once," James says. His smile is so sweet, and I can tell he senses how stressed I am. His concern is reflected in his heavy lids and the slight pout to his lips. I'm also pretty sure he knows that my state isn't about a paper. It's the same way I know our shopping plans are more about him spending time with Morgan than about anything retail related.

"Sure. Yeah. Text me," I stammer, hugging my unclasped bag to my chest with my work hurriedly tossed inside.

I somehow escape without seeing Theo again. I don't know how I would react if we made eye contact again. He has a spell on me, and it's more than a schoolgirl crush. I want to fix him, but to do that I need to travel back in time. And even if I could, I don't know what I would be able to do differently.

There were no warning signs of the ominous outcomes ahead. Anika was having an amazing night, then out of nowhere, she needed to drive into town. It was urgent, and she seemed panicked about something. She grabbed a set of keys and found the matching car. Morgan and Brooklyn literally hijacked me from the conversation I was having with Theo, insisting that the three of us go with our friend. Theo yelled for his sister to wait, and he was searching for his own keys, but Anika was already peeling out of the dirt lot by the barn. The three of us caught up to her before she hit the dirt road and piled in with her.

The rest happened so fast, I barely remember it at all. Only the vivid scenes. The nightmares.

Without even thinking, I make my way to Theo's secret door. I don't want to explain myself to my roommates right now, and I don't think I can contort my face into anything other than distress. I tug the door open and quickly shut it behind me, feeling for my phone in my pocket. Once in my hand, I turn on the flashlight and wind my way through the tables and desks until I get to the one in the back. I pull the chain for the small lamp and drop my bag on the desktop as I fall into the leather chair. My body slumped, I roll away from my homework and slowly draw my legs in to hug my knees to my chest.

I soak in the silence, not even a hum from the glowing bulb on the desk to distract me. I stare so hard and so long at my bag on the desk that it blurs. My mind doesn't even register what's in front of my eyes. All I see is the hard line of Theo's jaw, his plump bottom lip, his teeth—that beautiful view of him so close to me, wanting me.

I wipe away the tear before it makes it past the curve of my cheek just as my phone vibrates against the desktop. I scoot forward to scan the notification; the message is short enough I can read it all in the preview.

THEO: *Where RU?*

Chapter 18

Theo

LILY: *I'm right here.*

Some other girl, any other situation, I'd chalk that response up to playing games, being coy.

Not Lily.

That was honest.

She's right there—mine if I want her.

Mrs. Fuentes keeps glancing at my plate. Probably because, while her son and Cameron have completely cleared theirs and moved on to seconds, I've basically pushed cheese and sour cream around my plate for ten minutes.

"It's all right if you don't like it," she finally whispers.

I'm being rude.

"Oh, no. I have something on my mind is all. It's . . . it's good." I scoop up a pile and shovel it in my mouth and barely taste it. It smells amazing and I'm sure it's as great as everything she makes, but all I can taste is Lily.

All I smell is Lily.

My fingers vibrate with reminders of her skin. My head is so twisted trying to sort out this pull I have to her, along with the things she makes me feel. She makes me hurt, but she also makes me feel alive.

She's the one person in this entire world who gets my pain. And that's part of the problem. I see that pain in her, and I don't want any more of it.

"Should be a pretty easy game Saturday," James says, and it's obvious he's trying to guide the discussion to something neutral. Without it, though, we'd be sitting here having zero conversation.

"Don't take Augustine for granted. They're a good squad," his dad says, tapping his fork on his son's plate, then nods toward me. "You and he need to get that pass sequence down tighter. Too much room to get picked."

"We'll nail it," James assures, glancing across the table to me with his perfect-ass smile. My foot is bouncing under my chair while above the table I'm doing my best to swallow down forkful after forkful. At this point, I simply want to leave.

James leans to his side and slips his phone from his pocket, glancing down at it in his palm, which is hidden by the table.

"No phones at the table, son," his dad scolds and his son apologizes, putting it away and promptly turning his attention to clearing the table.

"That was the best meal I've ever had, Mrs. Coach," Cameron says, leaning back in his chair enough to lift the front legs from the ground as he rubs his belly. James' mom stands to help clear the table, stopping behind Cameron and giving his shoulder a pat. His gaze falls to her touch and lingers on his shoulder long after she's gone. Cameron doesn't talk about his mom, or his dad for that matter. His parents are off-limits, and a mystery.

While my roommate dismisses himself and returns to the

gaming console in the living room, I take the pile of plates from Mrs. Fuentes' hands and join James at the sink and dishwasher.

"Thanks, man," he says as I pile the dishes in and rinse while he loads them into the machine. We're removed from the others, enough that the tension between us is more obvious.

"That Lily? The text?" My ask is pretty fucking obvious.

James chuckles and glances my way as he bends down to drop in a plate. He quirks a brow.

"You know I'm not a dick, right? I'm just a nice guy. Or I try to be," he says.

I kill the water and leave the remaining pile soaking in the sink while I take a towel from the counter and dry my hands.

"That so?" *I'm not such a nice guy.*

He stands up straight, a few inches taller than me—*asshole*—and smirks.

"Yeah, Theo. It is. And you know what? Lily is a beautiful girl."

I shift my weight, my arms swelling with energy as my hands ball into fists. James shuts the dishwasher drawer, eliminating our barrier, and my chest puffs as he steps closer to me. I sway with angry energy as his eyes lock on mine, and when he pushes his finger into the center of my chest, I reinforce my position, not budging an inch. I'm acutely aware that his dad, my coach, is steps away, but right now I'm that irrational kind of pissed off, the kind when trashing my future seems completely fucking worthwhile.

We're close enough to kiss, sucking up the oxygen before the other one has a chance to breathe. James raises his chin a tick, enough to make his glare on me a hair more judgmental. I feel my nostrils flare.

"You wanna read my text? *From Lily?*" He's baiting me, patting his side pocket where his phone is.

"Fuck you, man," I seethe.

He lunges at me, and I flinch but brace myself. Part of me wants to get hit. A second later, though, he's backing away, laughing under his breath though his mouth is far from smiling. He pulls his phone from his pocket and slides it on the counter. It spins and stops so his messages face me. I glance at the temptation, my fingers itching to open the one labeled LILY.

"Go on. Read what has you so worked up and ready to fight me. See for yourself what an asshole I am."

I gnaw at the inside of my cheek and rap my fist against the side of my leg a few times before giving in and tapping the icon on his phone to open Lily's message.

LILY: *I'm sorry about that. Theo and I are complicated. Can you tell him where I am when he seems rational enough to talk? I'm in his stupid lair.*

My finger swipes to close her message and I stare at the blank screen while my skin tingles with humiliation. James palms his phone and slips it back in his pocket, then leans against the counter with his arms crossed.

"I get that you two are complicated." He breathes out a laugh. "Believe me, I got that almost the second I was in a three-way conversation with the two of you. And you don't have to tell me about the reasons for it. I know enough about you both. I don't need to dig on your trauma. Like I said, Theo, I'm a nice guy. Lily is my friend. And *I* *think* we're friends. And while maybe I'd be into her in another situation, I know when a girl is not mine. And Lily . . . she's taken."

My tongue poised behind my teeth, I breathe out once, harsh, and ragged, before my eyes blink their way to James. They burn, and I feel tears welling in their depths. I'm not going to cry, but the hurt and need pushing out from my insides is physically painful and it must go somewhere.

"I'm . . . sorry," I croak. I'm far from proud right now. I swallow hard and James shifts his stance, signaling we're no longer alone.

"Everything all right in here, gentlemen?" His dad's voice is a mix of parent and mentor, and I wish I had a man in my life who sounded like that. I did, once. A long time ago.

"We're all good, yeah," James says, reaching his hand out to me. I glance up to meet his eyes and he directs my attention to his hand. I grasp it and he pulls me in, patting my back with his other hand.

"Go tell her . . . whatever it is you need to tell her," James says at my ear.

I nod and pat his back in return before we break apart. I turn into his father and reach out my hand in thanks. We shake once.

"Thanks for everything, Coach. I was feeling some shit just now. James helped me work through it."

His dad narrows his eyes on me, then glances to his son before nodding.

"Good. Now work through your pass sequence."

James and I both laugh, and the release feels good, injecting a little life back into my arms and legs.

"Yes, sir," I say as I back out of the kitchen area and cross through the living room.

"I'll be in late," I say to Cameron as I pass. He pauses the game and shoots me a knowing look complete with the smug grimace he wears as an *I told you so*. He holds up a peace sign, then turns his attention back to game.

I snag my shoes from by the door and do my best to slip them on mid stride toward the library. I reach the door in less than a minute and slide the deadbolt in place after I enter.

Lily's head bobs up from the far desk where she's sitting with her things spread out, a small lamp the only light in the room. I'm not even sure she can see me from this far. I see her, though.

I see her.

Her brown hair is lit gold at the edges from the lamp's light, her cheeks red, probably from crying. She's too far to be able to tell, but her silence is telling. She knows it's me. Who else would it be?

"James told me you were here." My voice sounds raw, my throat still decompressing from wanting to growl with jealousy a minute before. I could not have spoken more obvious words.

"Are we done?" She flattens her palms atop her notebook and pencil against the desk and lifts her chin.

I pass through the rows of desks between us and stop a few feet short of her, dropping my hands in my pockets and letting her beauty literally punch me in the chest. I nod slowly.

"Yeah, Lily. We're done."

Her eyes stay on mine, even as they grow heavy and relief morphs into even bigger worries. If we're done—*if I'm done* —with this pulling away and being afraid nonsense, are we ready to step into something so public and fragile all at the same time?

"I wasn't trying to be mean," she says.

I smile on one side of my mouth and let out a single laugh.

"Yeah, you were."

She sighs.

"I was. But I'm sorry." She blinks slowly and her lips part with a tiny breath as if she's ready to say more. I love the way her top lip curls up, begging to be eaten.

"I deserved it," I say before she can apologize more.

Her mouth closes again, and her shoulders rise with a deep breath.

"You did," she utters, offering a soft laugh of her own.

I move to the desk and let my hand drag along the surface as I walk to the side. My fingers nudge her notecards, a few of them scribbled and torn. I try to force a ripped one back together and she steals it from me, sweeping it into her lap.

"That one's trash. I couldn't focus," she says, turning in her chair as I continue to round her desk. I stop with less than two feet between us, and she pulls her feet up into the chair, hugging her knees as her chin rests on top of them.

"James told me something . . . something I guess I needed to hear," I say.

She peers up at me through her lashes, her upper lip slipping free with a tiny breath. I think she may be at her prettiest in those small moments right before she speaks.

"And what was that?" Her head tilts to the right a hair.

"He said you were mine."

Her eyes flash wide, but only for a second. Her breathing becomes more rapid, her chest rising and falling in sync with mine. I drown in her eyes, staring so long I wonder if I've fallen into a trance and missed her response.

"I am."

As if a switch flips inside of me, all resentment and jealousy and fear sweeps away under a wave of need. I step into her and take her hands, cuffing them and dragging them up my chest to coax her to stand. She gazes up at me the entire time until we're inches apart while I hold her hands at my neck.

"I'm yours," she repeats, making her feelings abundantly clear.

Abandoning her hands around my neck, I slide my own

along her arms to her sides, lift her and turn so she's sitting on the desk, her note cards scattering to the sides and the floor. My palms move from her hips to flatten against the desktop as I lean into her and take her top lip between both of mine, sucking it in hard until my teeth find her tender skin and grip.

"I fucking love your mouth," I say, not even flinching at that slip. It's a good place to start in understanding my feelings—her perfect, delicious pink mouth. Lips like candy and tongue sharp and tart.

Lily leans back and opens her mouth more, deepening our kiss and grazing my lip with her own teeth. I want to tear into her yet savor every bite, and that war grows stronger as her fingers weave into my hair and grab hold.

Bracing her back with my right hand, my entire body rushes with adrenaline as my fingers find the bare skin at the arch of her spine. I lean into her more and her body shifts, willingly laying down. As she rests on the desk, her hair spilling off the back, my palm glides to her side. I nip at her lips and drag my kiss down her chin and into the crook of her neck as she arches into me.

My hand continues its path up her ribs until I find the braless curve of her breast and the hard peak of her nipple.

She whimpers at my first touch, and her body squirms with my second. My thumb makes slow circles around her tip, and I nuzzle my nose against hers to awaken her eyes. I want to see what this does to her—*what I do to her*. Her lashes lift and our gazes lock just as my thumb and finger roll her nipple with sweet pressure, pinching until I see her eyes flinch.

"Did that hurt?" I brush my lips to hers and she pushes her breast into my hand.

"Yes," she moans. "A good hurt."

Fucking hell.

My cock swells, and I want her to feel it, to know what she does to me. I tease her breast again, running my thumb over the hard tip with a feather-light touch while I bring my knee up to the desk so I can press into more of her. Leaning down, I take her mouth in mine and pinch her nipple hard enough to make her cry out while my hips rock forward, pressing my hard dick between her legs.

"Fuck," I groan, pushing into her again, needing the relief. I'm going to come in my goddamn jeans, and I don't care.

Lily's hands move from my shoulders to the bottom of her sweatshirt, and her golden eyes level me with the kind of look that's nothing short of a demand. She lifts the hem of her shirt up over her bare tits and I quickly help her pull it over her head, discarding it to the ground behind her. My mouth covers her left nipple as my right hand works the right, sucking and pulling her delicate skin into tiny, delicious beads. If she let me, I'd bite them off right now.

"Are you mine?" she whispers at my ear, her voice gritty and soaked with want.

"Fuck yes, I'm yours, Lily." I push my cock against her thigh, and she reaches up and grips my neck, pulling my mouth to her. I kiss her raw, my hand kneading her breast while I rub against her like an animal.

That's what I am. Lily strips me to my base core, until there's nothing left but my singular emotions, felt one at a time. Right now, it's lust. Right now, it's my dick wanting to dive into a wet pussy. It's a broken boy and a girl needing to feel something other than pain. To feel each other. To find ecstasy in the darkest of places. And as my dick swells and hot come soaks my jeans, I've never been more right to indulge.

Chapter 19

Lily

It's the first time the three of us have been in a car together since it happened. Brooklyn offered to drive; I think maybe she knew I wouldn't be up for it. Besides, she drives a G-wagon. It's a bit classier than an eight-year-old sedan.

"Everyone buckled?" She glances at me in the mirror, and I tug on my seat belt for proof. If there are three people on this earth who will *always* wear their seat belts, it's us. If it weren't for our safety belts, we would have smashed into the glass. There wouldn't have been any of us to save or do the saving.

I've never been in the car when Brooklyn drove, and I can't help but wonder if she's always been so fastidious or if she changed her habits after the accident. She's checked her mirror angles twice, at least, and I've never seen someone sit so upright behind the wheel. Her hands are at the literal ten and two positions.

She finally backs out of her parking spot and Morgan leans over to switch on the stereo. I'm not sure what Morgan was expecting to hear, but I for one wasn't prepared for her speakers to blast the latest financial reports from the exchange.

"Are you seriously that boring?" Morgan teases, and I hold a fist to my mouth to cover my puckered lips that are dying to laugh.

"Are you seriously that out of touch with the important things happening in our world?" Brooklyn has stopped us in the middle of the parking lane so she can look Morgan in the eye and have a brainy stare-off with her. It lasts an awkward four or five seconds, and Morgan eventually gives in and sighs.

"Oh, yeah," Morgan says, snapping her fingers and bringing her arms up. She sways in her seat and looks back to me. "Come on, Lily. Dance with me. Don't you love the beat of this report on, wait . . ." She turns the volume up and cups her ear.

Oil futures were up a half point today, and many economists credit it to the ongoing negotiations with Walden Bennett, the president's chief advisor, and refiners in . . .

Walden Bennett is Brooklyn's father. She was listening for news about him. Probably has been all week during her drive to her internship at the mayor's office. She turns the volume down quickly and presses a few buttons on her touch screen to pull up a play list with some real dance music.

"There. That better?" She glances to me in the mirror, and I shrink down into my seat. I feel like an asshole.

"B, I'm sorry," Morgan says, reaching out to touch her friend's arm.

Brooklyn merely looks at her touch then returns her focus to the road. I don't know enough about her life to fully understand why this is sensitive, but I'm guessing Morgan knows more. Maybe more trips like this will help me feel less on the outside. I'd like that. I want both to trust me with their secrets. Of course, I could start by sharing some of mine.

"I went to second base with Theo last night," I blurt out.

Brooklyn stops her SUV again, this time shifting into park. Thank God we aren't on the street yet! Within a second, she and Morgan are turned in their seats, faces shoved in the space above the console so they can stare at me.

"Repeat that, and maybe with less grade school slang," Brooklyn says.

My neck is hot, and sweat is building under my arms. Brooklyn seems to have moved beyond her tiff with Morgan of a second ago, though, so I guess this is worth it. This is how you get in, how you get close to people. Sharing the real stuff is something Anika was teaching me to do. No better time than the present, I guess, to practice her lessons.

"We've gotten . . . closer?" I eek out.

"Uh, yeah! Close enough for him to have his hands on your tits it seems," Morgan says. Brooklyn elbows her but returns her waiting stare to me for more details.

"Yeah," I breathe out in nervous laughter. "I mean, you know the issues. There's . . ."

"Baggage," Brooklyn finishes for me.

I nod.

"Baggage, right. And a lot of messy emotions. But I've always had this thing for him, and before . . . Anika."

They both nod, understanding what I mean without having to speak about it. It's a blessing that comes with our terrible shared history. Some incidents and references don't need mention to be understood.

"We were sort of talking, and we had this connection. Or maybe more that we *have* this connection," I say, feeling the smile stretch into my cheeks.

"You're blushing," Morgan says, tapping my knee. I bring

my palms up to my face and cover my hot skin. I smile behind them, though, the entire time.

"Guys, there were seriously some ugly words spoken, and some petty shit and behavior—*on both our parts*," I admit.

"But—" Morgan leads.

"But last night, after I walked out on my study session with James because Theo was being a jealous asshole, he came after me. We were in the archive room."

"You mean . . . *the lair?*" Morgan teases. We all giggle, and for a short slice of time, we're eighteen-year-old girls laughing about crushes and boys on a Friday night. Anika is with us. I feel it.

"Yes, the lair," I laugh back. "And oh, my God, the way he kisses!"

"Has it gotten better from when he was eleven? Because he smashed his lips on mine once in the playground and it was like kissing a helium balloon," Morgan says.

I didn't know about that, but the amount of time they've known each other, and their family connections, it makes sense that there would have been a youthful crush between them. There's a tinge of jealousy squeezing at my chest, too, but not enough to acknowledge.

"I'm gonna say he's probably had a lot of practice since then. Because girls . . . his hands, and his mouth, and—" I fan myself and curl up in the back seat with embarrassment.

"Look at you, our Lily, all grown up," Morgan says, tickling my knee with her long, glossy nails. "Girl, don't be shy about that shit. You tamed the beast. You wear that shit with pride. Theo Rothschild doesn't chase after anyone. But . . ." She taps her index fingernail at the hem of my skirt. "He chased you."

My grin stretches and I let my hands uncover more of my face.

"He did, didn't he?" Saying the words just now also forces me to accept it a little more. It still feels fleeting to an extent, and there's a truly damaged part of my self-esteem that doesn't feel worthy of being pursued by a guy like him.

"Yes, he did," Brooklyn says. They look at one another and exchange a glance, almost as if they've been in on this secret all along. Maybe they have. I'm sure my attraction to him has been obvious in many ways, and maybe they've seen things from Theo that I've been blind to or haven't been able to admit. I kind of think now that they've talked about us, maybe even nudged us toward one another in their own subtle ways. *Doing Anika's work.*

Brooklyn latches her seat belt again and shifts gears, finally pulling us onto the roadway.

"So how does he compare to those Ohio boys back home?" Morgan asks, rolling her window down and holding her palm out to catch the wind.

I consider her question and think about every kiss I've had before Theo Rothschild, and the comparison simply makes me laugh. Fumbling hands, tangled bra straps, drool, and braces.

"I think you summed it up with that one word," I say, meeting her gaze as she glances over her shoulder to me. "Boys."

We both smile and nod.

* * *

I've been through three stores and two hours have passed. I'd like to say the time has flown by, but I really do hate shopping. I haven't bought a thing yet, mostly because Brooklyn and Morgan want to get Theo's take on their favorite picks. I tried to convince them that Theo couldn't care less, but it's more about them torturing him and seeing if he'll break his icy character in front of them.

To be honest, I'm a little worried about how he'll do on this test. I meant what I said when I refused to be some secret. And I've learned that it seems things with Theo can change on an hourly basis.

The guys are on their way to Ashwood Mall, so we decided to grab some food and wait for them at the food court. I remember seeing Anika with the two of them sitting in this very spot during my third and fourth forms. It's nothing more than a large round table with some padded chairs—five to be exact. It always seemed as if this table were put here for their purposes. For their use only. Not that they were uninviting. The opposite. They were more on display, a destination point for other private school teens at the mall for the weekend. Popular cliques from other schools would stop by and it was like this meeting of the minds, or it seemed that way from an outsider's point of view.

Now, being on the inside, though? I realize we're simply sitting at a table, and we chose these seats because they're comfortable. And Brooklyn and Morgan? They know a lot of people, and they're friendly. I've met a dozen other girls who look and talk exactly like them in the twenty minutes we've been sitting here. Even stranger, I fit in.

"I talked to my coach today," I say, figuring now that I've shared the news about Theo, my decision to compete in a couple weeks seems uninteresting. Brooklyn doesn't take it that way, though, and literally spits out some of her drink before leaning across the table and putting her hand over mine.

"Lily, that's incredible! You know we'll come and support." A visual of her and Morgan waving signs and cheering my name passes through my head and it both excites and mortifies me.

I swallow.

"I'm probably going to get my ass kicked." I want to base their expectations in reality. I've made it across the pool a few times, and I've been winded. But it felt good to stretch my arms in the water and to push myself a little. I think if I spend the week conditioning, I won't be a total embarrassment in the water.

"I doubt that, but we will scream just as loud regardless," Morgan adds.

"Just as loud for what?" James' voice startles all three of us and our heads spin to find him standing behind Morgan, his hands planted on the back of her chair.

"Lily is going to swim again. She talked to her coach!" Morgan turns in her seat so she's sitting on her knees and facing James, and I watch him closely to see how he reacts. When he moves his hand to her shoulder for a friendly— *maybe more than friendly*—squeeze, I relax. He's going to score more points flirting with her rather than me, probably with her *and* Theo.

"I guess it's official then, huh?" Theo's voice floats above me and I look straight up to find him standing behind my chair, hands resting on either side of the back as he looks down. His hair is still damp from his post-practice shower, and he's wearing his Welles Football polo shirt that hugs his chest and arms like skin. All three boys are dressed the same, representing their team well. Theo, though, manages to make Dockers and a polo look a cut above.

"That's not the only thing that's official, so we hear," Brooklyn teases. She chews at the end of her straw and folds her legs up in her chair to get comfortable.

Theo chuckles and I study his expression, partly waiting

for it to turn hard and accompany some biting comment to shut her down.

"If you're talking about me officially pulling my head out of my ass, then yeah. That's official." He dips his chin and looks down at me again, offering a crooked smile that lingers with his gaze.

Morgan whistles.

"Really? All I do is look at her and that's got you going?" Theo jokes.

"Maybe I'm trying to provoke you, Rothschild." She arches a brow, like a challenge, and I laugh nervously. It's weird to have everyone talking so openly about me and Theo, as an *us*.

Before I'm able to truly crumble with embarrassment, however, Theo moves his hand to my shoulder, then my neck as he stares down Morgan and bends at the waist, pulling my mouth up to meet his as his eyes close and he kisses me in front of every single human in the Ashwood food court.

Morgan whistles again, but I barely hear it. My ears have gone mute. I'm drunk and floating. Theo's kiss drags on until Cameron finally can't stand watching us, and he throws his hat at his friend.

"Dude, you're being gross," he says.

Theo's lips leave mine and grin almost immediately. My heart is thundering in my chest. He runs his palm along my shoulder to my arm until, lifting my wrist, his fingers finally twine with mine. Then he picks up Cameron's hat from my lap and tosses it back to him.

"You sure you want to get into a discussion about which one of us is gross? You have penicillin growing under your bed."

Cameron shoots him a pointed glare as he slides his hat backward over his wild hair.

"It's one dirty dish, *Dad*," he quips.

I look to Theo and he mouths the word *four*, which makes me laugh.

"Come on, kids. We're here to outfit our girl. Theo, we want your opinion," Morgan says as she stands.

"Okay, naked. I choose naked," Theo responds as I get to my feet. I shoot him a wide-eyed look, then bury my face in his shoulder.

"Oh, my God," I say with my mouth on his sweatshirt-covered bicep. He laughs it off and Morgan chides him, calling him "classy" in her best sarcastic tone.

James and Cameron peel away from us before we get to the first store, and Brooklyn leaves us with Morgan in the women's section while she goes to check on a watch she's having engraved for her father. I let Morgan take control, gathering the choices she and Brooklyn decided were the best professional looks and leading me to the fitting room.

The outfits are literally ones I could borrow from her closet, but I guess it would be nice to have a few things to call my own. And I can't exactly wear the Welles skirt and sweat-shirt everywhere I go, though it's gotten me through five years at this place.

My first few outfits are ones Morgan picked for my internship, and I feel a little unlike myself in them. Theo's reactions sort of seals the deal.

"Looks fine," he says to the second dress I show off in. It's brown with small white flowers, and the only thing I like about it is that it doesn't cling to my hips. I'm relieved that he doesn't seem to think I look any better this way.

Morgan rests a hand on her hip as I shuffle my way back into the fitting room, though she tugs on the sleeve as I pass.

"I really liked this one," she whines.

"Then you wear it," Theo says, sandwiching himself into

the tight space. He's holding a yellow dress on a hanger, and he shoves it between Morgan and me. His gaze hits mine and his lips twist into the sweetest smile. "You look good in yellow."

"Nobody looks good in yellow," Morgan declares, pushing him out of our space with a palm to his chest. I've already taken the dress in my hand, though, and am heading back to my fitting room.

I step out of Morgan's pick and put it back on the hanger, then unzip the back of the dress Theo picked. It's more like me, plain but bright, with sleeves that hug down to the elbow. The fabric is stretchy, almost like my workout clothes but more professional. I step into it and work it up my body, then stretch to tug the zipper up my back, getting it most of the way up. I crack the door open a smidge and peek through in search of Morgan, but Theo steps into view first.

"Zipper?" I ask.

He looks to his side and holds up a hand, I'm guessing to Morgan, then checks the area around us before slinking into the fitting area.

"I don't think you're allowed back here," I whisper.

"I don't care," he responds. Of course he doesn't. My pulse jets up because breaking rules stresses me out. When he sweeps my hair over my shoulder and runs his hand up the length of the zipper, tugging it to its end at the nape of my neck, I decide rule breaking has its perks.

Resting his chin on my shoulder, he wraps his arms around me from behind and we both size up his pick. My hands run down the front to my hips and slip into secret pockets I didn't know where there. The discovery sparks an instant grin.

"It's perfect," I say, bunching the pocket material into my palms inside the dress.

Theo leaves his eyes on my reflection but drops a soft kiss at the curve of my neck. It sends a thousand tiny bumps down my spine, like cool ice and a breeze on top of it. I shiver in response, which makes him nuzzle his scratchy chin against my bare skin to tickle me more.

"Well?" Morgan shouts from a dozen feet away.

Theo backs out and I step in front of him and move toward my friend. Her arms are crossed over her chest and her mouth is screwed up to match her judgey expression. She twirls a finger in the air, directing me to spin, and I do, keeping my hands in their very cozy pockets the entire time.

"Fine, he's right. You look good in yellow. You should get it." She purses her lips, and I think she might truly be offended that Theo nailed this before she did. I don't care, though, because one, this dress has pockets, and two, I could get used to the way Theo looks at me in something he chose.

They both wait by the seats while I slip back out of the dress and into my school uniform. I check the prices on the two jeans I decided to get along with a sweater and the yellow dress, and my stomach clenches at the nearly seven-hundred-dollar total. I've never used the credit card my dad gave me for anything, though. And he tells me I should every time we talk—*when he responds to my calls.*

I leave the discards on the rack and head to the register with my friends. Brooklyn has caught up to us and James and Cameron are nearby entertaining themselves with the cologne samples.

"Your car is going to reek," I say to Theo as we both wait while the clerk scans my items and folds them neatly into tissue paper. I've never bought clothes that get packaged up like Christmas gifts before.

"Correction, Brooklyn's car is going to reek. I'm taking you home and they can all pile into the Mercedes with her."

"Oh, yeah?" I smile up at him.

"Ma'am, this card is declined." The clerk's voice breaks through my joyful haze and my chest tightens. I might be having a heart attack. My chest hurts, right under the bone. I can't breathe.

"That can't be. Can you try again?" I beg.

She levels me with a crooked grimace and slides my card again, not even bothering to look as she does. My mouth is watering with the desire to vomit. She shakes her head and holds the useless plastic out to me.

"It's my dad's. It should work. Let me just call him. He must have a lock on it or something," I say, fumbling with my phone. I swipe to my dad's contact info and press CALL. The phone goes to voicemail almost immediately, so I try again only to get the same result. I start to text him, praying to see those little dots that show he's responding, but my message sits there unnoticed. It only says delivered. It doesn't even say read.

"Ma'am, if you can't pay, I need to take the next customer."

Oh, my God. There's someone waiting behind me.

I glance over my shoulder and spot a woman and her daughter waiting with their arms filled with merchandise. This lady will make way more in commission off them.

"Use mine," Theo says, handing over his card.

"No, I can pay. Let me . . ."

He wraps his hand on top of both of mine, stopping them shaking as they grasp my wallet. I'm so embarrassed. More than that, though, I'm hurt. My dad only shows his affection by making a credit card available to me, and the one time I try to use it, it's quite literally useless.

The woman swipes Theo's card and he scribbles his name on the receipt. Once my purchase is bagged, we head over to where our friends are still sampling sprays and lotions. I feel like crying, and when Brooklyn asks me if something's wrong, I tell her I'm probably allergic to the toxic cloud James and Cameron have made.

It makes for a good excuse, but the pit in my stomach only gets deeper the more we walk through the mall. Once there's some distance between our friends and us, I thread my arm through Theo's and hug it, sure he can still feel me tremble.

"You didn't have to do that," I say.

He stops us in the middle of the mall, turns me so I'm square with him and he puts his hands on my shoulders. I can feel the pout swelling in my bottom lip.

"I wanted to," he says. I drop my chin, but he lifts it fast. He bends enough to bring our eyes level.

"Not because I wanted to shower you with presents or pamper you or whatever, but because I know what it feels like."

My eyebrows pull in.

"I get the pain of having a parent let you down. I know how it feels when other people are watching, but more than that, I get how it might seem everyone is watching even when they're not. I wanted to take you out of that situation because I care about you, and I know how it feels. And I don't want you to feel like that. Okay?"

The tightness in my chest drops to my heart, and though I can hardly breathe, I oddly feel like laughing at the same time. The madness kind of laugh. The kind that comes with extreme relief, with being seen.

"Okay." I nod, stepping into him. Theo wraps me in his arms and drops a kiss on the very top of my head. I imagined this. Well, not *quite* this, but the sentiment. I maybe wished for it. Turns out, he *is* that kind of guy after all.

Chapter 20

Theo

Today was a good day.

I think maybe accepting that I have feelings for Lily, and that they're real and valid and . . . well . . . allowed, tilted the universe scales for me. I aced my economics test. I caught every pass James threw to me at practice. And he and I honestly gelled, like a real friendship.

We didn't talk about what he called our 'come to Jesus moment' in his kitchen. He merely asked me if I made shit right and I nodded and shook his hand. I suppose as dudes we gloss over the details and bury feelings, but the outcome is what matters, and he and I? We're square. Solid, in fact.

Since Lily and I left the mall, though, I keep thinking about my biggest epiphany—that I'm *allowed* to have feelings for her. To care about her. To fall for her piece by beautiful piece. While I might not have been up for the heartfelt talk with James, I think Lily and I need to have it. Maybe it's a latent lesson from my sister stuck in my head, but I sort of feel as though Lily deserves it. Or perhaps I simply want to know if she feels like we're forbidden, too. It sounds stupid in my head, but it was a mountainous hurdle only a few days ago.

"You mind if we pull out somewhere and hang out just me and you a little while?" I glance at her and she sucks in her lips, tucking her hands under her thighs and pushing her skirt in.

I chuckle, realizing how that sounded. And now that the idea is mixed in with more gentlemanly reasons I wanted to hang out with her alone, I'm half hard and sure to fuck up anything important I want to say.

"I really did mean to talk. But—"

I grab the back of my neck and laugh. I'm the goddamn devil.

"I'd like that. Alone time doesn't feel totally alone in your lair, no offense," she says, her voice raspy and quiet.

"I could kill Cameron for that label. It makes me sound like one of those *Dungeons and Dragons* nerds." I pull off at the next exit toward the lake and realize Lily didn't laugh at my joke.

"Oh, God, wait. You're— You play that shit?" I hold a fist to my mouth and spit out a brief laugh before she swats at my arm.

"Says the guy with a He-Man credit card." She folds her arms over her chest and shifts to stare me down.

"Touché," I relent. I nod and hold my mouth shut, keeping the millions of questions I now want to ask her locked behind my lips. They're still in my head, though, and eventually, one of them slips out.

"So, were you like, a fairy or a warlock? Or . . . oh! A dragon?"

"I was twelve and you're an asshole," she huffs. I can tell by her tone she's not truly mad, though. Sadly, I've seen her earnestly angry with me. Both that time and this are my fault.

"So . . . dragon then?" I nod as I stare straight ahead and the roadway turns to dirt. We cross into a cover of trees. The car is quiet, but I see her shifting in my periphery, looking around at the landscape and thankfully not angry or nervous.

"Dragon princess," she finally responds.

Unrestrained laughter flies out of my mouth and I cough, likely choking on the foot I keep putting in my mouth.

She gets me back by reciting a few lines from the He-Man cartoons and by the time I pull us into the clearing, we're on playful and friendly terms.

I kill the engine and unlatch my buckle so I can pull up a leg and look her more in the eyes. She does the same, only keeping one leg tucked under the other. My eyes instinctually drift to the exposed part of her inner thigh, and my dick flexes its muscle to remind me it's still very much present.

"You look great in that dress," I say, clearing my throat as I steer our conversation into safe territory.

Lily looks down and bats her lashes as she tucks her bottom lip under her teeth.

"Thank you," she utters. "I really love it. I'm still embarrassed that you had to pay for it, though. I'll pay you back."

I shake my head and wave a hand.

"Please don't. Consider it me making us even for all the times I've been an asshole this term."

She lifts her chin and meets my gaze, seeming to study me for a few seconds. I wonder if she's trying to read how genuine I am. I think this may be the sincerest I've ever been. She seems to pull that quality out of me and multiply it.

"You weren't an asshole," she finally responds.

"Oh, I was. But thank you for letting me off the hook."

Our gazes lock again. After a few more seconds, her head falls to the side and her mouth pulls in, outwardly displaying her thought.

"You weren't an asshole," she insists. "You were grieving."

Wow.

My smile fades at her honest assessment, but I leave my eyes on hers. Her smile is soft, her eyes matching as they slope and display understanding.

I swallow hard.

"I was. Still am. Probably will be for—"

"Forever," she fills in.

I open my mouth to offer a different word but decide quickly that she's right. I close my mouth and nod in agreement.

Shifting in my seat, I sink down lower and rest my hands on the bottom of the steering wheel. Lily shifts too, and for a few minutes we sit in complete silence and look out at the stars.

"Can I say a bunch of things without you looking at me so I can get them off my chest, and will you promise not to think I'm weird?" I brace myself for her reaction, but it's a simple and quick *yes*.

I breathe in long and slow through my nose while I mentally sort my words. It's hard to express the mess in my head, but I need to for Lily and me to be able to have a real shot. Even if she doesn't need to hear it, I think I need to hear myself say it. Our family therapist would say I'm actualizing my feelings. I'm just trying to make sense of my own brand of crazy.

"I blamed you for Anika even though I knew it wasn't your fault. I'm self-aware enough to know I was transferring my own guilt and trying to find a reason for something that will never make sense." I let that first big confession sit out there in the open for a few seconds. I glance to Lily, and when I find her eyes still focused up on the stars and her expression relaxed, I exhale.

"I thought about you all summer. I haven't stopped thinking about you since those hours before it all went to hell. I thought about you when they asked me to identify my sister. I thought about you at the police station, and all the way home while I sat there speechless in my uncle's car as he drove me and my shit home for the rest of the term. I looked for you the moment I got to campus, and I scanned every classroom with this repressed hope that your face would be in there. I wanted you with me, near me, within reach or a phone call away. And I hated myself for wanting any of that."

I sit up tall in my seat and lean forward, resting my hands on the top of the steering wheel and laying my head to the side so I can stare at her. I'm afraid she's going to run from this car screaming or tell me I'm a liar. Or worse—tell me I'm alone in these thoughts.

"I hated myself for liking you so damn much. In my mixed-up head, my biggest worry was what other people would think. I didn't want people to think I was with you for Anika's sake, that I was trying to, I don't know, honor her or whatever. I didn't want them to think what I felt for you wasn't real, because it is."

Her lips part and I lift my head, eager to hear her react. Terrified.

"You didn't want me to think you were giving me some pity attention to make me feel better for failing your sister." She blinks a few times, then turns her head slowly until our eyes meet.

She gets it.

"Yeah," I croak.

We sit quietly like this for nearly a minute. It's strange that I never feel forced to look away. Even stranger that she never seems to either.

"My feelings for you are not because of any of those

things," I say, breaking the silence. My chest feels lighter with every thought I say out loud. I can breathe, and the difference enlightens me to how little I have been for the last several months.

"I believe you," she says. "And neither are mine."

Our mouths both curl into soft grins, and I think maybe for once I'm blushing, too.

"I've had a crush on you since I was a dragon princess, just so you know," she adds, breaking up the seriousness that was honestly starting to make me itch. She shifts in her seat again, tucking her skirt under her thighs with her hands, and like a trained dog, my gaze immediately follows.

I scratch at the front of my neck and lean back in my seat once more, stretching my legs out to give my dick more room. Thank God I'm not wearing a tie right now. I'd choke.

"When we were twelve?" I arch a brow, anxious to hear what she thought of my young, punk-ass self. I was not very crush-worthy in my memory.

"Oh, yeah. You know what sold me completely?" Her mouth twitches with a laugh, so I brace myself for whatever's coming.

"The cannonball during physical education." Her grin goes ear to ear and is completely serious. She blinks with wide eyes as she looks at me.

I slap my own face and run my palm down it at the memory. I leapt over the girls' class while they were sitting and listening to their teacher, and I angled myself just right so I could soak every one of them.

"You found that charming?" I peek through spread fingers.

"I found it annoying as hell. The water was so cold. But .. . the boy was cute." She bites her lip and shifts in her seat.

My eyes do their thing, checking the status of her skirt, which has risen another inch. *Fuck.*

If she hasn't caught me staring at her thighs yet, I'm going to have to get overt.

"White," I say, blinking my gaze back up to her face.

Her lips twist with her sideways glance.

"Your panties. I hope they're white."

Chapter 21

Lily

My panties are white. And my God, are they wet.

Before Theo has a chance to take those words back, I squirm in my seat, purposely inching my skirt up my thigh to expose more of my leg. I've heard the stories, and I know there's a lot of truth to them. I'm not the first girl he's parked in this car with out in the middle of nowhere. He's also not the only boy who's seen the color of my panties.

Ohio boys got nothing on Boston.

"You know, a lot of Welles girls talk about you and Cameron and your football friends," I lead.

"Oh, yeah?" He leans into the center console, placing his elbow on the leather arm rest while his hand lingers an inch or two above my knee. I suck in a quick breath.

"Yeah," I say, mentally willing his hand to lower. "They call you players and bad boys and all that." Truthfully, all Welles boys have a certain rap. They're not known for long-term relationships and commitment, which is probably why so many Welles girls date Augustine guys.

Theo's never officially dated anyone. He's taken girls to formal dances, and I've heard all about the make-out sessions and sex at parties. But when it comes to life on campus, he's never walked around holding hands with a girl or kissed her after a football game. Naïve as it is, I would like to be the first. He's already kissed me in the middle of the Ashwood mall.

Theo breathes out a laugh and scoots even closer in my direction. I clench my thighs together, feeling myself swell with need.

"I've never said I was a nice guy, remember?" His voice is deeper, husky in fact.

His fingertip brushes against my knee, almost like a test.

"Oh, I remember. But you *are* a nice guy, Theo. You're just also . . ."

His hand makes another pass, this time using the side of his knuckle.

"Also what, Lily?"

I shiver, fully aware of the tiny bumps now covering my legs.

"Not from smalltown Ohio," I mutter nervously.

He chuckles again and continues to run his knuckle along my skin. I glance up to meet his hooded eyes, then take in his chest and arms, breathing in his scent and wondering if he could get a little closer. I look down to my lap quickly, suddenly very aware of his erection and where this is going. Where I *want* this to go.

"Lily?" His voice is deeper somehow.

"Uh huh?" I croak.

"I'm not a player. But if you want, we can play a game."

Theo draws a small circle on my bare knee and instant shivers crawl up my leg and wrap around my body. He feels my slight flinch and his mouth curls ever so slightly into the faintest, most devious smile. His tongue stops at the edge of his teeth. I wait for his eyes to flit to mine. When they do, my core clenches.

"Am I making you nervous, Lily?"

Yes.

"I'm fine." My voice comes out in a barely audible whisper.

Alone with Theo, in his car, parked far away from anyone and everything with nothing but the dim light of the cloud-covered stars. I should be more nervous than I am. But I have wanted this for so long.

"How about this . . ." He breathes out a teasing laugh, his tongue resting back against his teeth. It's the most intoxicating expression I have ever seen. My hands are tucked under my thighs, my skirt's hem cutting a line across my thigh. My core pulses.

"I will write my name, my *full* name, on your leg with this finger." His touch leaves my knee briefly as he shows me his index finger before placing it between his teeth and closing his lips around it to suck it wet. He drags it free, then returns it to my knee, the touch cool. "When you would like me to quit writing, simply say *stop*. And I will."

My lips part and an audible though hushed gasp leaves them.

"You'll stop," I reiterate.

Don't stop.

His finger moves to draw the T in Theodore.

"I will," he says, his gaze holding mine for another second before returning to his invisible penmanship work on my thigh.

My attention moves to follow the gentle path of his finger. He's writing in cursive, every little sweep and dash like a feather that has me growing wetter . . . *bolder*. He reaches the hem of my skirt as his finger begins to slow down and draw the D. I glance up, my lips frozen in their barely parted position.

"Oh, Lily. Are you sure you're ready to be a bad girl?" His grin ticks up and my center pulses with need. Without pause, my legs part a little, inviting him in. His eyes blaze, but his gaze doesn't leave mine as his finger continues to draw along the curve of my thigh. The D, then another O. I fall back slightly and remove my own hands from the safe space under my thighs, letting my arms fall over my eyes as they blink closed and Theo continues to draw his way to the thin cotton strip of my panties.

His touch, again, feather light.

I moan and he teases his finger along the edge of the material as my legs fall open further.

"Would you like to play some more?" His mouth has moved close to my ear, his weight on the center console. I can only whimper my response, but my arm slides away enough from covering my eyes to allow our gazes to meet. I nod. He smiles and moves the center strip of my panties to the side.

My teeth grip my bottom lip and my eyes flutter shut uncontrollably, my body teeming with anticipation as one of his fingers teases the inside of my thigh while the others have curled around the fabric between my legs to expose my core to the cool air. My tender skin practically vibrates with the craving to be touched. He hasn't placed a finger on my center yet and still I'm on the verge of coming.

"They're white, aren't they?"

I nod at his whispered question, a tiny whimper slipping from my lips.

Almost as if it's a reward for him being right, his finger slides along my wet, swollen center, and I pulse against his touch. My breath hitches and he hushes me, pausing his fingertip at the most sensitive spot.

"Say it," he says in a hushed tone.

I whimper again.

"Please," I beg.

My thighs have spread as wide as the passenger seat of his BMW will allow and my skirt has bunched up to my waist. I spare opening my eyes for the smallest moment, and as soon as my gaze is met with the purest silver-blue eyes in the world, Theo's finger taps against my center and my entire body begins to pulse.

"Oh, God," I sigh out, bring my arms back over my face.

My need to orgasm is out of my control, but before I fall over the edge, Theo slides his finger against me again, driving my nerves wild.

"We'll get this one out of the way, yes?" I nod as his finger dips inside me, curling against my insides then moving in and out. My hips lift, my body wanting to rock with his touch and take him deeper, and when my orgasm peaks, I cry out, quickly muffling it by biting my own arm.

"Fuck, Lily. You smell like sex." His hand works my pussy, one finger increasing to two as he slips in and out, his thumb flicking against my clit while I writhe in his seat.

My arm falls from my face and my hand grabs my sweatshirt, bunching the material up as I desperately work to uncover my breasts.

"Fuck it," Theo growls. His hand leaves me and I sit up fast, but before I have a chance to beg him not to stop, he's left the driver's side and is flying around the front to the passenger side. He flings my door open and grabs my hand, tugging me from the seat and guiding me to the hood where he quickly picks me up and sets me down.

Theo's mouth covers mine in a hungry kiss as his palms grip my thighs, squeezing then sliding up to the band of my underwear. Without hesitation, his fingers curl around the sides and he pulls them down my hips and legs. I lay back on his hood and slip out of my sweatshirt as he tosses my panties to the side.

I'm wearing my nicest bra—white lace that exposes part of my nipple. It's the only sexy thing I've ever bought myself, and right now it feels like the best purchase I ever made.

Theo's hands caress up my legs, parting my knees enough for him to stand between them. His hands don't stop there, though, continuing their journey north over the curves of my thighs until slipping around my ass and squeezing me hard.

My center swells instantly with more desire, and my arms fall to either side of me, palms flat on his hood. I arch my back to push my tits toward him. I want his mouth on them. But Theo seems to want to kiss me somewhere else. His palms trace the curve of my ass and hips, my skirt now doing nothing to cover my most private parts. I move my arm enough to lay my eyes on his, and we hold our stare for the two seconds it takes for him to bend down and bring his mouth to my center. He sucks the moment his lips touch my swollen middle and when his tongue flicks against my clit, I come again. Maybe I never stopped.

My hands move to my breasts, and I squeeze myself as I arch, pinching my own nipples through the lace to satisfy this growing, unquenchable need. My own hands are soon replaced with Theo's. His tongue punishes my center with long, methodical strokes while he tugs down the cups of my bra and tugs at my rock-hard nipples.

"Say it, Lily," he says, his words muffled as he groans against my tender skin, and I buck against him.

"Please," I repeat, hoping it works like it did before.

Theo shakes his head, his lips moving from side to side against me, and I cry with the rhythm.

"No, say what you want. Tell me you want me to fuck

you, Lily. Please fucking say you want me to fuck you." One of his hands has moved from my breast and his body jerks between my knees as he strokes himself.

"Fuck me, Theo. Please fuck me," I say, without even having to think about it.

His mouth leaves one last suck behind as he stands and quickly pulls a condom from his wallet, tossing it to the ground and unzipping his pants. I lift myself up on my elbows enough to watch as he pulls himself out of his boxers and slowly rolls on the condom. It's almost laughable how much better he is at this compared to Michael Shipley, the boy who mowed our lawn and who took my V-card two years ago.

His hand runs up my center, pulling my skirt up my belly and holding me still as he moves forward and guides his tip into me. I can feel my pussy pulsing already and I fall back, readying myself for him to fill me completely. He starts slow enough, rocking his hips forward and entering me an inch at a time, but soon, he can no longer handle it, falling forward and resting his weight on his palms on either side of my face while his dick slides all the way inside.

"Oh, fuck," he groans, and I close my thighs around him, holding him to me and bracing myself for him to rock out and in again. The burn subsides as I stretch to fit him, and with each thrust, he grows bolder—*and harder*—sinking into me with more force.

My hands fly to his neck then wrap around his shoulders and back as I work to hold myself in place to meet every thrust. I'm on the cusp of coming again when his muscles flex and his breathing halts as he grinds into me so hard that my body slides several inches up the length of the car.

Theo pulses inside of me, his cock hot and skin damp. My hands cling to his back, silently begging him to push into me a few more times, which he does. His thrusts are more guarded, less about chasing his own orgasm now, but the fullness is enough to send me toppling again.

As his body blankets mine, I breathe in the hot air around us—made by us—and I smile because he's right. It smells like sex out here. And that's because I just fucked the hottest boy at Welles in the middle of a clearing. God, I want to do it again.

Chapter 22

Theo

Lily turns me into a rabid animal. I lose all reason.

That's not the way I wanted to have our first time, but I couldn't stop once my hand made it under her skirt and she whimpered at my touch. I had to taste her and damn, was she sweet.

I keep pacing from the locker room out to the field gate and back, and I don't even care how obvious it is that I'm looking for her. She said she would come to the game today, and I *want* her there. The only person I've ever cared about seeing me play is Anika.

I want Lily there.

When I step back into the locker room, I catch a few of the other senior players talking shit. They barely hide it by separating and instantly going quiet when I walk in. One of the guys, Oliver Raskin, has been doing a lot of whispering. He started the second I got back to campus. Probably because he loves to tell people about the sweet settlement he got when my sister stole his car and crashed it into a river. Insensitive fuck that he is, Raskin doesn't seem to quite get the tragic part of the story—*that Anika fucking died!*

"You ever get jealous of those guys who get to play their games under lights?" James pulls my attention to him, holding out a roll of tape for me to wrap his wrists. I take it but leave my glare on Raskin's profile. It makes me feel better knowing he's checking his periphery for me, to see if I'm still there.

I'm right here, you dick!

I stretch the tape and start wrapping with divided attention.

"Nah, Friday lights are overrated," I respond. Welles doesn't have lights. Our games have been on Saturday mornings for legit a hundred years.

"I think I'm gonna miss the lights. Don't judge me, bro," he says, taking over the wrapping now that I've gotten it started. I give up my stare-down and return my thoughts to more worthy things—*Lily.*

"That's cuz you're a quarterback. You guys are all about the glory." I roll my eyes and step closer to my locker so I can give my phone one more glance before Coach comes in and makes us all pay attention.

LILY: *We're here. Morgan put glitter on my face for this. I hope you're happy.*

I laugh quietly to myself and shoot her a gif of an overzealous stripper covered in glitter. She responds with a pic of the glitter lines under her eyes and my number, 88, on her right cheek.

ME: *I like the glitter better on you.*

LILY: *Aww, and I was about to offer you a pole dance.*

ME: *Wait!*

Her typing dots disappear, and I know I'm meant to be left hanging with that.

"Jesus Christ, are you going to be like this all year?" Cameron says over my shoulder.

I swipe my screen off, toss my phone into my bag, and push the locker shut.

"Your fault for looking at shit over my shoulder," I say, taking a test whiff to see if he'll be playing his first game high this season. He smells clear, which means maybe we might be half decent today. Cameron's fast, and his hands somehow catch everything thrown in their vicinity. Probably because he couldn't give two shits what happens to his body when he leaps into the air and lands on his neck.

"Gentlemen!" Coach Fuentes gets our attention, and we all line up on the rows of wooden benches.

For a private school with a serious endowment, our locker room is still stuck in the 1960s. After rolling a well-worn chalkboard to the front of the room, Coach runs through the key plays we worked on this week. I'm paying attention, but I'm not really listening. My focus has drifted to the back of Raskin's head, two rows in front of me.

My pulse has ticked up with anger, and I want to flick his red freckled ear that sticks out like a doorknob. After about ten minutes of review, Raskin turns to the side, and I'm right there waiting for him.

"Let it go," Cameron whispers at my side.

"I've never liked that asshole," I grit back.

"I know, but let it go," he repeats.

For such a wild human, Cameron's oddly a pacifist. He's sat back and watched me throw punches plenty of times over the years. And when I ask why he doesn't jump in and have my back, he shrugs and always says, "You're a big boy."

Deciding Raskin isn't worth it, I heed his advice for now and do my best to get into a competitive headspace. James leads us in a prayer, and I go along with it, figuring I could probably use some extra fortune. If I'm decent this season and manage to come out of the internship with some good recommendations along with an improved GPA, pretty much any school on the West Coast is in my cards. It's about three thousand miles from my mom's house to Stanford. That distance feels about far enough.

We all file through the hall, passing the trophy case that doesn't showcase any football hardware from this century . . . *yet*. The clacking of cleats along the concrete floor sounds like a rainstorm echoing off the walls until I break through the double doors. It's a short walk down a path cut through the grassy hill to the field. With the changing leaves hovering along the riverbank behind the home stands, the scene is almost plucked out of a New England Thanksgiving Card. The weather isn't quite crisp enough yet, but in a few weeks I'll see my breath during this walk. Some people hate the cold. I'm not particularly fond of it most times, but on game days? I live for it.

The Welles drumline pounds out the traditional drill beats that we always charge into the stadium to, and I glance to my right as we pass them, something seeming to draw my sight. Instead of focusing on the syncopated strokes of the snare drummers, though, my gaze goes right to the last person I want anywhere near me ever again.

My mother brought fucking Neil to my opening game!

I break from the team, shirking off Cameron's grip on my arm before marching up the grassy slope to where Neil is standing with his fat arm draped over my mom's shoulder. His polo shirt is too tight for his gut, and his Rolex looks out of place on his arm compared to his ill-fitting pants held up by a belt that must be made of magic.

"Why are you here?" My eyes bounce from my mom to Neil as I growl my words through the mouthpiece I left between my teeth. Good thing it's there because I'm close to cutting through it with my molars right now.

"Theo! We wanted to surprise you." My mom's voice is overly bubbly. She's putting on a show for me. This is how she sells a pile of shit to people with the hopes of convincing them it's gold. It's not. It's Neil—aka, a pile of shit.

"Surprise! Great, now tell your guest here to run along," I say, sweeping my hand in the air and shooing him. I wish that had a physical effect. I know what will—my fist in his jaw.

"Theodore, son." Neil's smoker voice gurgles through the words.

I point at him immediately and spit out my mouth guard, letting it dangle from my helmet.

"I'm not your son." I step in front of him so I don't have to see his face, and meet my mom's panicked gaze. She could not have possibly thought his would go well.

"What are you doing with this asshole? Why did you bring him? Ma!" My head is throbbing with my rising blood pressure.

"Theo, you're not being fair. We'll talk after your game. You must concentrate." She takes my hand and I let her because she's my mom, but I keep staring at her with an open mouth. She squeezes my palm and looks up at me with beggar's eyes, and the only response I can muster is ticking out a short laugh before walking away.

"Unbelievable," I mutter on my way back down the hill. The team has already run through the banner the student prefects made for opening day. By the time I walk through, it's nothing but shards of paper. I plop my helmet down over my head and jog until I'm standing next to Cameron.

"I've got a bad feeling about today," he says.

"Yeah? Why's that?" My tone is hostile. Even I hear it and cringe. I don't apologize for it, though.

"Just don't get kicked out. You can slash your stepdad's tires after the game," he says.

"He's not my stepdad. He's my mom's emotional crutch and an abusive son-of-a-bitch," I respond.

"Whatever. Don't deal with him on the field," Cameron says, popping his mouthguard in and running out for the first series of downs.

Left on my own on the sidelines with nothing but the defensive squad—including Raskin—I push my intense focus onto the team, sticking close to our coaches and shouting out things I spot as they unfold on the field. After a twenty-yard pass completion to Cameron, I get called in and get to put my aggression to work by blocking. It takes exactly thirteen seconds for me to get my first holding call. Seven seconds later, I get another.

Cameron grabs the front of my helmet when I come back to the huddle, twisting my head so we're mask to mask.

"I told you to let it fucking go!"

"I am letting it go! Not my fault these refs suck!" I shout back.

He lets go of my helmet and pushes the center of my chest as he walks to the other side of the huddle. I stare him down the entire time James runs through the sequence, and by the time we all clap and shout 'break,' I'm about as wound as a horny bull staring at a sea of red.

"Offsides!" The flag lands at my feet.

"Oh, fuck that!" I gripe.

"That's it! You're outta here!" The head ref's hand flashes in front of my face, and I'm clear-headed enough to get that he's ejecting me.

I begin to walk to the sidelines but turn back because this guy's been on my ass since the minute I started the game. I get two steps into my tirade walk before Cameron body hugs me and literally pushes my ass back to the sidelines.

"Cool off! You need this, and you're gonna fuck it up. Be pissed. Just be pissed on your own time, yeah?" He levels my shoulders with his heavy palms and pushes my ass down on the bench, my knees buckling because it's so unexpected. Also, I'm not used to Cameron being the grown-up in our friendship.

I take in a deep breath and rip my helmet strap off and spit out my mouth guard.

"Yeah, all right." I shove my helmet up on my forehead so I can get some air and catch the glare from Coach. He's pissed.

I pull my helmet off completely and set it on the bench next to me, then lean forward and rub my forehead. I stare into the dying grass at my feet, letting my focus drill down to the ants making their way toward the Gatorade table. I roll my head to the side and see my mom sitting on the edge of the first bleacher, Neil's fucking arm slung over her to show she's his property, and my stomach boils when he leans into her and talks in her ear—about me, no doubt.

Stretching to the side, I hold the back of the bench and scan the rest of the bleachers in search of Lily. Shame clings to my chest a bit. I didn't want her to see me like this. Even so, when I finally pick her out from the crowd, all it takes is her holding up a palm to calm my rage. I hold my hand up in return and indulge in staring at her for a few seconds.

"That's pretty wild, bro." Serenity is abruptly cut short by Raskin's voice, followed by the weight of his body flopping down on the bench next to me.

Don't start shit with him too, Theo. Not here. Not now.

Instead of responding, I simply grunt and pull my helmet into my hands. If he keeps talking, I'll put it on and muffle his damn voice. It takes him about a second to elbow me. He wants a response. *He wants attention.*

I swivel my head to look at him, but I can tell by the tightness in my jaw that I'm doing a shit job of feigning interest in anything he could possibly say.

"I mean Lily . . . and you. That's wild. Your sister be okay with you hooking up, you think? I mean . . . yeahhhh, probably. They were friends, right?" He leans back and stretches out his legs, letting his gaze drift out to the field. He's barely on the defensive squad. He'll be lucky to see minutes at all this season. *Asshole.*

My teeth grind and the noise fills my ears. Raskin has an enormous zit on the side of his left cheek. It's disgusting, and it's all I see.

"You ever find out why Anika picked my car? I mean, she could have grabbed anyone's keys. She could have taken your car. I mean, she tried to hook up with me a few times, but we never really—"

And that's enough. Before another word leaves his mouth and enters my ear, I swing my arms to the side and bash Raskin's face with my helmet. The bridge of his nose splits, and I might have knocked out a tooth.

"What the fu—" He stands, but I match his speed and my hands clutch his pads as I charge into him, knocking him off balance and into the Gatorade table.

The crowd's reaction is white noise in my ears while I work to stay on top of his big, clumsy body, straddling his hips while my arms fly at him, punching wherever I can. I land a few shots to his chin before he shoves me from him, and we both roll through the pile of orange ice quickly dissolving into the grass.

"Boys! Knock it off!" Coach's voice cuts through the chaos as he wraps an arm around my midsection and pulls me back. James and Cameron take Raskin by the arms and pull him back several steps. He spits blood on the ground and rolls his shoulders as he backs off even more. His pads are sticking out, and his jersey is torn. I wish I'd done more damage.

I'm seething, and spit and hot air flies from my mouth as I huff through gritted teeth. The refs must have called time on the game because a quick glance to my left reveals the entire Augustine team on their sideline while most of our guys are huddled several feet away from me. Only Coach, Cameron and James are near me now.

"You need to cool your head and get your ass in the locker room," Coach says, jerking me around to face him by the collar of my jersey. I feel his knuckles against my throat as I swallow hard, and he loosens his grip on my jersey but doesn't let go completely. Sweat drips into my right eye and I blink it away. Everything around me feels both bright and blurry.

I snapped.

"He was talking shit about my sister," I growl. My breath is still ragged, my lungs pumping with fuel.

"I understand, Theo. And I'll deal with him. But this is not acceptable. This can't happen on my field, you hear me?" He steps in close to force my eyes on him. He's literally all I can see.

I nod.

Coach unfurls his fist, letting go of my jersey, and James swings an arm around me, quickly leading me off the field.

"He was talking shit about Anika . . . and Lily," I explain.

"I know," James grunts as he keeps urging me forward.

"I fucking lost it," I say.

"You did," he agrees.

We get to the hill path and I stop, turning to scan for my mom and that asshole. They've started walking to the parking lot, away from me, and I don't know whether I'm glad my mom's leaving or hurt that she doesn't want to check on her son.

I shift my focus back to James, my bloody helmet dangling at my side in one hand while I grab a fistful of my own hair with the other.

"Fuck!" I rock from side to side. I'm so mad at myself, but also, I'm mad I didn't hurt Raskin more.

James steps in close and places his hand on my shoulder to steady me—to ground me.

"Hey, it's going to be okay. Everybody knows he had it comin'. It's going to be all right, dude. Just breathe."

I try to follow his advice, and tears prick the corners of my eyes. I'm still livid, but now that helpless sense is taking over space in my chest.

"Go dress out. Shower, or maybe go for a walk. Put some distance between this and you, for now. I promise, I've got your back." He moves his hand to the back of my head, and I meet his stare head on, nodding okay.

After two pats on my shoulder, James takes off back down the hill toward the team. I head straight to the locker room and strip out of my uniform and pads, stuffing everything into my locker after grabbing my phone and my T-shirt and sweats. I don't bother showering because the only sweat I earned was from knocking the shit out of my own teammate. I still firmly believe he deserved it, though. I'd do it again. I'm pretty sure I will always choose to do it again, no matter how much time passes.

I kick open the back locker-room door and head to the only place that feels safe—the archives. The door is cracked open by the time I get there, and when I step inside, I'm relieved to see Lily waiting for me. I tug it closed and slip the lock in place, then let her wrap me in her arms as we both crumple to the ground. I cry in her embrace in the dark until my head hurts and my skin feels raw from hot, salty tears. Lily never lets go. In fact, she never speaks. She simply stays with me and lets me feel it all.

I haven't told her this, but I hadn't cried for Anika yet. Not until right now. I don't think I knew how. But something about Lily makes it seem natural to be vulnerable. Being with her makes it all right to not be all right.

Chapter 23

Lily

Theo cried into my chest for ten straight minutes. I don't think he's ever let his emotions out like this. I had a sense he was more of the bottling-things-up type. His sister was like that, too. A lot of people who self-harm have that trait. It seems easier to physically hurt yourself than open up to others.

The game is probably over by now. I'm sure we won. The other team didn't look very good. None of that really matters to Theo right now, though. It's been several minutes since he spoke. I'm not sure whether his mind is on missing his sister, hating his stepdad, or the consequences he's likely going to face.

Threading my hand through his hair, I notice a small scar that runs from just behind his ear to the center of his head. I let my finger follow the line a few times, and before I find the courage to ask, Theo speaks.

"Neil caught me behind the wheel of his car about six months after he moved in with us," he begins, moving his hand up to touch the scar, as if he's reading its story. "I was just playing around like I was driving. I didn't have keys or anything like that, so it's not like I was really going somewhere. Our dad used to let Anika and me pretend to drive all the time. And, I don't know, maybe I was missing him or something."

"Neil loves that car. It's a classic. Sixty-five Plymouth Belvedere, candy-apple red." He looks up at me from my lap with a kid-like grin as he describes it. "Anika was with our mom getting her hair done for some party. I was supposed to be putting my suit on, but something about that car—it called to me."

"You were a little boy. Cars will do that," I justify.

He shoots me a crooked smile that fades fast as his gaze falls away.

"Neil grabbed the back of my zipper hoodie I was wearing and pulled me out of the car by it, lifting my feet up off the ground and shit. He held me like I was a cat he fished out of the pool, and my zipper caught the back of my ear and sliced a line across my head as I fell out of the hoodie. Turns out I was kinda heavy."

I can feel the dent in my forehead, and I try to erase it before Theo looks up at me, but he catches it and presses his finger into it, rubbing small circles.

"Nah, I was fine. Don't fret." He shifts to sit up and pulls my head toward him, kissing my worry line.

"He hit you a lot?" I ask.

He nods then shakes his head, sort of giving a double answer.

"I don't remember them all. Like, most of the time it was a smack to the back of the head. He was pretty strict and, well . . . you've met me."

I let out a sad, airy laugh.

"Imagine if you were Cameron," I respond.

We both chuckle quietly. Theo swivels around to sit next to me, pulling his knees up to hug them. I do the same. We're wearing near-matching outfits of Welles sweatshirts and gray sweatpants. Mine is covered in the glitter I've shed from my face, though. I pick a few of the sparkly pieces from my pants and Theo joins me.

It's such a sweet, simple act, and I'm not sure whether that's what cracks open the guard I've carefully put around my old wounds, or maybe it's this need for him to understand how deeply I understand. But I want him to know me—demons and all.

"So, those scars you probably saw on me—the ones right here." I open my knees and trace along my inner thigh. Theo continues to pick glitter from my sweatpants but shifts his gaze to my hand and nods.

"When my dad asked my mom for a divorce, he offered to take me with him. He wasn't being noble or anything. He wasn't even really being an invested dad. He liked the tax write-off, and maybe he felt a little guilty leaving me behind. My mom is rather high-strung. I've learned, through *a lot* of therapy, that she's probably the way she is because my grandmother was a cold and abusive woman. And I'm sure if I dug deeper in our family history, there would be a long line of psychopathic types who lack empathy and see children as a check box and status symbol as well as a nuisance and an albatross."

"Big words," he whispers, quickly adding, "Sorry."

I laugh softly.

"Don't be. A little humor is good when you're talking about dark shit."

He nods and glances up at me, our eyes meeting for a brief second. I see myself in him. I see Anika too, and all the ways we're the same. I swallow down my nerves and blink my gaze back to my hands, that are now picking at my cuticles and the skin along my fingernails. The compulsion is always there. Stress draws it out.

"My mom slapped me across the face for the first time in the checkout line at our neighborhood grocery store. I asked to get a pack of cookies, the kind my dad always got for me when we went to the store. She smacked me and told me she knew he always liked me better."

I give him a sideways glance to assess his reaction. His smile is soft, gentle, and understanding. *Neil* is a lot like my mom, I'm guessing.

"It was usually verbal, the abuse. Almost always in public or in front of Drew, my stepdad, and his son, Levi. I would instantly feel small, and even though Drew tried to make it better, it only ended up making things worse. She'd come right back at me with accusations for trying to steal her new husband. Not in *that* way, but she has this sick jealousy of people liking me better. And my stepbrother . . . wow!"

"Does he hurt you?" Theo's concern comes out fast as he turns into me and touches my chin. I shake my head to quickly dismiss that idea. Levi is harmless, if not arrogant.

"No, nothing like that. He simply revels in my demise. My mom puts him on a pedestal, which I've learned is her passive aggressive way of punishing me without doing it physically or directing her words *at* me. Levi gets whatever he wants. His car is brand new, and mine barely passed emissions this summer."

I return my attention to the inside of my leg, placing my palm over the skin that years later still feels freshly wounded in my mind.

Deep breath.

"I was eleven the first time I cut myself." I swallow hard and my eyes close automatically. It's easier if I'm not tempted to look Theo in the eyes. "I was ashamed the second I did it. It's messed up, but that shame was better than the way I felt when my mom humiliated me. When the first wound healed, I did it again."

"Anika had scars like that," Theo hums.

I cry a little, tears pushing through my eyelids. I blink them away and curl my mouth into a painful, familiar smile steeped in heartbreak. I nod.

"That's how we met. I . . . got her pain. But having your sister in my life, and I think maybe with her having me in hers, that darkness faded. The urge—*compulsion*—it wasn't as strong. I leaned on her. And in her own, crazy way, she leaned on me."

"My sister really loved you," he says through broken laughter. I chance a look his way and our eyes meet, both glossy, and I'm sure mine are just as red.

"It's going to be okay, what happened today." I shrug and shake my head. Theo levels me with a doubtful look.

"Don't ask me how I know. Call it my gut, or whatever. But it's going to be okay. Sometimes, the good guys get to win." I inhale a hard, cleansing breath and plaster the most convincing smile I can muster on my face. I almost believe the words I'm saying. The worry lingering in the back of my head is loud, but I refuse to give it voice. I can't lose Theo. Not now that I've only just got him.

He reaches forward and places a palm on my cheek, running his thumb along the raw, hot skin under my eye.

"You are . . . exceptional."

I cry out a soft laugh, the kind that blubbers on my lips. It's hard to take compliments sometimes, but this one—it hits me in the center of the chest with the weight of a bowling ball.

I lean forward and take his face in my hands, staring into his crystal blue eyes. I think I love this stupid boy.

Pressing my lips to his, I move forward until I'm curled up in his lap with his arms wrapped around me. I hold him tight, even after our kiss breaks, and I stay tucked in the safe space under his chin and between his arms for the rest of the afternoon.

Chapter 24

Theo

A two-game suspension seems fair. I was expecting expulsion.

Mediation, however? I'm not vibing with this. I received a text early this morning to report to the headmaster's office. I figured they'd let it go on a Sunday, but this isn't the Jesuit Welles it once was. There are no days of rest when there's a possible stain on the school's reputation. Right now, I'm that stain.

They put me in a room with Raskin about ten minutes ago. Some counsellor or mediator or whatever is running late. They called a guy in from Harvard. Probably a former Welles student getting his PhD and needing hours. Our headmaster probably should have kept me and asshat separated until that someone was here in the ring with us—I mean conference room.

I will admit I'm getting a rise out of staring at him. We're separated by a polished stone table, and we're both leaning back so far in our chairs that our toes are close to touching under the table. Raskin is trying his best to act aloof but swiveling in his seat nervously is giving him away. So is his inability to hold eye contact. I haven't looked away once. I may not have even blinked.

"Gentlemen." As our headmaster walks in, Raskin sits up straight and folds his arms over one another on the table and looks to him. I don't move an inch, and my glare is staying fixed where it is.

"I'd like you to meet Holly Asplund. She's here to help us work through whatever conflict seems to be happening here." Our headmaster sounds like he's reading from a script, check-boxing keywords, like *conflict*.

"The conflict, Ms. Asplund, is that Oliver Raskin thinks it's okay to talk shit about my dead sister." I leave that comment on its own and remain perfectly still, laser eyes on Raskin's increasingly defensive expression. I can almost predict his words. *What? I didn't do anything.*

"Sir, ma'am. He's completely misinterpreting. I didn't say anything." *I was close. I guessed the gist.*

"You want me to repeat your words for you?" I ask.

"Fuck off, Theo. You're talking out of your ass." He winces at his own lack of control, and I let my mouth rest in a smug grin.

"Right, well. It appears we have our work cut out for us." Ms. Asplund drops a set of packets on the table between us, then takes a seat at the head. Her hair is jet black, cropped in a razor-perfect line at her chin. Square, black-rimmed glasses match her angular face perfectly. She glances over her shoulder, motioning for our headmaster to leave the room. He does, though begrudgingly, and when the door is closed, she morphs into perhaps the coolest adult I've ever met.

"Look, guys. You aren't getting out of here until there is some sort of mutual agreement to not make headaches for the administration. We can get there two ways. One, we can go through this packet of ice breakers, most of which will have you rolling your eyes and hating me. Or . . . you can let me level with you, as I see it based on what I know of the situation. We can clear this up in minutes if you two decide to set aside the bullshit that comes with being eighteen-year-old privileged private school boys and hear what I'm about to say and internalize it, honestly. Because we all know I'm going to have this, right? And arguing more is just posturing and puffing up chests to prove your manhood, and I am . . ." She sighs and rolls her eyes. "So over that."

I chew at the inside of my mouth through my lopsided smile and shift my focus from Ms. Asplund to Raskin, who seems to be giving her proposal equal consideration. I nod at him, and he does the same.

"Deal," we both say in unison.

"Excellent," she says, bringing her hands together in a celebratory clap. She drags the packets back toward her and rolls them in her palms, like a visual aid.

"Oliver, you don't know how to behave around Theo. What happened to him, to his family, and to this school, is tragic. Things like this often leave an awkward environment in their wake, and because you all are, well, not adults yet, you have trouble navigating interactions. You may have some leftover hostility over your car. Or, perhaps, you are embarrassed about your history with Theo's sister. Maybe you have regrets of your own, wishing you treated her better."

Ms. Asplund sits back in her chair, crossing her legs and folding her hands in her lap as she studies Raskin. He's red, but not the angry kind. He's embarrassed because she hit some hot spots with her assessment. She's not far from the truth. In fact, as she was talking to him, I realized her explanations applied to a lot of people on this campus since I've come back. And maybe a little to me and how I interact with my mom. I don't know how anymore. I kind of think I haven't had a good handle on it since our dad died.

"What do I do with that? Am I supposed to apologize when he's the one who broke my nose?" His voice is stuffy, and the bruising on his face is nasty. I don't think I actually broke his nose, though. I've broken one of those before, and it makes a certain sound.

"You take it in, and you think about it—honestly," she responds. "And yeah, you probably have some things to apologize for. Doesn't mean Theo is off the hook."

I shift in my seat and tighten my mouth into a hard line. I liked it better when she was talking about Raskin.

"All right," he says, hesitantly. I flit my gaze to his and he reciprocates, our eyes briefly meeting a few times while we navigate this weird space.

"Theo." She calls me to attention. Unlike Raskin, I'm not willing to sit up tall. I'm still a little pissed off, and I think it's better if I simmer and slouch. I'm probably a better listener by not faking it. I do turn to meet her stare, though. She offers me a sympathetic smile, her maroon-tinted lips ticking up on one side.

"You're grieving. And yes, a lot of your behavior can be forgiven because of your circumstances. You are under an extraordinary mental weight. Your emotions are likely on a pendulum, as is your ability to trust. When we lose people who are close to us, it brings our own mortality, and that of everyone we care about, to the forefront. You don't know who you may lose next. And you realize, even if below the surface, that you have zero control over any of it. Because of that, you try to control what you can. What people say about your sister is an obvious start. But you need to get a handle on what your emotions do to trigger your physical reactions. You can't go through life punching people."

Pity. But she's right.

I nod and tuck my chin, looking down at my outstretched legs. I hit Raskin hard. And if I'm being honest with myself, in my mind, I wasn't hitting him. I was hitting Neil.

"I was out of line," I admit.

I glance up and catch her gentle smile, her eyes crinkling on the edges behind her glasses. She leans her head to her right, and I follow her lead, meeting Raskin's gaze with a tad less antagonism. I repeat my words to him, stopping short of an actual apology. Baby steps and all. His tongue pushed into his cheek, he nods in acceptance.

Eventually, Ms. Asplund invites our headmaster back into the room, and after signing a series of documents that basically let Welles off the legal hook and promise we will not cause further violent disturbances or break the bullying policy on campus, we're dismissed. We never shake hands but the ice in the glares we shoot each other melts, at least for me. I vow to be indifferent to Oliver Raskin until I graduate. If I see him on the street any time after, however, he's fair game. And I'll probably punch him in the face.

* * *

By the time I make it to the fieldhouse, Lily is just finishing up for the morning. She had planned on swimming early, and I was going to go with her. That's the rule—she swims, I watch. Nobody drowns.

The headmaster's call put a snag in our plan, so I called James. I don't want my issues to derail her from overcoming hers. And maybe I also wanted to show some personal growth by insisting James be her guardian.

He's sitting on the small set of bleachers at the opposite end of the pool when I walk in. I saunter over, watching

Lily's arms make perfect strokes along the top of the water in my periphery.

"I swear I was standing closer at first, but she told me I was a distraction, and the girl is intense when she's in swim mode." His eyes widen with his words.

"By intense, you mean scary," I say.

"Yeah. She's scary," he deadpans.

I chuckle and return my gaze to the pool. Lily's locked in today. I don't even think she's noticed I'm here. That's for the best because I have some amends to make with James right now.

"Thanks. For . . ." I stop, not knowing quite how to put into words everything James has done for me. I shrug and lean forward, arms on knees, and look at him sideways.

"For dragging your ass off the field? No problem." He snaps the gum in his mouth and winks at me, which eases the tension some.

Cocky fucking quarterback. Damn him, he is a good guy.

"Raskin's got some hits coming his way, just so you know. Practice isn't going to be easy for him next week."

I nod, a little ticked that Raskin still gets to practice. He got suspended for the next game, while I got two games out and no practice for a week. Feels cruel given that being on that field is the one thing holding me together. Well, maybe not the *only* thing.

Lily slaps the edge of the pool and howls as her head comes out of the water. James and I both stand and start clapping.

"You see that? I wasn't slow!" She pulls the cap from her head and tosses it up on the deck before climbing out of the pool.

Funny, when I was thirteen and fourteen, I thought the bikini was the sexiest swimsuit alive. The way the black racing suit hugs every curve and shows off Lily's toned shoulders, though, has taught me otherwise.

"Damn, girl. You weren't just not slow. You'd kick my ass," James says.

"That's not saying much," I add as he walks backward to Lily. He turns around and scowls at me before laughing.

I follow behind him, my lungs full and chest a little lighter. It feels good to be able to joke with him, to be able to let go of the jealousy. And it feels good to walk right past him and pull my soaking wet girl into my arms and kiss her smiling face.

She pulls back briefly but lets me keep my arms around her. Her arms are beading up with chills from being out of the water, so I rub them with my palms.

"How was your meeting?" Her brow is pinched, and I can tell she's a little worried.

"I may want to change my college major from business to psychology," I answer.

She steps back and screws up her mouth, confused. I wait while she picks up her towel to dry off her hair and wrap her body.

"Typical Welles intervention. Brought in some alumni from Harvard. She knew her shit, though. Pretty much nailed my psychological profile in two minutes, after reading my file." I stop short of telling Lily everything Ms. Asplund said. I'm not up to sharing my issues with James yet. He's had enough of me for one weekend. Maybe for a month.

"But you aren't facing anything . . . bigger?"

She means expelled.

"Nah." I take her towel so her hands are free to slip into her sweatpants and gather her things. "My mom might have a lot of flaws, but nobody's kicking her baby out of school. She'd bring down holy terror on them, and they don't want that. It would be a bad look on top of everything else my family's been through."

Lily pulls her mouth in for a tight smile and James paces away a few steps. I can't help but consider what the mediator said this morning—*people don't know how to interact with me since Anika's death.*

"Speaking of my mom, I think I have some unfinished business there too. I don't suppose you would be up for a trip to Charlestown?" I can tell by Lily's instantly frozen features that the thought of meeting my mom today terrifies her.

"Even if it's just for the ride in. I could use the company, maybe practice my speech before I confront her and my stepfather." *And maybe have a getaway driver on hand if I decide to toss Neil from the balcony.*

"I'll go with you. And if you want me to wait in the car, I will. But if you want me to go in with you, I'll do that too." She tugs her bag up on her shoulder and slips her feet into her slides before reaching a hand to me. I squeeze it tight before loosening my grip, a silent thanks for her willingness.

We leave the fieldhouse with James, and he ditches us when we get to Hayden Hall. I follow Lily inside and sit on her bed while she searches through her basket of laundry for a pair of jeans. Morgan and Brooklyn are each sitting on their beds with headphones on, but it's rather obvious by the way they alternately pick up and put down their phones that they're texting about me. I pull my phone out and send a message to them.

ME: *I'm in the room if you want to ask me anything.*

I rest my phone on my leg and scoot back on Lily's bed while they both pick up their phones at the same time then flip their heads up to look at me. I smirk and wave.

"We didn't want to be nosy," Morgan says, slipping her headphones down to her neck.

I laugh so loud it pulls Lily out from the closet to see what's going on. I point to Morgan, still laughing.

"She didn't want to be nosy," I say.

Lily smiles and laughs.

"You guys! Stop, that's not nice. It's not like I'm in everybody's business," Morgan protests.

Brooklyn's headphones are off now too, and the three of us exchange glances before finally breaking into hard laughter.

"Ugh! Fine, I don't care what happened to you today. I hope you got kicked out and then shipped overseas to some zoo." She finishes her tantrum off by sticking out her tongue and pulling her headphones back on.

I glance to Brooklyn.

"I'm not in any big trouble. I have this get out of jail free card," I say, forcing a crooked, sad smile on my face.

"For what it's worth, it was nice to see Oliver Raskin get his ass kicked," Brooklyn says.

"What do you think? Am I *meet-the-mom* appropriate?" Lily steps out in her Welles sweatshirt and a loose pair of jeans. My mom will probably like the lack of holes in them.

"You look gorgeous," I say, pushing up from her bed and crossing the room to pull her in front of me and take a selfie of us in the girls' full-length mirror.

"*And* . . . time for my headphones to go back on," Brooklyn says, making a fake gagging sound. Lily pushes her friend's knee, and they share a short laugh.

I hold on to Lily's hand as she grabs her wallet, phone, and keys and leads me out the door. I pull her close to my side as we walk down the hallway to the stairwell, and I kiss the top of her head before we open the door.

"I like seeing you that way with your friends," I say.

She sucks in her bottom lip and smiles up at me.

"Me, too."

* * *

It's an hour drive to my mom's house. Sunday traffic is light. I run through a few talking points with Lily during our trip, but I'm still not fully prepared for confrontation when we pull up outside my mom's house.

"Is that the car?" Lily asks, gesturing to the bright red classic sitting near the house. It's been covered for months. Neil left it here that way. The fact it's not now means he's been driving it, which means he's here a lot. Probably *more* than a lot.

"That's the one." I kill the engine and lean back in my seat, giving the car a long, hard stare.

"We don't have to do this. Not if you changed your mind." She's reassuring me and it's sweet, but I think we both know I'm not going to be able to focus much this semester if I don't take care of this thing with my mom and Neil.

"Ready?" I shift my gaze to her, and she reaches across the console, placing her hand on my mine and squeezing.

I lead Lily around the side of the house to the garage, where I punch in the code to open the door. As it starts to rise, Neil's voice calls out from inside.

"Can I help you?" His tone is loud and full of authority, and I instantly tighten everywhere, ready to fight. This isn't his fucking house. It never was.

"It's me," I grit out. Lily squeezes my hand again, reminding me to keep a level head. *I'll do my best, Lil. I'll do my best.*

"Oh. You know you can come through the front door like a normal person," Neil grunts. By the time the garage door is raised enough, we get the view of him turning around and pulling his pants up over his belly as he hobbles back toward the door.

"I could, but not really into ringing my own doorbell. Call me weird."

Neil shoots me a glare over his shoulder, pulling his glasses down on his nose to look over them. That move used to scare the shit out of me when I was young. Now, it's an achievement to make him do it.

He shuffles his way forward eventually, giving up on picking a fight here in the garage, and Lily and I follow him inside.

"Your mother is in the kitchen making tea. You know you made her feel like shit yesterday." Every word that leaves his mouth sounds like a grunt.

"That's why I'm here." I sigh.

"Good. That woman deserves a real apology." He gestures toward the kitchen, as if I don't know where it is, then continues down the hallway to the sound of his TV. He's watching football, which means maybe I'll get some time alone with Mom.

"You weren't exaggerating," Lily says in a hushed voice. I pull my mouth into a tight line and shake my head. If anything, I probably went light on the Neil details. The man is the actual devil.

"I was thinking of heating up that leftover stew for lunch. What—" She was expecting me to be Neil. My mom stops stirring her tea when her eyes spot me instead. "Oh."

"Oh," I repeat, shrugging with a lopsided smile.

Lily clears her throat at my side.

"Right, uhm . . . Mom, this is Lily," I say, holding a hand out as if I'm presenting her like some prize on the *Price Is Right*.

"Yes, Lily. I . . . well, we haven't met, but I do know you.

You knew Annie. And I know you were with her—" Mom's words trail off and she glances down at her tea and begins to stir. She called my sister Annie most of her life. She's the only one who could. Anika loved it. It reminded her that our mom was ours before she was with Neil.

"Nice to formally meet you," Lily says, stepping forward and reaching out her hand. My mom puts her spoon down on the counter and leaves her cup to shake Lily's hand.

Neither of them tries to fill in the blanks where my mom left off. It's a learned behavior in our house, not speaking about what happened in full sentences. Lily's one of the few who understands how those strange rules work.

"What brings you both here? I'm sorry; how rude. Would you like some tea?" My mom's hand is trembling as she picks up her cup, so I take it from her and move toward the table.

"I'm fine. Lily, you want any?" I know she doesn't, but it's polite to ask.

She shakes her head and moves to take the chair on the other side of me.

My mom sits down and brings her cup to her lips with both hands, blowing on the steaming surface. She's notorious for burning her tongue, unable to stop herself from sipping too early.

"Looks hot," I warn as she proceeds to test it despite me. Her lips barely meet the liquid before she pulls the cup away and continues to blow.

"You're right. It is."

I chuckle lightly.

"You hush," she whispers.

I twist in my chair to bring my feet under me and fold my hands together to rest them on the table as my mom continues to cool her tea, eventually taking a sip for real. It's still too hot, but she will never admit that.

"I want to talk about Neil," I begin.

Her brow furrows.

"Oh? And not about that embarrassing display you made of yourself at the game yesterday?" Those aren't her words; they're his. I recognize some of his favorite things to say —*embarrassing display*.

"Sure, we can talk about that too. It's all wrapped up in the same shit tortilla, Mom."

"Your language," she chides.

Lily's leg nudges mine under the table, so I sit back and take in a deep breath. I must pace myself.

"Okay, yes. I would like to apologize to you for my behavior. I never meant to embarrass you or our family," I say.

"It's your father's name, Theo. Shameful." She takes another sip of her tea, settling in now. My mom is good at conflict. I've often thought she needs it to survive, as though it somehow replaced all the joy she had when dad was alive.

My eyes flutter closed, and I fight to stay focused and not go off the rails with her.

"Like I said. I apologize. I'm sorry you had to see that."

She slides her hand across the table toward me and I sit forward to meet her halfway. Her warm palm slides over my knuckles and she pats the top of my hand twice.

"Thank you, Theo. That means a lot. You should probably apologize to Neil too."

I can feel her eyes on me, but I keep mine firmly planted on the top of her hand. This is going to get ugly.

Lily's foot slides next to mine and she leaves it there. I let my shoulders relax with her show of strength.

"That's what I want to talk to you about, Mom. Neil. Why is he here?"

Her hand slides away from mine, back to the comfort of her warm teacup. She cradles it where it sits on the table and levels me with her well-practiced indignation. Pursed lips, narrowed eyes, elbows in close—this is her defensive stance.

"Because he's my husband, Theo. And we've decided to work through things and be here for one another." She doesn't even blink as she says those words.

I suck in my lips, then let them go with a pop and a sigh.

"Ohhhh-kayyy. Mom, I can't do this." I get up from my chair and pace halfway around the table, ignoring Lily's warning stare. I need to move. Moving is the only thing keeping me from saying hurtful things.

"You threw Neil out, Mom. Less than a year ago. You threw him out. Do you remember?" My voice is raised, but I can't help it.

"Couples fight, Theo," she defends.

"No, Mom." I shake my head and grab the back of the chair across the table from her. I hold the carved knobs in my palms and squeeze so hard I could snap them off. I stop short of picking the chair up and slamming it back down in frustration. "This wasn't a fight. You kicked Neil out because of something he did to Anika."

My mom starts shaking her head, so I start rubbing mine.

"You're mistaken, Theo. Honey, you don't know everything that goes on in my life."

"Maybe not, Mom. But I know a lot about my sister's. And I know she was the reason you sent Neil away." I glance to Lily, and she nods once to give me courage.

"Do you mean that journal she had?" My mom's response rips me right back down to earth, and I drop my gaze to her.

"What journal?" I seethe.

"Ha, you don't even know about the journal. Theo, you're tired. And I got the call from the headmaster this morning so I know you've gone through the disciplinary meeting. That's where this is coming from. You're stressed."

I shake my head through her entire speech.

"No, Mom. That's not what this is. What journal?" My pulse is rattling my ribcage, my heart an angry beast trying to break out.

"Annie had an active imagination, and she wrote these stories. I found the book a day or two before the accident, and I warned her about having stuff like that written down. It seemed she was blaming Neil for a lot of her issues in school, the drinking and the wild behavior."

"Mom," I utter. I rush to the chair on her other side and slide it close to her, sitting down and forcing her hands into mine. "What did you do with that journal?"

My body is buzzing with adrenaline, and my knee is bobbing at my mom's side.

"I tossed it. The things she said in there, if someone saw them—I was afraid what they would think of her. I didn't want her to look like—"

"A victim," Lily mutters.

We both flash our focus to her. She coughs a little and looks up from the table.

"I'm . . . I'm sorry. I shouldn't have—"

"No, it's okay," I encourage.

My mom's hands have grown stiff in mine. She doesn't like that word, and that's what this is about. My mom refusing to accept that bad things happen, that some men aren't good, and that she was right to kick Neil out of the house.

"It's not my place," Lily says.

"You're right. It's not," my mom fires back.

"No, Mom. It is. Lily and Anika were close. And she confided in her." All of this feels like a betrayal to my sister. She isn't here to tell her own story, but it doesn't make her story any less valid.

"She was dealing with a lot of, uhm . . . emotional scars." Lily struggles to pick out the right words. Her love for my sister is genuine, and she doesn't want to say anything that makes Anika seem less than the amazing woman Lily found her to be—*than she was.*

"When did you throw her journal away, Mom?" I'm hopeful that maybe it was recent. Maybe, I could go out to the back of the house right now and retrieve it. Maybe I could read Anika's words and be her voice, saving my mom from the monster she's married to.

"That night. I . . ." My mom's eyes fill with instant tears, and she pulls her hands away from me as she looks down at them. "I sent her a text letting her know I threw it away. I told her I did it to save her, to keep her business private. It's the last thing—"

That's what Anika left the party for. She was rushing home to save her truth. She was coming here to save Mom.

"You told her Neil was coming back, didn't you?" My voice is soft, almost a whisper.

My mom doesn't respond. Through her sniffles and lack of words, I glean everything I need to know. My stomach aches and bile crawls up my esophagus. I look over my shoulder to the dark hallway where whistles and commentary blare from the TV.

"You can't let him stay here, Mom. You deserve better."

She remains silent.

I look across the table to Lily, and all she can manage is the same sad eyes I'm sure I'm wearing. I chew at my lip and look over my shoulder again, my inner debate a pendulum between rushing the monster and tossing him out myself or giving my mom time to do it herself. If I throw him out, she'll likely open the door to let him back in.

"Anika's accident . . ." I swallow down my emotions.

Right now, I'm the adult. Right now, I am the glue. "It wasn't anyone's fault, Mom. She had a seizure."

I stop before tumbling down the road of choices and consequences because I know I won't be able to help myself from pointing out my mom's bad decisions, and blame is not my intent. Blame will not erase the past. But truth can fix the future.

"Lily and I need to get back to school. I wanted to make sure you were okay, and like I said . . . I wanted to apologize." I stand and my mom turns in her seat, standing and reaching only three quarters of my height. When did I get so much taller than her? She used to seem like this invincible giant.

I wrap my arms around her small frame and inhale the lavender scent of her perfume. I'm sure she went to church this morning. I'm sure she went alone.

"I'll come visit more. And we can talk about things whenever you want."

She nods against my chest, and I let her go. She turns to her side, hiding her face from me, but I know it's damp with tears. My mom is lonely. She's been lonely since dad died, and it's worse now. One day, though, she won't be so lonely anymore. And she'll find strength, and I'll be here to support her. Neil isn't permanent. I won't let him be. My mom deserves better.

Chapter 25

Lily

Anika had her secrets. She and I shared plenty of unspoken ones. I recognized her abuse. It came out in little ways, not just the self-harm. We both flinched at loud noises, and we spent one Friday night comparing bruises we've had. Neither of us said where those bruises came from; we both knew.

I sensed more darkness for Anika too. She had a line she wouldn't cross when we talked about our family lives. She referred to her stepfather as lots of things, none of them nice. Only once did she say he made her feel uncomfortable, and she seemed to want to erase it the minute the word slipped out. I didn't draw attention to it, and I never asked questions. If she wanted to share, I would listen. If she wanted to ignore that corner of her mind, I'd distract her.

I can tell Theo wants to ask me what I know about his sister's experiences, but so far on our drive home, he hasn't. I don't know that I'd have much to tell. And I'm not sure I would if I did.

We pull over at a major truck stop and jog inside to

escape the sprinkles starting to fall. It's gray today, the cloud cover like a heavy blanket dripping on the people below. The humidity has made my hair wavy, and I thread my fingers through it in an attempt to tame what I refer to as *floof*.

"You're beautiful. Stop," Theo says, pulling my hair into his hands and parting it over either shoulder.

"My hair looks like an airplane pillow," I joke. It's not a big exaggeration.

Theo pulls at the sides, making it bigger, and I force my eyes far to the right to watch it grow.

"It's a little big, yeah. But still . . ." He moves his hands to cup my face, then leans forward to kiss me. "Beautiful."

What is this life? Part of me knows Theo is forcing himself to exude happiness. What we just went through was heavy, and even through his smiles and sweet gestures, the lines on his forehead show how worried he is for his mom.

"Hold my things while I run to the restroom?" I hand over my pile and he takes it, exaggerating how heavy my keys, phone, and wallet truly are. I probably should get one of those cross-body bags or something, but it feels as if that's just adding one more thing to my body, and I carry enough.

I wait through two people in line to get my turn in the restroom, so I skip the plan of braiding my hair while I'm in there. If Theo thinks it's beautiful, so be it. When I leave the restroom, he's hovering just outside the door, under an over-hang, talking on his phone. The rain has picked up, so I run out and grab my wallet from him so I can get a coffee.

I decide to get two, figuring if Theo doesn't drink his, I always can. Maybe I'll make two trips to the pool today and work off the caffeine buzz.

When I exit, Theo is waiting in the car, the door propped open despite the rain probably pelting his side. That mask he was working so hard to cultivate has morphed from a peaceful expression to one weighted with concern. His eyes droop, and the corners of his mouth are arrows pointing at the ground.

"What's wrong?" I ask, quickly slipping into the passenger side. I don't bother fishing for an answer. We're past that point. Theo . . . he's my person.

His phone is still in his palm, the screen on an ended phone call. I lean toward him, placing the coffees in the cup holders while I read the number. It isn't anything familiar.

"I just got fired from *The Affiliate*." He blinks a few times then shifts his gaze to me. My mouth is hanging open. That's not the news I was expecting.

"Why?"

I brace myself for him to tell me it's because they found out about his fight on the field or his slip-up in sales last week.

"The CEO wants a story about you and Anika, and they said you didn't seem interested in writing it. He called me personally and asked if I was ready to have the 'byline of my life.'" He breathes out a short laugh through his nose.

My stomach sinks. I hoped the conversation I had with Abby would simply vanish; that she'd forget about the idea completely. I had no intention of ever bringing it up again, but maybe that was a bad idea. I never thought she'd try to get Theo to do it. Unless she doesn't realize who he is?

"What did you say?"

The fact they fired him tells me it was probably a hard no. I'm just not sure *how* hard.

"Something to the effect of fuck you, you fucking fuck." He scrunches his nose as if he swallowed something bitter, and I smile with clenched teeth.

"Do you think maybe they don't know she's your sister?"

My question draws a bigger laugh from him.

"You see, now, that's what I was hoping. Turns out,

though, that's exactly why they asked me. In fact . . ." He claps his hands together for emphasis and forces his mouth into a tight-lipped grin. "That's exactly why they hired me in the first place."

That's why they hired both of us.

He doesn't have to say that part. He might not even know it or be thinking it, but it's clear to me. It worried me when Abby proposed the idea, but I dismissed it. I earned this internship. I interviewed and fought for her attention.

Or did I?

Theo elbowed me. I tripped out of my borrowed shoes, and before that I tried to get them to hire him instead of me, out of guilt. What do I really bring to the table—besides my story?

"I should have told you Abby approached me with the idea. I wanted it to go away, and I was hoping it had." I sink back in the passenger side and Theo pulls his door shut. He turns sideways, resting an arm on the steering wheel and studies me. His expression is hard to read—I can't tell whether he's upset about being fired or mad that I didn't stop this from happening.

"You should write it," he says. My stomach drops as though I've just gone over the edge of a rollercoaster.

"No," I respond immediately.

He nods, though, to combat my refusal.

"You should, and I know this seems spur of the moment, but Abby approached me about this last week, too. Like you, I figured maybe it would never result in anything."

I feel sick. I'm not ready to put what happened to me— what happened to Anika—on paper.

"Theo, I don't want to. They can fire me, too. I'll get my work hours done in the mail room at campus. I don't care."

He shakes his head.

"Can't. I've got that job now," he jokes.

My head falls to the side, and I stare at him, willing him to be serious.

"Lil, they're going to write this story one way or another. I'd rather it be you driving the narrative."

"How can they? I'll refuse to talk." It would be easy for me. I haven't been quoted once, anywhere, about what happened. When reporters called, I let them go to voicemail. And when my mom and Drew had people show up at our home in Ohio, they took their cards, sent them away, and promptly tossed them in the trash. That's one silver lining to my mom's cold shoulder toward me: she hates the idea of me getting any attention.

"I thought you've read *The Affiliate* for years," he says. "You know they don't need the subject to talk to tell their story. They'll find others to quote. Welles will put pressure on your coach, wanting the positive spin. Good press means donations and new students."

"I won't swim, then. I'll quit." I fold my arms over my chest and literally dig my heel into the floor of his car.

Theo leans forward and unravels my hold on myself, taking my hands in his and working his fingers through mine one at a time. He looks at them like they're special. He looks at me like I'm special.

Shaking his head, he says, "You have to swim, Lily."

My eyes burn. I shake my head.

"No."

He lets go with one hand and wipes away the tear that escapes down my cheek, leaving his hand there for support. His stare is so potent, so clear and honest. The scowl has disappeared from his forehead, probably because he's resolved to this being the only way. But I'm not. It isn't fair.

"You've worked too hard to break through that cage, Lily.

You're almost free of a huge fear. You can't give up on that because some greedy media mogul wants to capitalize on it. Besides, you know they'd only change the headline."

WILL SHE EVER SWIM AGAIN?

I can visualize the bold letters in my mind, along with the photos taken from that night. They'd use photos from the Welles student paper, and clips from the *Ashwood Courier*, the local paper that covers literally everything that happens in town. Someone would probably give them a yearbook, and I bet my old roommate Angela would beg them to be quoted in the story out of spite.

"I'm going to be fine. I'm not expelled, and I get to play football in two weeks. I said my piece to my mom today, and I'm prepared to play the long game when it comes to Neil. Lily, I've never been surer about the things in my life than I am now. I love you, and you have to do this."

Our eyes flicker at that word, but rather than maintain eye contact, we quickly look away—Theo's gaze darting out the windshield and mine dropping to my lap, to my kneading hands. He doesn't repeat it, and I don't respond. Not to that, at least.

"Okay," I murmur.

I love you, too.

"I'll do it."

Chapter 26

Theo

Is it weird that despite parts of my life unraveling, I'm exceptionally okay right now? I'm even all right with the fact I told Lily I loved her. Not really the way I wanted to say it, all innocuous and buried like that, but it was so easy to say. I don't want to label it an accident, but it wasn't planned or purposeful. I haven't really thought about it in terms of that level of feeling. But even after only weeks, the word is easy and accurate. There isn't a single thing I've come to know about her that I don't love.

Anika was right.

I wonder if I tell Coach I love him if that will fast-forward this uncomfortable meeting we're about to have? Probably not.

Even James was clueless what this meeting is about. I texted him right after his dad called me this morning and told me to meet in the headmaster's conference room before my first hour. I've been in this room more in the past two days than my entire time at Welles. I'm not very fond of it, either. It's overly ornate, which I think is supposed to impress wealthy donors—riches beget more riches, or something like that. But from my perspective, it's tacky. Why so much wood paneling? And why so . . . dark? What's wrong with windows?

"Theo, thanks for starting your day a little early for this," Coach says as he walks in behind me and interrupts my mental spiral down my own HGTV show.

"I mean, we could always write a note to my econ teacher if I have to miss first hour." I flatten my palms on the table and grin at Coach as he sits down.

He laughs dismissively.

"I'm afraid this won't take quite *that* long."

Damn.

"Look, I asked the headmaster if I could handle this, so you can relax a bit. It's just us," he says.

My muscles ease, but my palms are still sweating. I think maybe I've hit my emotional wall for the week.

"I got your punishment reduced to match Oliver Raskin's," he says.

My mouth falls open and I lean forward, a jolt kick-starting my energy. I can practice. That's all I want. I just want to practice and be on that field and forget the rest.

"Coach—"

"Before you thank me," he interrupts. "I think it's impor-tant you know that the reason it got reviewed and rolled back is because Oliver wrote a letter on your behalf. I mentioned offhandedly in my one-on-one with him yesterday that I was going to see what I could do, and then before dinner, he slipped this under our door. The headmaster has a copy, but I thought maybe you'd like to read it."

He slides a folded paper toward me, and I take it hesi-tantly, peeling up the corner to glimpse how long it is.

Damn. He even hand wrote it.

I begin to unfold it but before I can, Coach stops me.

"You can read it when we're done if you want. It's weird to have someone staring at you. Besides, I have this one other thing," he says.

I flatten the letter again as my heartbeat quickens with anticipation. I'm not sure whether to prepare myself for good news or bad. This conference room baffles me.

"I don't share this with a lot of people, but I had a sister." Coach meets my gaze for a beat, a painful memory tweaking the corner of his eye. I squirm a bit in my seat but leave my palms flat on the tabletop. "I was your age, almost exactly, when Savana passed away. She was a year younger than me, and the circumstances were different. My sister was sick. But her death was sudden in that we always expected years together. We were going to raise our kids close to each other and host barbecues and take vacations together. We got that from our parents and cousins growing up. The Fuentes clan is big and loud and so much fun."

He glances up and a faint smile stretches his mouth. He's lost in the memories for a moment, but his expression shifts back to a sort of blankness as his head falls forward and he looks me in the eyes again.

"It's never easy to lose someone you love," he says.

I nod, my stomach tightening with that hard truth.

"A sibling is something rare and precious, and I wanted you to know that I get it, your pain and grief."

"Thank you, Coach," I say, fidgeting nervously with the edges of Raskin's letter.

"One of the best things my family did to honor my sister and to help us heal was set up an endowment for scholarships in her name. It isn't much, maybe enough to give money to two or three students a year. If you think your mom would be open to it, I'd love to share the name of the scholarship we give at Welles with your sister."

"Wow." I'm stunned by the offer. I know that Coach and his wife aren't from the same kind of money most families at Welles are so the gesture carries even more weight. Not a lot of Welles parents would want to share credit for their scholarships. People around here are all about status and symbols to brag about.

A major perk of coaching and teaching is that a kid gets free tuition at institutions like ours. The public school James played at before here wasn't exactly well-funded. Apparently, they were good at sports but bad at academics—and commitment. From the little James has shared about his old team, it seems his dad struggled to keep kids eligible. A third of the team dropped out by the time they reached mid-season his junior year.

"I'll talk to my mom about it, but I can't imagine she'd say no. That's . . . wow." I laugh a little and rub my chin. Anika would get a real kick at the idea that someone would be going to school on a scholarship with her name.

Are they majoring in secret tattoos and piercings? I imagine her saying.

"Good. We'll get it done, then. Now, I expect I'll see you at practice today. That's part of the deal, you put in the work."

He stands, so I scramble to my feet to shake his hand.

"Yes, sir."

He holds my hand for an extra second, his grip squeezing a little tighter for a moment to make sure I feel it. He lowers his head a tick as our eyes meet and I nod, getting it.

He understands me.

"Thank you again, Coach," I say as he taps the table then pushes in his chair.

"Don't let me down, Theo. And read that letter."

I wait until he leaves before sitting down again. I flip open the letter and read the opening line.

To Whom It Concerns:

I am writing this letter to vouch for Theodore Rothschild and kindly request that you allow him to practice with our team immediately.

I chuckle a little and read the line again. I wonder what girl he conned into helping him make this sound . . . smart.

I check my phone for the time. I still have twenty minutes before my second hour, so I continue reading in private. The second I see Cameron he is going to pester me about this meeting and what went down. Two days ago, I would have shared this letter with him so we could make fun of it. Now, though? Maybe I see Raskin's sincerity for what it's worth.

I don't expect special treatment because of this letter, though if you would like to reduce my punishment, I won't argue with you. It would be magnanimous.

I laugh out loud at that line. He definitely got help with this.

It doesn't seem fair that Theo's punishment was more severe than mine simply because I bled. I'm not proud of this, but I gave Theo plenty of wounds, too. They just aren't physically visible. I was cruel in embarrassing ways. Maybe it's the fact he was able to step right in and get a starting spot on our team without going through the same summer camp conditioning the rest of us did. Or maybe the counsellor the headmaster brought in was right and I don't know how to interact with people dealing with trauma. I'm not sure what either of those reasons says about me. I'm either petty and jealous or a cold-hearted narcissist. But the fact I'm willing to put that in writing should be worth something. I'm asking that you show some grace to Theo. Show more than I did. At least punish us the same. He gets what he did was wrong. I get what I did was wrong. And no, this isn't going to make us instant friends. But maybe it will make us better men.

Sincerely,
*   Oliver Raskin, Jr.*

I pop my jaw as my mouth hangs open and I revisit the most potent parts of his letter. Even if he got help crafting the narrative, his heart was behind the intent. His actions sit heavy in my soul. This should make me feel better, and in a way it does. It also makes me feel ashamed. I can't read these words without taking a hard look at myself. And not only what I did to Raskin, though yeah, I seriously assaulted him with my helmet. I'm thinking about Lily, though. How I treated her. How I poured toxic acid on her invisible wounds.

Cameron called me out on it days ago.

"Imagine how she feels," he said.

Even now, as far as we've come, I haven't really gotten it. What Lily went through? She must have been terrified the entire time. And after, knowing she couldn't do it all—that Anika didn't make it.

I fold the letter back up and open my leather portfolio to slip it into the back pocket where it won't fall out. I'm going to need to thank Raskin for this. He deserves praise for this kind of self-reflection. But first, there's someone a lot more worthy—and a whole lot more attractive—who deserves some grace.

April, our headmaster's secretary, has always had a soft spot for me. When I was younger, I charmed her with my class-clown ways, making her laugh. The older I got, the more I relied on my charm to get me out of trouble when I was maybe late for a morning meeting with my advisor or desperate to use the office printer for one of my papers. I may need to turn on the smolder for this ask, though.

"Hey, April," I say, sliding up to her desk. I rest my arms by the visitor logbook and play with the pen. "I'm done in the conference room so you can lock up."

"Okay, sugar."

She loves me. It's go time.

"Do you think you could do me a quick favor? Oh wow, is that a new color?" It's a new color. She isn't a redhead, but she is now.

She smirks and leans on her desk, weight on her palm while she waggles the keys for the conference room in the other as her finger points at me.

"I see what you're doing. Don't think you're sly. I mean, I'll take the compliment and thank you for noticing, but you don't need to butter me up. What do you need, Theo?" April was born and raised in Georgia, and her accent is priceless. She could tell me off and it would sound sweet.

"Do you think you could call Lily Beachem out of first hour a few minutes early so I can apologize to her?"

Her head tilts to the side and her brow ticks up.

"What did you do?"

I know she means to scold me, but it still sounds sweet. That accent is magic.

April has been here for years, and as much as she loves me, Anika was possibly her favorite student of all time. April was also the person who coordinated the counselling services at Welles after the accident. She knows the details—the part Lily played in everything and how cold I was to start the semester.

Rather than respond to her question, I offer a contrite smile and silence, which she quickly interprets.

"Oh, honey. Cut yourself some slack," she says, reaching forward and patting the top of my hand.

April picks up her phone and makes a call, winking at me, and I leave the office and head to the main lawn where Lily's classroom lets out. My tie is still rolled up in my jacket pocket, so I pull it out and thread it around my collar while I wait for her. Less than a minute after April calls her out, Lily's rushing down the steps of the main building and pulling her phone from her satchel. She glances up mid-text and stops in her tracks when she spots me.

"Hi," I mouth, holding up my hand.

Even several yards away, her smile beams. Her hair is parted down the center, curly waves twisting in the breeze over each shoulder. She hugs her body as she cuts through the grass toward me.

"They just called me to the office. What are you doing out?" She scans the area around us before stepping up on her toes and giving me a quick kiss. I take her hands in mine and rub them to keep them warm.

"You're not really needed at the office," I say through a crooked smile. She squints at me with skepticism and maybe a touch of worry in her eyes.

"Are you getting expelled after all?"

"No, nothing like that," I reassure. "The opposite, in a way. Coach wanted to meet. He managed to cut my sentence. I get to practice today."

Her eyes widen.

"Amazing!" Her chest fills with relief, too. I appreciate her sympathy because yeah, I've had a pretty shit run of luck this last few days.

"What's amazing is the reason my punishment was reduced. You have to read it yourself. I'd never be able to do it justice." I open my portfolio and pull Raskin's letter out, handing it to Lily. I study her expression as she reads, and her response mirrors mine.

"Wow. He wrote this?"

I laugh as I take back the letter.

"I think maybe he had help, but yeah."

She sucks in her lips and lifts her brows in awe. I have no letter to give her. But I have things I need to say. I check the time on my phone again, wishing I had more than a few minutes for this. It can't wait, though. She's gone long enough not hearing it from someone who matters. And I hope I matter.

To her.

"I wanted to talk for a minute, before second bell. Walk with me?" I pull her knuckles to my mouth and press a kiss to her cold fingers. A smile flickers on her lips.

"Okay," she agrees.

Our fingers intertwine as we head in the direction of the math and science hall. Our second hours are at opposite ends of the same building so I can make the most of this short time.

"I don't think I've said this out loud to you, and well . . . I should have. For sure by now, but honestly . . . probably months ago," I say.

"Okay," she says, her voice wavering. I squeeze her hand

for reassurance. I stop us just outside the science building by the statue of some rich dude who paid for it fifty years ago.

"I'm sorry." There's a whole litany of items I could add after those two words, but I stop short of overwhelming her with all the things I regret and wish I could take back.

I'm sorry I blamed you.

I'm sorry you got hurt.

I'm sorry you had to grieve alone.

I'm sorry you ever felt guilty.

I'm sorry I made you.

The apologies run through my mind as I stare into her puzzled eyes.

"You're so nice that you don't even realize what I'm apologizing for," I say through a breathy laugh.

"Gah!" I look up at the sky and smile, both because I'm lucky and because I don't deserve Lily's affection.

I drop my head back down and cradle her face in my hands, bringing her forehead to mine as I close my eyes.

"I'm sorry I was a dick. More than that, I'm sorry for what happened to you, Lily. I'm sorry you went through something so awful."

Her lashes flutter against mine.

"It's okay," she whispers.

I press my lips to her forehead.

"No, it's not. And none of it was your fault. I need you to hear that—I need you to believe it. Anika—that night—it wasn't your fault."

Her body quivers and I can tell she's crying. Her hands cling to the lapels of my jacket.

"It wasn't your fault," I repeat.

I say it again, softer. And again, almost without sound.

I'll say it in her dreams until she believes it. I owe her that.

Chapter 27

Lily

I've wanted to hear those words for so long. I would have given anything for them months ago when the nightmares were at their worst. And the weeks before I came back to Welles, when doubt kept telling me I wouldn't be able to handle it—I needed those words then too.

But fate nudged Theo at the right time.

It's my first team practice, and I'll be in that water for real competition in a few days. It's hard to swim fast when you're dragging an anchor, and I have been. It was impossible for a while. It drowned me, beckoned me to the bottom of the pool and tempted me to give up. To stop.

It wasn't my fault.

Hearing it in his voice was vital. I needed it to be him who broke through the noise in my head and make me believe. Theo is the only one who could.

He didn't say he forgave me. There was nothing to forgive. Still, I feel forgiven somehow. I think I've forgiven myself.

I'll be swimming the two-hundred free event on Wednesday. It's an easy race against a weak field, and our coach thought it was a good place to break back into competition. I've managed to swim two dozen laps with the team today, and I've kept up. That's all I need to do—keep up. My personal goals are simple. And while it's sweet that my friends and Theo think I can win, I'm not intending to. I want to finish.

I'm still not sure I want to write about any of it, though. A little late to back out now, I suppose. I emailed Abby after promising Theo I would. She was thrilled. I was sick. I feel used, which is painfully accurate. I *was* used.

"Lily, great work today." It's hard to tell if my coach is being encouraging because I didn't suck or because I told her *The Affiliate* will be sending a photographer to cover our meet. I realize everyone has an angle, and sincerity might be dead for ninety-nine percent of the human race.

"Thanks, Coach." I towel off and pack my gear, ignoring my teammates whispering to my right.

They're talking about me. They don't think I deserve this attention. I don't want this attention.

I focus on my bag, rolling up my towel and tucking it in the corner, fitting my cap and goggles in, pulling out my slide shoes and sweatpants. The entire time, I hear them. Their gossip is like an air leak, this annoying little buzz. I squeeze my eyes shut.

"She's not even that good," one of them says, her words clear despite her attempt to whisper.

"Okay!" I break when the criticism gets to be too much. I straighten from my bag and march toward my teammates. Coach is on the other side of the pool, so it's just me and these two fifth forms who frankly half-assed their way through practice.

Arms crossed over my chest, sweatpants clutched in my

right fist, I jut out my hip and push my tongue into my cheek, giving them a hard stare. Their lips pucker with their effort to contain their laugh. Great, me standing up for myself is funny to them. I've been a wallflower and a pushover for too long.

"What's your problem?" I call them out and stare into the girl on the right's eyes until she looks directly at me. Her smug grin breaks down the second she does, and I move on to her friend. This time, I take a step or two forward to make her even more uncomfortable. She squirms on the bench and breaks eye contact with me repeatedly, looking to her friend to save her.

McKenna and Jade. I know their names but that's all I know about them. Most of that is on me for not being great at socializing, but that works in both directions. They don't know me, either. Not really.

"We were just wondering about *The Affiliate* photoshoot. That's all. Coach mentioned it—"

"Uh, that's a lie. I spoke to Coach, and you two overheard it. It isn't a secret. Most of the team overheard it. So go ahead and ask me. What are you *wondering about*?" I add my brand of sarcasm to my question, feeling my backbone grow.

"We weren't really *wondering*. More curious, or . . . uhm . . ." The taller one, Jade, fumbles her words. I have a feeling she's the follower in their friendship. McKenna's the one who said I wasn't very good.

"Go on," I press.

Jade looks to her friend. McKenna looks down then pops her gaze up to me, that Welles style of entitlement hazing her eyes.

"It would be nice if they paid attention to the team. You're not even . . ."

She trails off but I finish for her.

"Very good, yeah. I heard that little bit from before."

She swallows but sits up straight, hardening her position. I wonder how much money her family gives to this school. I'm guessing a good chunk of change. Money buys that level of cattiness.

"I guess *The Affiliate* was really drawn to my character. You know that thing that sets you apart from others? Like, for example, *you're* a bitch. You whisper behind people's backs, and probably not only mine. In fact, I bet you do it to her, too, when she's not around." I waggle my finger between the two, and Jade looks horrified. McKenna, though? She looks pissed. I think that means I nailed it.

"That's your character. The kind of person who picks at any acknowledgement someone else gets after they've survived a life-altering trauma, one that involves fucking swimming, and yet they are still willing to get their ass back in that pool. Not sure there's a media outlet looking to cover that. Perhaps you can start that magazine—*Entitled, Inc.*"

I twist my lips and blink slowly, leaving my verbal smackdown as it is. I've said enough.

"Whatever," McKenna finally says, standing and pushing her feet into her slide shoes. She leaves her "friend" behind, and when she's out of earshot, Jade looks up at me.

"I'm really sorry," she mutters. Her eyes resemble those on a beaten puppy. I let my arms fall to my sides, softening my stance. When Jade drops her chin, I reach out my hands and call her in for a hug.

She clings to me. And as much as I don't love hugging people I don't know very well, Jade's embrace feels nice. Her apology felt nice.

* * *

I brought Morgan and Brooklyn up to speed before I messaged Abby that I would do the story. Now they're fully engrossed in this project with me. Probably because I'm digging my heels in and deleting every sentence after I type it.

"Maybe you should write it like a journal. Or even better, do you *have* a journal? Maybe you can plagiarize from yourself?" Morgan suggests.

I lean over my bed and pull out my rainbow kitten backpack and slide out the spiral notebook that is full of my journal entries. I toss it over to Morgan.

"Knock yourself out. If you think there is anything worthwhile in there, tell me. But those are all assignments from my telemedicine robot psychologist, and I don't recall being honest about real shit in a single one of them.

Morgan skims through and pauses about ten pages in, flipping the book around and holding it open to face me.

"Is this a picture of a duck?"

I squint to see what she's pointing at.

"Oh, yeah. No, that's how I draw cows."

She spins the notebook back around and stares at it.

"Lily, that's not a cow," she says, shutting the book and tossing it back to me. "And you're right. This is useless."

I flop back in my bed and shove my laptop to the side. I'm not sure staring at the blinking curser on the blank page is going to motivate me.

"Would it help if I interviewed you? We could record it and maybe you can listen back and find some words to use." Brooklyn sits next to me and pulls my computer into her lap. She begins typing so I prop myself up on my elbow to read.

"What was that headline you said the first time? Fish something?"

"Fish out of water," I answer.

She types it and hits return.

"There. It's a start," she says.

"Great, four words down. Seven-hundred-ninety-six to go." An eight-hundred-word feature, that's what Abby wants. Minimum. I can't imagine being in such a groove that I squeeze out more than that.

"Why don't you interview us? Ask us for comments you can put it in the story. You need outside perspectives, right?" She twists my laptop toward me, and I chew at my lips, giving it thought.

"Okay, that might help." I sit up and take over the computer, turning and facing Brooklyn.

"What do you think about me swimming on Wednesday?" I stare at her with a blank face, hands poised to type. Brooklyn scowls.

"That's your question? I thought you wanted to be a sports journalist. Lily, that's not probing or introspective. You aren't going to get great sound bites with a question like that."

I sigh and snap my laptop shut.

"That's the problem. I know! You're right! But I don't want to ask probing questions to you. To Morgan. To anyone! I don't want to ask myself the probing questions. I don't want to capitalize off your trauma," I bark.

"*Our* trauma," Morgan pipes in.

Brooklyn and I both look to her. She puts her homework to the side and scoots to the edge of her bed, folding her legs up and holding her ankles.

"We all went through this together. And what you did that night, Lily, was heroic. I know you hate that word. It's half the reason I never bombard you with my gratitude, because you have a lot of mixed emotions about that term. But you saved my life, Lily. You saved Brooklyn's. We were not getting out of those seat belts without you. We were not getting to the riverbank without your strength pulling us to the surface."

Brooklyn stretches out her legs and rolls up the right pant leg of her sweats, showing the scar on the side of her knee.

"I have two pins in there. It hurts when I stand longer than fifteen minutes. I'm supposed to wear the brace until the first of the year, but I can't stand the sight of it. It reminds me, and I hate that I feel weak. But Lily, I couldn't move. I tore tendons with names I've never heard. And while I am working through constant feelings of inadequacy and failure —work I know will require years of attention—what you did for me was the most selfless thing I've ever seen. You were human to your core. You acted out of love. And like Morgan said, if I didn't know how much you hate hearing it, I'd tell you every day—thank you. Thank you, Lily."

Brooklyn's eyes glisten and she wipes them dry with her sleeve.

My mouth feels heavy on the corners, and I swear my frown is dragging my cheeks down to my shoulders. I'm not a hero. I was terrified. They don't understand.

"Whatever you're thinking right now, write that." Brooklyn reaches over and pulls up my laptop screen.

I look at the headline she retyped for me.

FISH OUT OF WATER.

There has never been a truer statement. That is what I am, what I've always been.

My hands hover over the keys for a few seconds and I start to type. I type my last thoughts. And then I type more, capturing the things Brooklyn said. Before too long, I'm asking better questions and sharing thoughts and feelings with my friends. And the longer we talk, the more things come back to Anika and how, though she's gone physically, she is the nucleus of all we do.

Then it hits me. My eyes jet up from the screen and my typing halts.

"It's Anika," I announce. "That's the story. I mean, it's about me getting in the pool again and yadda, yadda, but Anika—she's the reason. This story, it needs to be a tribute to Anika." I'm grinning. I feel the strange stretch on my face. And Brooklyn and Morgan's smiles are just as bright.

Brooklyn rushes to her dresser and pulls a box out from the bottom drawer, dumping the contents on my comforter and spreading them out. Dozens of photos, even one that I'm in. It was from that night; a selfie Anika took of the four of us before we headed out to the abandoned barn. Four young girls, vibrant and full of possibility. We were talking about boys then—I was talking about Theo.

I pick up that photo and hold it between my thumb and finger.

"Where did you get this?" I ask.

"Theo's mom emailed me the photos in Anika's cloud. She thought I might want them. My mom had them printed at one of those online photo places, and she put them in this box. I decided to put all my Anika things in here in case I ever needed to remember her."

We spend the next two hours sorting through photos, most of them Brooklyn's and some of them Morgan's. I find things on my phone that fit the story, and by the time we're done, we've painted a picture of our friend with our snapshots and text strings. She almost feels alive. It feels as though she's here with us.

I start to write at midnight, and I lose Brooklyn and Morgan to sleep at about two in the morning. I don't stop until my phone alarm rings, and my eyes sting with the need for sleep. But I'm done. It's my story, but it's more than that. It's Anika's story. It's the lessons she taught us all. I wrote it as if someone were interviewing me along with my friends. I wrote it with two purposes. One, to honor my friend. And two, for Theo.

I type the byline at the top.

Story by Theodore Rothschild.

My lungs fill and my heart pounds in my chest. I'm exhausted, yet I want to race to the train. I'm going to print this at the office and leave it for Abby to read. I don't want the email trail coming back to me, and it will take some convincing to get Theo to send it from his account. But when he sees what we've done—the girls of Hayden Hall—Triple B —I think he may be willing to let me put his name on it.

I did what he asked. I controlled the narrative. All I ask of him is that he also let me control the record, the author.

Chapter 28

Theo

Turns out, I'm good at answering phones. It's making the phone calls that I suck at.

I convinced our headmaster to let me get my internship hours in at the front office. It's not necessarily in line with any career goals, but I like hanging out with April all day and I'm decent at giving campus tours. Granted, it's only been one family so far, but they enrolled for next year. I'm pretty sure it was my tips on how to get the best side dishes in the cafeteria that sold the twelve-year-old prospective student on begging to attend Welles. Or maybe it was my quick trip through the fieldhouse during the girls' volleyball practice.

Lily was quiet after her internship yesterday. I don't think she wants to rub it in, but I'm over it. Yeah, I like that business. I think I'll be great in a broadcast booth one day. But I'm not very good at answering to authority, or so I've learned. And I'm definitely not a favorite of advertisers, charm or no charm.

Coach let us out of practice early today so we could all go

support the women's swim team. It was James' idea. I had to run a quick errand first, so I told him to save me a seat at the end of lane five. That's Lily's lane.

My phone buzzes as I walk into the fieldhouse, so I tuck the flowers I got for Lily under my arm and back through the doors as I read the message.

JAMES: *You better hurry. This place is packed and Morgan is threatening to sell your seat.*

ME: *Just got here. Be there in a second.*

I shove my phone in the back pocket of my jeans and spin around with a bit of a sprint. Not fully looking where I'm going, though, I smack right into a woman, knocking her purse from her shoulder and scattering whatever was inside in all directions.

"Sorry, I wasn't even looking—"

"Theo! I'm glad to find you."

I look up from the floor where I'm gathering up lipsticks and keys and a tin of mints, and am met with a familiar yet unwanted face.

"Abby. Nice to see you," I choke out. My words are sour as they pass my tongue. Maybe I'm not quite over it.

"Don't worry about that stuff. I'll get it," she says, holding her palms out for me to hand off what I've picked up. Despite my urge to simply drop everything back on the floor, I pass it to her.

"All right. Well, I'll be off, then." I can't quite spit out a 'nice to see you.'

"Wait!" She grips my arm and my eyes dart to her unwanted touch. She lets go, but she doesn't seem to be backing off.

"I wanted to thank you for reconsidering. Your story, Theo. It's . . ." Her palms open as she holds them out to her sides and shakes her head, mouth agape. "Wow," she hums quietly.

"My . . . story." My chest hurts. What is she talking about?

"Yes, and I understand that you didn't want to overstep and assume anything, but Theo, you could have delivered it yourself. I can't wait to show it to Michael. You and he didn't meet on the best terms, but he really is a fan of great writing, and your story, Theo. So much honesty."

I nod and do my best to inch up the corners of my mouth. My tongue is dry and I'm about a breath away from choking when I spot Lily pacing in the background, her earbuds in as she shakes out her arms.

"I'll get back to you, Abby. I need a second," I say, holding up a finger before abandoning my sudden fan.

Lily glances up when I'm a few steps away and her smile beams with what I hope is relief to see me. My stomach twists because I love that she looks at me like that, *but what did she do?*

"Hey! James saved you a seat," she says, sliding her hand around my side and to my back as she steps up to kiss me. Her lips are cool and electric. She's popping with nerves, but she seems so ready for this. My questions can wait, at least thirty minutes until her race is done.

"I brought you flowers." I hand them to her, and she pulls them to her chest and inhales. "They're lilies because, well . . ."

She giggles.

"Yeah, I get it. Clever." She eyes me but smirks. My brain is split in half, one side happier than it's been in months, the other full of shouting and questions.

"I should get to my seat," I say, extracting myself before

the skeptical half of my brain talks the part of me that's in love into ruining things.

"I'll find you after the meet. Thank you so much for coming." She clutches her bouquet again and bats her lashes over her smile. She's as confident as she is ever going to be, and I can't wreck that.

I dash through the long hallway to the other end of the pool and duck inside the doors to sit with our friends. James waves me over and I take the seat in front of him and next to Morgan.

"Didn't think you were going to make it," she says.

"Oh, yeah. I'm here." My hands knot together as I lean forward and rest my elbows on my knees. My eyes scan the deck until I spot *The Affiliate* photographer. Abby is right next to him, and I can't help but lock onto her while her words play over and over in my head.

Morgan's arm brushes against mine as she leans forward to join me.

"Of course, Morgan. I wouldn't miss this for the world," she says, putting on a deep voice.

"Is that supposed to be me?" I ask, not pulling my gaze away from Abby.

"Yeah, Theo. That's what you were *supposed* to say," she retorts.

I blink and shake my head, turning to meet her waiting stare.

"Sorry, I'm— Something came up just now, and I don't know what to think about it. But . . ."

"Ohhh," she says in a hushed voice, sitting up straight and flitting her gaze toward the photographer and Abby.

"Oh, no," she adds on.

"You keep saying that, and it doesn't sound good. Wanna fill me in? What's *oh, no?*" My focus bounces between her and Abby, and finally I shift so I'm squared with Morgan.

She reaches into her purse and pulls out her phone, scrolling while holding a finger up to me as if I'm supposed to be patient. Meanwhile, visions of pushing Abby into the pool drift through the back of my mind.

"There it is," she says, holding her phone screen against her chest then looking me in the eyes.

"You need to know that Lily is going to show you this. Like, as in right after this meet. She wanted to before, and she went back and forth, but frankly, I talked her out of it. I mean, I think she was mostly set on waiting until she knew for sure, but given how *off the handle* you can fly before all the facts are in—"

"Morgan." My voice is stern, and she snaps her lips shut before her eyes shift to the side, toward the pool. I pinch the bridge of my nose. "I'm sorry, you were rambling, though."

"You need to read the entire thing. Don't say a word until you're done. And then please, Theo, let Lily tell you on her own. Pretend it's the first you've heard about this. And have whatever reaction you decide you want to have then. But do her that courtesy," she says, turning her attention back to me.

"What courtesy," I say, leaning my head to the side.

"The one of letting her be open and honest with you, and the courtesy of considering her intent with this. This is an act of love. Lily, she's full of so much love. And she loves you."

I breathe in through my nose and study her expression. Morgan and I go way back, and if there is anybody whose face I can read like a book, it's hers. We've survived the same society circles. We have our own secret code. She's being straight with me right now.

I nod and she hands me the phone. I cradle it in my palms and Morgan gives me space as I read.

. . .

FISH OUT OF WATER
  A story by Theo Rothschild

I glance to Morgan in a flash, but she's clapping and ignoring me. I return my eyes to the screen and continue to read. The further I get into what Lily and the other girls have constructed, the more I see; the more I understand.

This is a love letter. She's right. But it isn't to me—it's to Anika. It may be a gesture done *for* me, but the recipient is my sister. My heart swells with every new revelation.

It's all there. Lily and Anika's bond, in so many words, yet still respecting my sister's privacy. Those who know will know, and those on the outside will see a special, blossoming friendship. All of Anika's gifts, her value and worth shining brightly in the quotes from Lily, Morgan, and Brooklyn. She included pieces from older articles, words from my mom that were in the local paper.

It takes me twenty minutes to finish the piece, and I go back to read certain sections again. I don't know how Lily managed to write something from my perspective, as if she were examining herself from above. It's a gift. Even more, though, is how accurate she is with my voice. It's everything I have wanted to say. It's better, and I don't deserve this credit.

Morgan leans into me.

"You finish?"

I hand her phone back.

"Yeah."

We both stare out at the calm waters, swimmers getting to their blocks while Welles students cheer behind us. My chest is heavy, but it's different from the guilt and pain it's been carrying. I don't feel worthy of having a girl like Lily do something so selfless for me. I'm grateful for the way she saw my sister, though. For the way she memorialized her and gave her credit for everything she's about to do.

"You won't tell her I told you." Morgan isn't asking.

I answer anyway.

"I won't." And I'll beg her not to give away this credit.

My heart thrums, my lips and hands and legs numb.

"There she is," Morgan says, nudging me to look off to the right where Lily is walking in, a photographer trailing her.

She's still listening to her music, but her features are stiff, her gait stilted and robotic. Her nerves are back. The attention is swallowing her.

"Come on, Lily," I mutter.

"Come on, girl," Morgan says at my side.

They announce the swimmers for her race and when they call her name and she holds up a hand, every single person in the stands screams. We're all rooting for her, but I know how she's interpreting this. She sees people here for the show, and yeah, a lot of them are. But there wouldn't be a show if she weren't so goddamned brave.

She bends down and dangles her arms, stepping up to the edge of the pool and stretching to touch the edge. She flexes for a moment, then rights herself and pulls her goggles down over her eyes. Her body is sleek, ready to cut through the water. Her heart and mind, though, they're jagged.

"Swimmers, take your mark."

I hold my breath, and the room grows quiet. Lily's face remains down, her eyes on her feet, on the spot where her fingertips graze the pool's edge. When every other racer's head pops up to look out on the lanes ahead, Lily's remains down. And when the beep sounds to dive in, Lily is frozen.

"Theo." Morgan squeezes my arm.

"Come on, Lily. You can do it," I say. The room is filled with people cheering her name, begging her to hurry, willing her to race for them.

"Do it for you, Lily. Just finish. Remember, you only want to finish," I say.

"Dude, this isn't good," James says over my shoulder.

My stomach roars with acid and my heart sinks as Lily rolls her body up to stand and she pulls her goggles up to her forehead.

The fieldhouse echoes with chants, her name on repeat. I doubt anyone else sees it, but I notice the way her body cringes with every mention of her name. Every word pierces her, cutting her down, breaking her resolve, and pulling her back into the hole she worked so damn hard to get out of.

"Watch my stuff," I say, emptying my pockets and pulling my shoes from my feet. I tug my Welles polo over my head and toss it to my empty bleacher seat and rush out to the end of lane five.

Without pause, I dive into the water and swim toward her. I stop about halfway and tread water, holding her gaze, willing her tears to stop.

"Just make it to me. That's all you have to do is make it to me," I shout.

She shakes her head so I swim closer, cutting the distance in half.

Her lips quiver with a fearful laugh and her gaze scans the room. She's feeling the pressure of it all, the attention crushing her, the embarrassment stamping her skin.

"We're all behind you, Lily. Nobody cares if you win. We know you can do this. *I* know you can do this. Just make it to me."

My jeans are growing heavy so I kick harder to keep my body afloat and my head above water. Some of the other swimmers have stopped, realizing what's going on. The ones on the end lanes continue to race. The water is choppy.

"I'm here, Lily. I'm not getting out of this pool until you cross it with me." I hold out a hand, legs whirling in the water beneath me to keep me from sinking.

Lily nods, the movement slight but there. She pulls her goggles from her head and tosses them to the side and wraps her arms around herself, rubbing her sides as she stares at me.

"You can do this, Lily. We'll do it together. You can finish," I beg.

She nods, her eyes seeming more ready this time.

I will her not to look around the room anymore, slapping my palm on the water and pleading with her silently to let go of the fear. To ignore the pangs of judgement that aren't there.

She leaps into the water feet first and paddles slowly toward me. I want to meet her halfway again to cut her distance, but I also know how she'll feel if she makes it this far. Rather than moving forward, I kick my legs to swim away from her. She's gaining on me, but she's moving farther with every stroke.

"Come on, Lily!" A swimmer from Augustine has joined me, swimming next to Lily in her lane. Soon, the swimmer on the other side does the same, and three of them are heading my direction.

"We're almost there," I shout, kicking to get closer to the other side.

Lily catches up to me about a dozen feet from the pool's edge, and she grabs my hand with hers but continues to claw through the water, ensuring we reach the side together. She grips the edge and pants, not from being tired but from enduring a panic attack while pushing through one of the toughest barriers in her life.

"You made it," I whisper into her ear. I wrap an arm around her and cradle her head with my open palm, kissing her temple. "I'm so proud of you, Lily. You did it."

Still breathing heavily, she turns her head slowly until our eyes meet.

"I want to finish," she says, and the flash of determination returns to her eyes.

"I'll go with you," I offer, but she shakes her head.

"You already have," she breathes out. Her body turning toward the open water, she looks at the twenty-five meters of water that stand between her and the other side. And then she's off.

With every stroke her body breaks freer, her muscles working harder, feet kicking with more power, picking up speed. There isn't a single swimmer not in sync with her. This has become about more than winning points in a swim meet. This is about lifting other people up. This is faith and kindness.

I pull myself up to the side of the pool and cheer from the edge. Morgan comes to sit beside me, and together we count each lap.

Four.

Five.

Six.

When she coasts away from me for her final twenty-five meters, the building is vibrating with a collective voice. I scramble to my feet and run to the other side so I can be there when her hand smacks the deck for the final time. *The Affiliate* photographer kneels beside me when I get there, his camera whirring with a constant hammering of shots. Frame-by-frame, he captures Lily's journey.

Her hand glides the final distance to the pool's edge, and

every competitor has pulled back, collectively conceding this race to her. Some things are more important.

I flatten myself on the deck and Lily reaches up and holds the sides of my head. I reach down to support her, lifting her enough to be able to press my lips to hers.

"I'm so proud of you," I shout. Even this close, it's hard to hear each other. The cheering inside the fieldhouse is deafening.

Lily drops her hands and rests them on the deck, laying her forehead on the backs of them to give herself a small moment of privacy before turning around and smacking the water with her open palm. She sends a small tidal wave across the water.

"Woo-hoo!" she shouts, and our friends all rush to the other side of the pool to raise their arms and scream along with her.

I get to my knees and when Lily turns again, I hold out my hand to help her out of the water. Morgan tosses her towel to her, but she wraps herself in me instead. Getting dry is useless. My clothes are soaked, and these jeans have fused to my legs.

The photographer snaps closeups of us as I praise her over and over, one hand behind her head, the other at her back. Nose-to-nose, we laugh near maniacally. Her eyes are spilling tears, her body shedding the stress that nearly toppled her. I kiss her forehead then rest mine on hers, never letting my arms leave her as she sobs in front of everybody.

"You did it, Lily," I say.

"I finished, Theo. I finished."

I nod, my head rolling against hers, our noses grazing.

"I fucking love you," I say, part of me wishing I'd saved the word for this moment.

"I love you so much," she says in return, leaping onto me

and hugging me koala-bear style, all arms and legs wrapped around me tightly.

My arms shift to hold her weight and I spin slowly, not wanting to leave this moment. I end up carrying her to the bench where the rest of her team is waiting, all of them clapping in unison. Lily looks each of them in the eyes once I set her down, her smile growing and cheeks reddening, the good kind of blush. This is pride.

"You guys," she finally says. "I did it!"

She starts to run in place, pounding her feet on the wet concrete, fists punching the air. Her team joins her, and I peel off to let her have this moment, standing to the side as she celebrates. An hour from now, she's going to have to live this all again, accepting a medal that she's earned more than most. And after that, she's going to tell me about the story she wrote. She's going to use all the reasons to convince me why I deserve my name on it, but in the end, I won't let her do it. I can't. Because I don't, and it would be wrong.

This is Lily's story. Hers and Anika's. I'm merely grateful to be in it.

Epilogue

Lily

Theodore Rothschild is bossy.

I've said it to his face a dozen times today, and probably a million times this year.

"I know. Now just read that file and get ready for the next interview," he says, sliding a packet across the conference table to me before winking.

I scowl at him, but I can't stay mad for long. Especially when it's just play mad.

"Fine," I huff, pulling the next scholarship candidate's profile into view.

"You love me," he says.

"Yeah, yeah," I dismiss.

I do, though. I love him so fucking much.

Theo asked me to do these interviews with him. I insisted he invite his mother instead, but he denied that request as soon as I made it. Just like he made *The Affiliate* take his name off the story I wrote. I tried to compromise with a shared byline, but when I wasn't paying attention, he pulled Abby to the side and had her make the change in edits.

He did get to rejoin *The Affiliate*, though. And not in sales. We're both finishing our second semester in editorial, staring down the final days of our final form before we head off to college.

Theo was hell bent on going west, far away from his mother. I wanted to go farther east, for similar reasons. Somehow, though, we both ended up in Louisiana. I got in at Tech and Theo will be at State. He's thinking about walking on for football, but only if that's where James decides to commit. I think he should play no matter what, but that's because I like watching him. And kissing him after a game is pretty nice too.

Things between Theo and his mom are still strained. I applaud him for his patience, though. Neil isn't well, and it feels wrong to root for someone's demise, but when the person is so toxic, it's more than tempting to justify it. I think Theo is waiting for Neil to die. He won't say it, though he has maybe uttered it a time or two after drinking some Jack in his lair. Maybe then he'll get his mom back, and he can begin mending their relationship.

I've given up on mine. My mom didn't even read the story in *The Affiliate*. My stepdad did, and he even had me sign it when I went home for Thanksgiving. He said my mom was proud, but the way she turned her nose up at the mention of it says otherwise.

I sent a copy to my dad, too. Two, in fact. He never received the first one. He sent me a photo of the second, but that was it. Visual proof that my mail made it to him was all I was going to get. Maybe I'll send him his credit card back next time, especially since I found out he never activated it. A gift he sent and immediately forgot, like me.

But I don't need love where I am unwanted. I have so much here. Triple B is back and unbreakable, even if college is going to pull us to different corners of the country. My year with Brooklyn and Morgan meant more than any award or recognition I may graduate with from Welles. I'm leaving this place with lifelong friends. They're family, and I know any of us would drop everything and rush to help the others.

We are what Anika wished for us to be. Maybe she was clairvoyant. She always insisted she could see it all, our future. Me, her, and the girls. Me and Theo. Her gut never led her astray. The cruel universe simply took her too soon.

"Are you reading?" Theo taps his pen on the table next to me.

"Yeah, yes! Geesh, okay," I whine. I wasn't reading, though. I was reminiscing.

I go to work on the file, and the first thing I notice is the photo. Nose ring, ear cuffs, and purple hair. The girl is from Long Island. In her self-reflection essay, she wrote that she never felt as though she fit in.

The Anika Rothschild and Savana Fuentes private school scholarship is made for girls like this, the outcasts and misfits. It's for people needing a place to grow and an opportunity to be more. Welles has its flaws, but I am so grateful for its gifts. Being here has opened doors my public school in Ohio never could have. It's also given me love that I would never have known.

"Maive Whitford. I like her name," I say.

"I have a feeling about this one," Theo says.

Just then, the door opens. Blue eyes with hints of gray, clear like crystal, and a smile that stretches from freckled cheek to freckled cheek.

"Sorry I'm late." Her voice is raspy and her bright-colored jacket matches the pink on her lips. "I got a little lost on campus. No, wait."

She looks down and smiles before glancing up through extra-long lashes.

"Your marching band was jamming in the commons, and I couldn't help but dance. Sometimes when life gives you music, you have to listen."

I glance to Theo and I can tell instantly from his dimple and crooked grin.

We've found Anika.

THE END

Preorder Rebel and Habit Now!

The Boys of Welles continues with Rebel and Habit, books 2 and 3 in the series. Coming fall 2022!

Rebel

Cameron and Brooklyn's story

The Boys of Welles Book 2

Free in Kindle Unlimited

Habit

James and Morgan's story

The Boys of Welles Book 3

Free in Kindle Unlimited

If you enjoyed this series, you might also like:

The Varsity Series

A New Adult Sports Romance Trilogy

Free in Kindle Unlimited

Begin Your Binge with Varsity Heartbreaker

Lucas Fuller is a lot of things.

He's the boy next door.

He's the first crush I ever had.

He was my first kiss.

He's also the only person who has ever broken my heart.

For two years, I've wondered what happened to the us I used to know.

We were best friends, and then suddenly...we weren't.

I tried to run away from it. I even changed schools just to make the hurt disappear.

But no matter how hard I tried to not think about Lucas, I just couldn't stay away from the high school quarterback with perfect blue eyes and so many secrets.

I'm back. We're seniors now. We've grown—all of us. And Lucas Fuller might be different, but I'm different too.

This is my time to take risks, to experience life and to fall in love for real.

I want Lucas Fuller to be a part of my story, but I know for that to happen, I need to know the truth about our past.

BUY NOW ON AMAZON

Acknowledgments

Thank you so very much for spending time on my words. I can't thank my readers enough for giving me this chance to do what I love to do, which is create twisty, angsty, realistic worlds and characters I hope you want to be friends with (or kick in the face when they deserve it, *haha*).

This book was hard for many reasons. I had a story I wanted to tell, and it meant I had to let myself go places and touch raw hurt and pain without falling in too deep. This book was inspired by many experiences and struggles by people I love and have known for years and some I've recently met. The themes of this book touch on abuse and self-harm, which I know is a difficult subject for many. Mental health, more importantly the normalizing of *talking* about our mental health, is a passion of mine. It's a vital step in helping those who need us. It's hard to ask for help in a room that would rather not hear such words. Be open. Be accepting. Show grace. Give love. Support and champion. And if you feel alone and need somewhere to turn, please look to your family and friends. And if that's not an option, please reach out to the warm and embracing individuals who work and volunteer for NAMI (National Alliance on Mental Health).

https://www.nami.org/help

1-800-950-NAMI (6264)

helpline@nami.org

If you are in an abusive situation, no matter who it is that is the abuser, you can contact the National Abuse Hotline 24/7.

Call 800-799-7233

SMS: Text START to 88788

https://www.thehotline.org

I have so many people to thank for helping me to kick this series off and get this book into readers' hands. Enormous love to my husband and son for always understanding my odd writing habits, the late night typing, and the laptop that has to come to the ballgame sometimes. Brenda Letendre, you are the net for my trapeze artist ways. You are the most amazing editor and friend, and I am so grateful for you. Mom, your eyes on my words and support for what I do is everything to me. You make me better in so many ways. Autumn . . . oh girl. I know I say this with every book, but you really are my fuel and fire. This year was a struggle train, but you kept the steam roaring and ensured my wheels remained on the tracks. Thank you, for everything. Not just the bookish stuff. Love you.

Readers - you are the reason I get to live my dream. You are the reason I type until my fingers are stiff and crackly (they do get that way sometimes). I love hearing your reactions, reading your reviews, seeing your graphics and posts. It's all I need. If you enjoyed this book, please feel free to drop a review or do any of those bookish things we all enjoy so much. It's good publicity, yes. But also, it makes my ever-loving day.

Now, off to write about a hot stoner boy with a penchant for danger ;-)

About the Author

Ginger Scott is a *USA Today, Wall Street Journal* and Amazon-bestselling author from Peoria, Arizona. She has also been nominated for the Goodreads Choice and RWA Rita Awards. She is the author of several young and new adult romances, including bestsellers Cry Baby, The Hard Count, A Boy Like You, This Is Falling and Wild Reckless.

A sucker for a good romance, Ginger's other passion is sports, and she often blends the two in her stories. When she's not writing, the odds are high that she's somewhere near a baseball diamond, either watching her son swing for the fences or cheering on her favorite baseball team, the Arizona Diamondbacks. Ginger lives in Arizona and is married to her college sweetheart whom she met at ASU (fork 'em, Devils).

FIND GINGER ONLINE: www.littlemisswrite.com

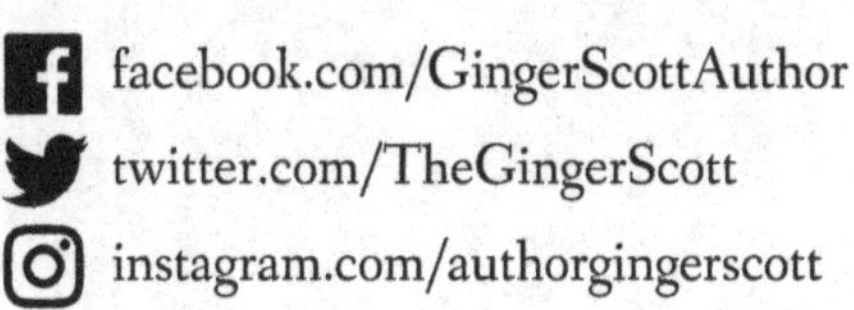

Also By Ginger Scott

The Boys of Welles

Loner

Rebel (fall 2022)

Habit (fall 2022)

The Fuel Series

Shift

Wreck

Burn

The Varsity Series

Varsity Heartbreaker

Varsity Tiebreaker

Varsity Rule breaker

Varsity Captain

The Waiting Series

Waiting on the Sidelines

Going Long

The Hail Mary

Like Us Duet

A Boy Like You

A Girl Like Me

The Falling Series

This Is Falling

You And Everything After

The Girl I Was Before

In Your Dreams

The Harper Boys

Wild Reckless

Wicked Restless

Standalone Reads

Candy Colored Sky

Cowboy Villain Damsel Duel

Drummer Girl

BRED

Cry Baby

The Hard Count

Memphis

Hold My Breath

Blindness

How We Deal With Gravity

www.ingramcontent.com/pod-product-compliance
Lightning Source LLC
Chambersburg PA
CBHW011131190726
48289CB00012B/2995